# eve's men

## also by newton thornburg

A MAN'S GAME

THE LION AT THE DOOR

DREAMLAND

BEAUTIFUL KATE

VALHALLA

BLACK ANGUS

CUTTER AND BONE

TO DIE IN CALIFORNIA

KNOCKOVER

GENTLEMAN BORN

# newton thornburg

# eve's men

a tom doherty associates book   new york

This is a work of fiction. All of the characters and events portrayed in this novel are either fictitious or are used fictitiously.

EVE'S MEN

Copyright © 1998 by Newton Thornburg

This book is printed on acid-free paper.

A Forge Book
Published by Tom Doherty Associates, Inc.
175 Fifth Avenue
New York, NY 10010

Forge® is a registered trademark of Tom Doherty Associates, Inc.

Design by Sara Stemen

Library of Congress Cataloging-in-Publication Data

Thornburg, Newton.
Eve's men / Newton Thornburg. —1st ed.
p.   cm.
"A Tom Doherty Associates book."
ISBN 0-312-86399-3 (acid-free paper)
I. Title.
PS3570.H649E95   1998
813'.54—dc21   97-29857
CIP

FIRST EDITION: April 1998

Printed in the United States of America

0   9   8   7   6   5   4   3   2   1

**To Kris and Mark and Doug,
in whom their mother's beautiful spirit
lives on.**

# eve's men

# chapter one

They were not your average couple rattling along a Colorado blacktop in a dirty pickup at three in the morning. For one thing, they were not high on liquor or drugs. Nor were they in any way average-looking, in fact could easily have passed for a pair of New York models a decade past their prime earning years, the woman appearing to be around thirty, the man forty. Also, despite the late hour, they didn't seem to be tired or sleepy but intensely alert, the man maintaining an expression of unbending determination in the face of the woman's obvious disapproval as he guided the four-wheel-drive Chevy through the genteel horse country north of Colorado Springs. Every so often she would look over at him, glances that could scald, given their source, the beautiful green eyes with their sculpted lids and long lashes, their look of cool intelligence. The woman's hair was dark brown, thick, and unkempt. Her teeth were very white and even. Her mouth, barely rouged, was full and strong.

"You're really going through with it, then," she said.

The man did not look at her. "Why else would we be out here at this hour?"

"We could pull over and neck."

"Big thrill."

She sighed in regret. "It just seems so stupid, Brian. So wasteful. You'll go to prison and they'll make the goddamn movie anyway."

"Yeah, it's a bitch."

At that, she settled back, looking out the passenger window at the small ranchettes sliding steadily past, an occasional horse clearly visible in the moonlight. Out the other window, past Brian's curly head and the pines along the road, she could see the ghostly white peaks of the front range running across the horizon, like a rip in the sky. But it was her lover's face she settled on, the carefully fashioned mask of sardonic amiability that never quite worked for her, never quite hid the pain underneath. Even now, as grimly determined as he was, she found it impossible to see the mask, its surface handsomeness as usual undone by the character of the man. Improvident and reckless and hopelessly honest, Brian Poole had the scars to show for it, including one running from his ear halfway down his flat cheek, a memento of six months spent in a Mexican jail fifteen years before. Nasty as the scar was, she knew it was as nothing compared to the one that had brought them here on this night, so far from home, if L.A. could be called a home.

The truck suddenly slowed.

"It's just up ahead," Brian said.

The woman sighed. "It's not too late, you know. We can still turn around and go home."

He looked at her. "And just live with it, right? Just accept it? Buy into their fucking lies?"

"They're not going to use your name, you know."

"No—just my life."

There was no sense arguing. And anyway, she could see it up ahead now, the night lights burning in the darkness, barely illuminating the newly erected outdoor set: a street and storefronts, with the exterior of a modern log cabin hideaway set off to the side. Running straight back from the blacktop was a row of equipment trucks and trailers and a couple of prefabs, one with lights on inside.

"What if it's not here?" she said.

"The bulldozer? It was this afternoon. But if it's gone, then there'll be a fire."

She smiled ruefully. "My hero."

"Not now, okay?"

He swung into the driveway and stopped in front of a heavy gate chain with a No Trespassing signboard attached. Close to the road, on the near side of the open street area, a huge yellow bulldozer was parked.

"Good, it's still here." Brian slid the gearshift into park, then turned and looked gravely at the woman. "Remember, Eve, you just back out and leave. You don't wait for me. I don't want you being an accessory."

And I don't want you being a criminal, she thought, but didn't say it. Not this time, not this late in the day. Instead she slipped her arms around him and kissed him. He gave her a quick hug and got out of the truck.

"Remember," he said, "you don't stay."

But she did. She got into the driver's seat and started to back into the road, then stopped and killed the truck's lights and sat there watching as Brian stepped over the chain and headed across the rutted, open area toward the lighted prefab. He called out something, and a middle-aged uniformed security guard appeared in the doorway of the prefab. Brian had told her that he was going to plead car trouble, ask to use a phone inside the small security building. And that was what he appeared to be doing now, talking, smiling, putting the man at ease. Then, as they went up the short stairway toward the doorway, he suddenly grasped the man's right arm and pushed it up behind his back, at the same time clamping him around the neck and forcing him on inside.

Eve's eyes filled with tears. In frustration she began to pound her fist against the truck's plastic dashboard and was still pounding when Brian appeared again, taking the three stairs in one stride and running across the open area toward the bulldozer, carrying a ring of keys in his hand. He had explained to her that in his wanderings after Vietnam he once had worked as a ranch hand in West Texas, clearing chaparral with a Cat dozer. So she was not surprised as he clambered up into the protective cage atop the huge machine and within seconds had its diesel engine clattering loudly, spouting black exhaust. Next, he raised the Cat's blade, then turned the dozer on a dime and started across the rutted open space—a space undoubtedly cleared by that same machine—toward the row of storefronts.

Eve couldn't help reflecting on how stupid it all was: Brian about to bulldoze a row of facades, shell buildings, when the real ones—the real town, the real cabin—existed only a few miles away. But the real thing evidently just hadn't looked real enough for Hollywood. So now Brian would destroy not the hick bar he once had been thrown out of, nor the bank and grocery where the lady, the burned-out star, was refused service, nor the cabin where they had lived on coke and she had died of it, of overdose. No, Brian would destroy the *images* of these places—though not without reason, she knew. Because it was here on this set and in Hollywood that their two lives—his and the late Kim Sanders'—would be permanently altered, probably defamed, certainly diminished, in order to fit the enduring "reality" of film.

That was what Brian wanted to destroy. And he set about it now. Clanking across the camera track, he came to the corner of the set, an old-fashioned gray stone bank, a dual facade, front and side, with a hick-town covered walk in front. Next to the bank was the grocery, then the bar, followed by a couple of other shops, unimportant to the movie. After raising the blade a few feet higher, Brian shoved the bulldozer into gear again and the huge machine cut effortlessly through the walkway roof supports and into the bank itself, buckling its fake stone corner and shattering the front window, which had been lettered in gold leaf: the First National Bank of Black Pine.

With the bulldozer half on the walkway and half inside the "buildings," Brian continued down the street as walls and roofs, bars and counters, groceries and liquor bottles, cascaded all around him, even covering him in his cage for a short time, like a burrowing mole. Then he clanked into the open again, with the street a shambles behind him. Halfway to the log cabin, he stopped and looked back toward the gate. Seeing that Eve was still parked there, watching him, he gestured angrily for her to leave. And finally she did so, backing the pickup all the way into the road and starting forward, moving slowly, watching to see if he had begun on the log cabin yet. But he had not. And she suspected that he was waiting not only because he wanted her away from there, safe and free, but also because he wanted to be alone when he demolished this last shell, this Hollywood version of the place where he and Miss Colorado had briefly lived and loved. And used. And died.

When the phone rang, Charley Poole was lying awake in his king-size bed in the comfortable bedroom of his comfortable home in the comfortable Chicago suburb of Flossmoor. Earlier, at six, he had awakened briefly at the alarm, feeling Donna slip out of bed and head for the bathroom. Before he fell back to sleep she was already bounding along the treadmill in the alcove, keeping body and spirit hard for the labors ahead of her, always considerable on Sunday in the real estate business. And now she was back upstairs again in the master suite, as she called it, having already showered and dressed and breakfasted on coffee and cantaloupe. As he listened to her in the bathroom, putting the finishing touches on her face and hair, he reflected that he was probably in deeper trouble than he had thought, not even able to look forward with any enthusiasm to a round of golf at the club with Harry Duncan and Joe and Jack McAllister, three of his oldest friends.

First, it had been the family business, the real estate brokerage his grandfather and father had passed on to him and whose operation he gradually had turned over to Donna, for the excellent reason that she loved it and he did not. Then there was the hobby he had turned into a thriving enterprise of his own, buying certain problem homes cheap and creatively remodeling them for resale, usually quite profitably. But even that had begun to pall this past year. And now the last straw, not even wanting to get out of bed to play golf with best friends.

Looking at the matter objectively, he couldn't help wondering if he wasn't getting a bit too fussy for his own good. It seemed that if life didn't shape up pretty soon and get a helluva lot more exciting, old Charley Poole just might have to show it a thing or two. Why, he might even have to pull the covers up higher and burrow into the pillow a little deeper. For a real go-getter, there was always a way.

It was as he was thinking this, trying hard to kid himself out of the funk he was in, that the phone began to ring. In the bathroom, Donna gave her first order of the day.

"Charley, would you get that, please."

He did so clumsily, almost pulling the cradle off the nightstand before he was able to growl hello. The voice he heard, however, brought him sharply awake. It was a woman's voice, husky and smooth, a performer's voice.

"I'm calling for Charles Poole," she said.

"This is Charley Poole."

"My name is Eve Sherman. I'm a friend of your brother's. I hate to bother you so early, but I'm afraid he's gone off the deep end. He's in jail here in Colorado Springs."

"Colorado, uh?" Charley didn't know what to say. His brother had been in jail before.

"Yes. You see, Hollywood's making this movie, *Miss Colorado*, about Kim Sanders' life. As you may know, Brian was living with her when she died—when she overdosed—in her country place north of here. Anyway, Brian doesn't want the movie made. So last night he bulldozed the outdoor set where they were going to shoot the exteriors, starting tomorrow."

"That was smart."

"I know. I feel the same way. But the point is, whatever they set his bail at—we don't have it. His Venice condo is mortgaged to the hilt."

"That's hard to believe."

The woman ignored that. "But just as important as the bail, Charley, I think he could use your influence right now. I really do. You're the one person he looks up to."

Charley smiled slightly. "Is that a fact."

"No, I mean it," she said. "Maybe not the businessman–family man part, but what you *are*. Your character. Brian always said that you got all the brains and character while all he got was the curly hair."

"Among other things."

"Well, that's what he says, anyway."

"Just so I get this straight, you are—what?" Charley asked. "An old friend? A new friend? His fiancee—what?"

"I've been living with him for three years now. Why? Is that important?"

"I suppose not. Just curious. And another thing I'm curious about—why didn't he call me? Why you?"

"The bail money. He just couldn't ask you himself."

"I don't see why not. But let's move on. What's he charged with? What's the specific charge?"

"Felony destruction of private property and first-degree assault."

*"Assault?"*

"Yes. He handcuffed a security guard while he did the bull-dozing. Then he let him go and stayed there while the man called the police."

"Well, that's a plus anyway. And just how much damage would you say he did, dollarwise?"

"I'm not sure. The set probably cost three or four hundred thousand to build. But the big item will be lost production time, keeping the crews here while they rebuild the set or sending them all home and bringing them back later. That kind of thing."

"Which means bail will be substantial."

"I suppose so. But Brian wanted me to make it clear that he isn't asking you for a gift or loan—he just wants to sell his interest in your company. That's the only way he'd let me call you."

Charley didn't know what to say to that. When his parents died in a car crash nine years before, he and Brian had each inherited half of the estate. And Brian had promptly sold out to Charley for four hundred thousand dollars, payable over ten years at 8 percent interest. Which meant there was only forty thousand and change left to pay on the contract. So Charley couldn't help wondering where the rest had gone. As far as he knew, Brian had worked fairly steadily in Hollywood, in recent years as a production assistant of some kind, before that as a stuntman or stand-in, not to mention his stint as "personal manager" to a superstar.

"That sounds like him," Charley said, not without irony.

Which Eve Sherman missed. "He's a proud man. And with good reason, I think."

It had been three years since Charley had seen his brother, and while he was not inclined to accept the woman's assessment of him, neither could he accept the idea of Brian behind bars. Even now, after all their years apart, he felt yoked to him in a way he was to no one else, not even his wife. The bonds of childhood were simply like no others.

Then too there was the matter of the funk Charley was in, his own little midlife crisis or whatever the hell it was. Flying out to Colorado would mean getting out of the round of golf and the vodka tonics afterwards, followed by a spate of yardwork at home and maybe a nap, then Willis Tate's retirement party at the club, all the pleasant little tortures of the good life.

"All right, I'll fly out as soon as I can," he said now, picking up a pad and pencil. "Tell me where you're staying."

By then, Donna had come back into the bedroom, looking every inch the take-no-prisoners lady executive, from her carefully mussed blond coiffure down to her Ferragammo shoes. Though he knew she was in a hurry to leave, she stood waiting by the bed until he had hung up.

"Colorado?" she said. "What's all this? You're going to Colorado?"

"Brian," he explained. "He's in jail for bulldozing a movie set.

That was his current lady friend. She says he needs bail money, not to mention my sterling presence."

"Well, you're not going, are you? My God, Charley, we send him almost fifty thousand a year."

"I'll just make the final payment, that's all."

"But it's not due for six months yet."

"So I'll deduct six months' interest. It's no big deal." Getting out of bed, Charley put his hands on his wife's padded shoulders. "The kid's in jail," he said. "I can't know that and just go on out and play golf, as if everything was okay."

"He's not a kid. He's forty-one years old, for Christ's sake."

"And in jail."

"You could send the money from here."

"Yeah, but I'm not going to. I'm flying out there today."

"And what about Willis Tate's party tonight? I want that listing, Charley, and he's your buddy a lot more than mine—old Floss-moor family and all that bullshit."

"My dad's buddy, Donna. Not mine."

"That dump of theirs will go for a good seven hundred."

"Probably. But don't worry—you'll get the listing, as you always do. If you can't charm the old bastard, browbeat him. It usually works, doesn't it?"

He had gone too far. She was looking at him with pure hatred. "Go to hell," she said.

He smiled sadly. "I'm sorry, Donna. That was just jealousy talk-ing. I've always envied you, what a closer you are."

"Sure, you have." She was not an easy sell. "All right, then—you go on to Colorado and help your little brother. He's been a screwup all his life, but don't let that discourage you."

"I won't."

"Meanwhile, I'll try to hold down the fort."

Ignoring the sarcasm, Charley kissed her lightly on the cheek, knowing her makeup would still be slightly sticky. She did not return the kiss. At the doorway, she looked back at him. "You'll call tonight?"

"Sure. And have a good day—Brian might need the money."

"I'll keep that in mind," she said.

The only nonstop flight Charley could get a seat on did not arrive in Colorado Springs until a few minutes after eight in the evening. Though the flight took almost three hours, Charley was so lost in thought he later would have almost no memory of it. All those miles across all those endless plains, he squinted out his little window at the still-dazzling sky and thought about his brother and their life together, what different paths they had taken, what totally different men they seemed to have become. And the irony of it was that for the first twelve years or so people were always getting them mixed up, saying they looked so much alike, an assessment neither of them ever agreed with. The truth, Charley figured, was simply that people got their names mixed, not sure which of them was Charley and which was Brian.

The older by nineteen months, Charley was also taller, thinner, and if not smarter, certainly a much better student. Brian, on the other hand, was a much better mischief maker, in fact was pretty much a world-class pain in the ass from infancy on. There just never seemed to be a temptation he could resist, whether it was the playing of an innocent trick on a classmate or creating general havoc at home. And when he was caught, which was most of the time, he would simply fall back on his good looks and warm smile to disarm his victim as well as his guardian at the moment, whether parent or teacher.

By the time he was in high school, though, he put away such childish things and became more seriously delinquent. He never studied, wouldn't listen to his parents or teachers, and was a constant truant. He drank excessively, smoked marijuana, and became so dedicated to making out that any girl seen with him was assumed to be a slut, when in reality she was probably only in love with him. At the same time, he never quite lost his love of mischief. Leader of the beetle patrol, as he called it, he and two of his friends took upon themselves the task of upending Volkswagen beetles, which were a great favorite of the underpaid teachers of the time. While his cohorts would stand on either side of him, pressing against the roofline of the car, he would take hold underneath the door, and the three would begin to rock the homely little vehicle so violently that finally all it took was a word from Brian—and a sudden surge by all three boys—and one more beetle would tumble helplessly onto its back.

The three were reputed to have struck the spotless yellow VW of Miss Mellinger, head of the English department, on three separate occasions, an overzealousness that resulted in their expulsion from school for two days. It was a punishment that Brian endured in style, however, cruising the school grounds with his friends in someone's bright red Chrysler convertible, drinking beer and smoking cigarettes and waving to the kids inside, as if he were a hero instead of a miscreant.

Nor was the beetle patrol Brian's only achievement in high school. Looking out the jet's window, Charley couldn't help grinning at the memory of his brother pretending to try out for the track team when he was a sophomore, chugging toward the finish line in the mile run with a lit stogie clamped between his teeth and a trail of blue smoke drifting out behind him. Even the coach, old "Second Wind" Sarff, had joined in the laughter that afternoon. And oddly, Sarff was not an exception. Despite the fact that Brian was known to be a problem student and general troublemaker, he always seemed to be well liked by the faculty, probably because his attitude was never surly or hostile. And then there was that winning smile.

Even that couldn't help him in college, however. Enrolled as a probational student at Illinois State, he found all his courses to be remedial: bonehead math, bonehead English, bonehead science. Terminally bored, he dropped out within a month and enlisted in the marines just as Richard Nixon was being drummed out of office. A year and a half later he came home on crutches, with the back of his right leg a quilt of shrapnel scars that he belittled as spent-metal wounds, barely deep enough to bleed. They were enough, however, to return him to civilian life, staying at home in Flossmoor for all of two months, until he had no more need of crutches. Then he was off again, taking odd jobs here and there—including lumberjack and stevedore, according to his postcards—before he found something more to his liking: the tail end of the counterculture movement, a ragtag army of diehard hippies and acidheads trooping up and down the West Coast, living on handouts, drugs, and sex. Through the rest of the seventies, Charley would receive occasional battered letters from him—from Vancouver and Mazatlan and places in between—usually asking for money, sometimes containing snapshots of him and his friends, beaded, bearded, barefoot, all grinning like idiots.

In time, though, Brian settled down in Hollywood, "doing a little of this and a little of that," as he said during one of his rare visits home to their parents' place at Thanksgiving, with Charley and Donna and their little boy Jason there too. Brian had brought a very sexy blonde along with him, a movie starlet so quiet he referred to her as Harpo. Though the girl was obviously in love with him, that was the last they ever heard of her. Then, on a Christmas afternoon six or seven years ago, Brian phoned Charley from Nashville, where he said he was staying with a friend who wanted to say hello. The friend turned out to be the country singing star, Kim Sanders, and she had much more to say than hello.

"I just wanted to tell ya, Charley, I'm sorta in love with your badass brother and one of these days we gonna go and git ourselves hitched, we are. I just love the mean old sumbitch, I really do, and I wanna tell ya I never been happier." She had laughed then, with the lilting huskiness that probably had much to do with her success as a country music singer. "And just between you, me, and the fencepost, Charley, I gotta admit right now I'm higher than a turkey vulture. Merry Christmas, y'all!"

Brian reclaimed the phone and confirmed what the singer had said, that he was traveling with her on the road and that they would be getting married "one of these days." He said that he was her "semimanager" now and that if he wasn't careful, he might have to learn one or two things about the music business.

"She thinks she's pretty hot stuff, Charley," he said. "But I can lick her. Most of the time, I can lick her."

In the background Charley heard the superstar's whoop of laughter. And in the years that followed, Charley would occasionally come across a newspaper or magazine item about the singer, sometimes about a performance or new song but more often about a narcotics arrest or some nightclub brouhaha. And in the accompanying photographs, Brian was usually there, standing behind her or off to the side.

Then, just four years ago, TV and radio flashed the news that Kim Sanders had died of a drug overdose—while her companion, Brian Poole, dozed beside her.

Thinking of that unhappy night and the rest of Brian's life, Charley could only shake his head at how greatly it contrasted with his own. All those years, Charley had pretty much just sailed along. A good student and fair athlete in high school, he made the National Honor Society and lettered in basketball and track, running a fairly respectable half mile. In his senior year he was even voted prom king, an honor bestowed on him, he figured, because he was then dating the prettiest, most popular girl in class, herself the inevitable prom queen. At the University of Illinois, he majored in English Lit and minored in world history, both against the wishes of his father, who wanted him to study business administration. And like the nation's current president, he hated the war, demonstrated vigorously against it, and did his best to dodge the draft. He also smoked pot, though more daringly, actually inhaling the stuff. And he did his share of womanizing too, until a girl named Donna Sunderson showed him the deeper joys of monogamy, including almost endless sex. To lessen his chances of being drafted, they married in their senior year—only months before Brian was wounded and shipped home. And twelve months later they had their first and only child, little Jason.

Through his twenties, Charley worked for his father, selling houses in the posh Flossmoor and Olympia Fields areas. But the real content of his life then, other than his love of Donna and the baby, was the game of tennis. He became so consumed by it that he played every day at the club, often for three and four hours, with the result that by age twenty-four he was one of the best amateurs in the Chicago area. He even briefly entertained the notion of turning pro, until Jimmy Connors came to town one week, visiting friends, and needed local players to practice against. Even though Connors' serve was supposed to be the weakest part of his game, Charley found it almost impossible to return. Sadly, he accepted the conventional wisdom that he had come to the game a decade too late in life. That, however, turned out to be only a minor disappointment.

Two months later, when he was thirty-one, he suffered the

only real blow in his life, when his mother and father were killed in a car-truck accident on the Dan Ryan Expressway. The hole that left in him, in his life and in his heart, had never really filled in, but like most people he simply carried on, running the business as best he could and trying to be a good husband and father and friend. And in time, as Donna proved so much better at selling real estate than he was, he gradually turned the company's operations over to her and concentrated more on his hobby, buying select old houses and, after redesigning them, rebuilding them with his crew of semiretired carpenters and masons, artisans all, old-timers who could make, among other things, flawless brick arches and curving balustrades.

The area was full of thirty-thousand-dollar houses sitting on two-hundred-thousand-dollar lots. So the opportunities were there. And the profits. And for years he had enjoyed the work, the feeling of actual, tangible accomplishment, not just the making of money. Lately, though, even that had begun to pall for him, just like Saturday morning golf with his old buddies. Instead, he seemed to want to stay in bed mornings, or go for long, solitary walks, or watch some crummy late show on TV, just him and a bottle of Absolut or Scotch.

He accepted it that the root of the problem was his marriage, that he and Donna simply didn't connect anymore, that day by day they seemed to be turning into perfect strangers. But he preferred not to think about it, since it seemed insoluble, a fact of life as immutable as aging.

In any case, here he was, easygoing if not overly happy Charley Poole, sailor of smooth seas and walker of the worn path, on his way to rescue his little brother, who seemingly had been everywhere and done everything, almost none of it safe and sane. About all Charley could do was smile sadly at the prospect. Fortunately or unfortunately, he had a strong sense of the ridiculous.

**W**hile she was still on the phone, Eve Sherman had offered to pick Charley up at the airport, but he had told her that wouldn't be necessary, knowing that even if he stayed only a few days, he would want his own transportation. So he rented a Ford Thunderbird at the airport and headed north. He had been in Colorado Springs twice before, the first time to attend a realtor's convention at the Broadmoor Hotel and the second time on vacation with Donna, so he had some knowledge of the city, which sat at the foot of Pike's Peak at an altitude a good thousand feet higher than Denver.

To the west was the great wall of the front range, to the east a flat wasteland so desiccated all it seemed capable of growing was tumbleweed and housing, mile after mile of crackerbox condos and apartment buildings so drearily the same that Charley elected to take the freeway to Brian's motel rather than the shorter beltway, Academy Boulevard, which cut through the heart of the wasteland. Normally Charley was not that sensitive about his environment, but in the last few years, as he redesigned more and more homes, he had come to loathe boxy architecture, even to the point of considering it responsible for much of the country's social ills. Boxes, he believed, were for dead bodies.

So he was not overjoyed to find that Brian's motel, the Goodland, was itself a box, an oblong two stories with patios and balconies on the side facing the mountains, and a swimming pool, parking lot, and entrances on the other side. It was located just off the interstate, almost as far north as the Air Force Academy, which made Charley wonder why Brian had chosen it, a place so far out of town. Then it occurred to him that the motel was probably one of the closest to Black Forest, where the movie set had been built.

After parking, Charley had just gotten his luggage out of the back seat of the car and was closing the door when he saw the woman up on the second floor, standing at the walkway railing, looking down at him. She was a striking brunette, slim in jeans and a green jersey turtleneck. He was about to look away from her, reluctantly, when she smiled slightly and lifted her hand in a tentative wave. He smiled back at her, then spoke as he drew closer to the building.

"Eve?"

She nodded. "I'm so glad you came, Charley."

He gestured toward the office. "I've got to check in."

"I'll come down." She was already moving along the walkway, toward the stairs.

He waited for her there, outside, still holding his luggage, a suede suit bag and an overnighter. But as she came into view, smiling more warmly now, he almost dropped the bags in his confusion as to whether he should kiss her in greeting or just shake her hand. Fortunately, she solved the problem, taking his hand and turning her cheek up to him, for either a kiss or an air buss, as he called them. He chose the kiss.

"Did you have a good flight?" she asked.

"Yes. Uneventful."

"I've reserved your room," she said. "Just two doors down from us."

"Good."

After he had checked in, she led the way, carrying the overnight bag, graciously insisting on it. In his room, she opened the drapes and the sliding glass door, letting in fresh air and the last of the sunset, a mosaic of reds and purples burning above the ridge of the mountains.

"Great view," he said.

She smiled. "Yes—great view, lousy everything else. I hope your heater works better than ours."

"That's right. It gets pretty cold here at night, doesn't it?"

"*Very* cold. Even in June."

Having hung up his suit bag, he went out onto the balcony. "Before it gets dark, I've got to see more of this."

She followed him out. "Yes, it's really breathtaking, if you over-look the foreground."

"Oh, I don't know," he said. "At night, even a freeway can look okay."

"Brian said you're an optimist."

"You sure he didn't say a Pollyanna?"

"I'm sure."

Beyond the freeway, up in the foothills, it was still light enough so Charley could make out the Garden of the Gods, as it was called, steepled rock formations that looked at that hour, and at that distance, like a village of monstrous teepees, a home of the gods. Next to him, Eve was lighting a cigarette.

"How's he doing?" he asked.

"I'm not sure. All I did was talk on the phone with him this af-ternoon. We can't see him until the arraignment tomorrow at ten." She shook her head in amazement. "Did you know it was on the network news tonight? The bulldozing? CBS, with Bob Shieffer."

"You're kidding."

"No, I'm not. But Brian wasn't the real news—he was just the crackpot, the villain. The big story's the movie—the filming being interrupted. And of course 'Miss Colorado,' how even in death she's vulnerable to this particular crackpot."

Charley shook his head. "Brian must've loved that."

"I don't know if he even saw it. Unless his lawyer told him."

"Who'd he get? Someone good, I hope."

"A public defender, that's all. Brian says the more expensive the lawyer, the higher his bail will be."

Though he knew that was nonsense, Charley didn't quite say so. "I'm not sure he's right about that. Maybe we can get him someone else in the morning. Some old courthouse hand, a crony of the judge. Maybe that's the way to go."

Eve smiled ruefully. "I don't know. Brian says the case is open and shut. He did it. He waited right there to be arrested. There's no question of his guilt."

"He's not going to plead guilty, is he?"

"No, he says he wants his day in court. He wants everyone to know *why* he did it."

"Well, that's something anyway. If he pleads guilty, he goes straight to prison."

"Yes, he knows that." Eve's eyes suddenly filled. Then she shook her head, as if to wake herself up, snap herself out of her unhappiness. "Listen, you must be starved," she said. "There's a nice little place across from the parking lot. We could walk there."

"Well, I am a little hungry," Charley admitted. "For that matter, I could probably use a martini."

"Fine. Why don't you get settled in here, then just come by. We're two-oh-three, two doors down."

After she was gone, Charley unpacked a few things and washed up, but he stayed in the clothes he had on, an old herringbone jacket, gray slacks, and an open blue shirt. Idly he found himself speculating as to whether Eve would go as she was or would change into something different: say, a light, short dress. He couldn't help wondering if her legs were as beautiful as the rest of her.

The restaurant was a cozy place with wagon wheels at the entrance, Remington prints on the walls, and tiny wood tables lit with candles burning in red glass jars. Charley ordered a steak sandwich that proved to be both generous and tasty. Even better, the bartender was not stingy with the Swedish vodka, which was what Charley called a martini: straight Absolut on ice, with an olive. He had two of them before the food came and a Bailey's coffee afterwards, while Eve made do with a single Scotch and water.

Like him, she had not changed clothes, and he wondered on the walk over to the cafe why he had cared, since her stonewashed jeans amply displayed the excellence of her legs. More to the point, he was embarrassed that such a stupid speculation would even cross his mind, on this particular evening, in the company of his brother's girlfriend while the brother himself was in jail. But then Charley was never greatly surprised at his capacity for sexual woolgathering. He often thought that on his deathbed, all wired up and gurgling, he would still somehow find the strength to observe and compare the nurses' buttocks. In this instance, however, he judged he wasn't entirely at fault, since Eve was in no way just another good-looking woman. He ran across good-looking women all the time. In fact, Charley's own Donna was one of them. But Eve was different. She was one of those rare *perfect* physical creatures, like a leopard or eagle, with everything just the way it should have been, from any angle. He imagined that wherever she went, she turned heads and stopped conversations, set men fantasizing about sex and women about murder.

Even now, as she finished telling him about the bulldozing and went on to other things, Charley caught himself paying as much attention to her eyes and mouth as to her words. Still, he learned that Eve was indeed an actress, a failed one. Jewish on her father's side, Irish on her mother's, she had been raised in comfort in Santa Barbara, where her father was a prosperous tax attorney. After studying theater arts at UCLA for a couple of years, she married a lawyer colleague of her father's, divorced him a year later, and seriously set about becoming an actress. Getting nowhere in New York and London, she returned to Los Angeles, got a new agent, and landed a few parts in various cable TV movies.

"And other real dreck," she said. "Bikini and beach stuff. Even a cavewoman epic. My fanny's been on screen more than my face."

"That's a shame," Charley said, adding, "I think."

Eve gave him a wry look. "Well, it was. At least for my so-called career, it was."

"Well, I suppose you have to do movies like that in the beginning."

"Maybe so. But I just couldn't hack it—the cattle calls and the humiliation. In the end, I wound up pretty much like Brian. Maybe the business didn't want me, but the stars did."

Charley made no response to that, waiting for Eve to elaborate. But she apparently preferred to leave the matter as it was, which made him wonder why she had brought it up in the first place. There were many things Charley wanted to ask about Brian, particularly his long-standing problem with drugs, as well as the state of his finances, considering that his bail was likely to be substantial. But Charley didn't want Eve to feel that he was pumping her, so he sat back and let her continue to take the conversation where she would. As he expected, she never strayed far from Brian. Regarding his use of drugs, Eve claimed that he no longer used them at all except for alcohol and tobacco. And even with these, she said he tried to minimize their harmful effects by strenuously working out. In Venice he ran the beach and swam in the ocean; here he swam in the motel pool for thirty and forty minutes at a time.

He was in great physical shape, she said. Unfortunately she could not say the same about his attitude, his outlook on life.

"More and more, he just seems to do things with no thought to their consequences. And I guess the making of *Miss Colorado* was simply the last straw. I mean, here's his onetime lover, this has-been star and longtime drug addict, and they're going to portray her as a helpless victim in the clutches of a cruel, drug-pushing boyfriend."

"Which was not the case," Charley said, unsure what the truth was.

"Definitely not. My God, when Brian first met the lady, she was doing heroin as well as coke and just about everything else. She'd been a hype for years, and everyone knew it. At least Brian got her off heroin for a while. Yet the script has him the big villain, like Ike and Tina Turner, for God's sake."

"Can't he get an injunction? Can't he sue?"

"No, they're not using his name. And anyway, it's just a movie, they say. Just entertainment, not history."

"Except to the young and the unread, which means practically everybody."

"That's for sure."

"How is he with you? I mean, has he changed there too?"

Eve shrugged. "I guess—to a certain extent anyway. He's quieter and scarier, and I'm unhappier. His attitude says it's time for deeds now, not words. And he seems—I don't know—almost relieved about it all, as if he's finally found his way, finally knows what his life is about."

"That doesn't sound too good."

"No, it doesn't."

"So what's he going to do—keep trying to shut the movie down?"

"He says not. But I don't know." Eve's eyes, filling again, looked faceted in the candlelight, like a pair of emeralds. "I don't know what he's going to do. I'm not even sure I know him anymore."

Charley smiled sadly. "I remember the feeling."

Walking back to the motel with Eve, it bothered him that he could not see Brian's bulldozing of the movie set as she did, as a noble, hopeless blow struck against the forces of darkness, all the Hollywood scum more interested in ticket sales than in the truth. But then Charley knew he was operating under a handicap, having grown up with Brian and having learned the hard way that his brother's grand gestures of rebellion were usually more grandstanding than anything else. Charley couldn't help thinking that if Brian felt anything as he bulldozed the movie set, it was probably pure animal pleasure, the joy of destroying so much so easily. Worse, Charley would have bet that if the movie studio suddenly offered Brian a job—say, as executive producer on the film—he would have pocketed the money in an instant and eagerly pitched in, whoring up the movie right along with the best of them.

Charley said none of this to Eve, however. He wanted her to think well of him, and he judged that such a cold dose of fraternal cynicism would not have been to her liking.

# chapter two

It was already close to noon. The charges had been read, Brian had pled not guilty, bail had been set at forty thousand dollars. And Eve was still waiting, sitting on a bench now outside the county clerk's office. Like the old stone building it was in, the office was from another time, its interior walls gleaming cherry wood with large glass windows that rattled every time a truck climbed the hill outside. Through the glass, Eve watched as the men inside struggled through the red tape holding up Brian's release. She could have joined them. Charley had even held the door for her, but she had declined. The clerk, a chubby mess of a man, was a cigar smoker, and his office smelled like it. Even though she herself smoked cigarettes and knew that she probably reeked to nonsmokers like Charley, she still could not abide the odor of cigar smoke. Enough of it and she would surely have gagged.

Of the six men, two seemed to be mere spectators: the burly Chicano deputy and the public defender, who looked as if he'd been selling vacuum cleaners for the last thirty years. The others—Brian, Charley, the bail bondsman, and the clerk—were sitting at a table, signing and shuffling papers. Of these, the bail bondsman looked the happiest, smiling almost constantly under a pencil-line mustache. With his greased-down black hair and bright blue suit, he looked as if he were auditioning for the role of slimy bail bondsman.

In time the clerk got up and went over to his desk and the others followed, standing around while he stamped and stapled. And Eve could not help comparing the brothers as they waited, Brian standing with his arms folded, looking superior and aggressive while Charley seemed almost to hover over the group, slightly bent and head cocked, like some kind of latter-day Cooper or Stewart, his very stance a gesture of kindliness and accomodation to a shorter world. Though Brian as usual was the best-looking man in the room, Eve had to admit that Charley cut quite a figure too in his single-breasted beige suit—an Armani, she would have bet—set off with a blue button-down and a wheat-colored silk tie. As Brian often said, his brother obviously wasn't hurting for money.

Finally Brian came out into the corridor, followed by the deputy and the public defender, who went different ways, the PD toward the front entrance, the deputy in the other direction. But Brian stopped him.

"Hey, chief!" he said. "Listen, I want you to thank the sheriff for me. I've really enjoyed my little stay here, especially those unforgettable nine hours I spent in the pigpen with all your relatives."

The deputy glared at him. "Better watch it, asshole, or you goin' right back in."

"Hey, I meant it as a compliment, chief. I was referring to the noble descendants of Cortez and Quetzalcoatl. So what, they drink paint thinner and carve on each other's private parts? Nobody's perfect, right?"

The deputy dismissed Brian with a wave of his hand and went on up the hallway. Eve was not amused.

"Do you have to do that? Always baiting the people who can harm you the most?"

"It's called standing up to the enemy."

"He's not the enemy, for God's sake. He's just a cop."

"Right, the enemy," Brian said. "Listen, don't you want to hear how it went in there? We're in clover, baby. Charley made the last payment on the business—over forty-five grand."

"Didn't you have to use some of it?"

"No, and the sweetest part is I can cash it today. He'd already phoned his banker at home and they certified it by wire or something like that."

"Well, what about the bail?"

"Charley put the four down and signed a note on one of his houses—one he's rebuilding. Some complicated reason he had to buy it outright—I don't know. Anyway, he brought the deed with him, so it's all taken care of."

Eve wished she felt happier about the news. "We should all have a brother like Charley," she said.

But Brian didn't share her gratitude. "Come on, it's like I told you. Him and that barracuda wife of his stole me blind. I should've held out for twice what they paid me, and they know it."

"Twisted your arm, did they?"

Brian gave her a look. "Hey, who the hell's side you on anyway?"

"*Who's side?* You mean Charley's the enemy too? After what he's just done?"

Brian grimaced, as if her obtuseness caused him exquisite pain. "Drop it, okay?"

"Why not?"

"We might as well go face the fucking reporters," he said, starting down the corridor toward the front of the courthouse. "Otherwise they'll be chasing us all day."

Eve followed. "What about Charley?"

"He'll catch up."

On the broad stone steps outside, the media were gathered like a flock of vultures patiently waiting for some poor creature to breathe its last so the feast could begin. As usual, the TV crews were at the front, the cameramen sitting or squatting, for the moment letting the courthouse steps bear the weight of their equipment. At Brian's appearance, though, they scrambled to their feet, hoisting lights and cameras. And to Eve's surprise, Brian went straight over to them, smiling slightly, as if he were somewhat embarrassed, like a hometown hero arriving at the train station to bands and bunting. The reporters barked out their questions, then thrust their mikes at him like a phalanx of swordsmen.

"Why did you do it, Brian? What did you hope to accomplish?"

"Why did you plead innocent? You did it, didn't you?"

"Did you do it for Kim, Brian? Are you still in love with her? With the memory of her?"

Brian raised his hands if he were a candidate quelling the overenthusiasm of his troops. "Look, this is no big deal," he said. "I went out there—I don't know why—maybe just to see where they were going to shoot the movie, I don't know. And then I guess I went into some kind of weird fugue state, something like that. All I know is, I have no memory of the incident. It's all a blank in my mind."

The chorus erupted again:

"Are you serious?"

"Is that your defense, then, Brian?"

"Do you really expect people to believe that?"

At that point Charley had come out onto the portico too. Seeing him, Brian immediately began moving in his direction, pulling Eve along. When one of the cameramen got too close, practically striking them in the face with his camera, Brian shoved him away, then caught the man before he fell, even smiled benignly at him, still playing at the role of hometown hero.

"Hey—sorry about that," he said, turning then to Charley.

"Where's your car, man? Let's go!"

And the three of them did, running as fast as they could from the hungry flock behind them.

An hour later Charley and Eve were standing at the walkway railing at the motel, looking down at Brian in the pool, swimming tirelessly from one end of it to the other, with his face submerged except when he would draw a breath on every fourth stroke. At each end of the pool, he would flip under water and push off, like a competition swimmer.

"He in training for the Olympics?" Charley asked.

"Sometimes I think so." Eve lit a cigarette.

They were both hungry and wanted to go out for lunch, but Brian had insisted that he swim first.

"I've got to wash that shitty jail out of my soul," he'd said.

"You've got fifteen minutes," Eve had told him. "After that, we leave."

"So be it." In his trunks by then, he had hurried out the door, heading for the pool. Now, twenty minutes later, he was still going strong.

"Why don't we just leave without him?" Eve said.

"Oh, I think I can probably last another few minutes. Why don't you try to reach your friend Rick again?"

Rick Walters, an acquaintance of hers, was assistant to Damian Jolly, producer-director of the movie *Miss Colorado*. Charley had discussed with Eve some ideas he had about Brian's situation, things he might be able to do in return for Jolly's help in getting the charges dropped or at least reduced, and she was enthusiastic. Charley thought it would be a good idea if he and Brian could meet Jolly and talk things over.

Through other Hollywood friends, Eve had learned Rick's Colorado Springs phone number—Jolly's number actually—and had tried earlier to reach him, at the time not quite sure why. Now, having a reason, she had phoned twice in the last hour, not getting him either time, however.

"I guess once more can't hurt anything," she said, heading for her room.

"Good. Meanwhile I'll go down and see if I can drag Esther Williams out of the pool."

It took another hour, however, before the three of them were sitting at a restaurant table, waiting for their food over drinks, a beer for Brian and martinis for Eve and Charley. The restaurant, the Firebird by name, sat on a cliff above the interstate, which ran along the base of the foothills, roughly dividing the city from the mountains. Indian rugs and pottery and other artifacts crowded the wood-and-glass structure, whose windows offered spectacular views of the area, ranging from the sprawling city itself and the distant Air Force Academy to Pike's Peak and Cheyenne Mountain, in whose depths were the still-unpressed buttons of the Cold War, doomsday at a touch.

"So you got in touch with Jolly's loverboy," Brian said.

Eve sighed. "None of that, all right? If Rick's able to arrange a meet with Jolly, you put a lid on your precious homophobia, understand?"

Brian smiled ruefully at Charley. "It's so handy to live with your warden, you know? You never have to wonder what you can and can't do. They just tell you."

"Like with the bulldozing?" Charley said.

Which made it Eve's turn to smile. Sitting next to Brian in the booth, she gave him a playful shove. "What's this? No comeback? We're waiting, dear."

"Jesus, is this the way it's going to be? Two against one all the time? I'll get paranoid."

*"Get?"* Eve said.

Brian looked at her, then at Charley across the table. "Seriously, if Jolly gives us a meeting, what the hell good is that? What can I say? Can I make restitution? Not unless I win a lotto jackpot or something. Or do I just say I'm sorry as hell, and he lets me off the hook? Don't be stupid. The hairy little monkey is overjoyed at all this. He not only gets to bankrupt me and send me to prison, but he gets all this free publicity besides. He'll want to help me about the same time Pike's Peak out there turns into Old Round Top."

"Bad as all that?" Charley said.

"Yeah, every bit that bad."

Eve gave Charley a look, as if to say, Well, here goes. "Charley has some other ideas," she said. "A different approach."

"Like what?"

When they were kids, Charley often had found himself interceding on his little brother's behalf, sometimes winning him pardons that the stubborn little bastard refused to accept. Though Charley suspected that he was headed down that same garden path now, he went ahead anyway.

"Well, first there's the insurance," he said. "Jolly and the studio are probably totally covered for what you did, including downtime. So they've got no reason to press for restitution. What you said about the free publicity, I think that's the key. When the movie opens around the country, what if you were to start making all the talk shows, maybe even criticizing the movie from your angle, saying it wasn't true, wasn't the way things actually were. I don't think Jolly or the studio would care, as long as they were getting the publicity."

Having just lit a cigarette, Brian was blowing a cloud of smoke toward the ceiling. "Let's see if I've got this straight," he said. "You want me to enter into some sort of agreement with Jolly to promote his fucking movie about Kim Sanders and me—the same movie I just tried my damnedest to shut down. You don't see any hypocrisy in that?"

Eve blew. "Hypocrisy, my ass, Brian! We're looking for a way to keep you out of prison, that's all! Can't you get that through your thick skull?"

"Trouble is I do get it. You think I'm a total flake and what I did was bullshit."

"I didn't say that."

"No, but that's what you think. Unfortunately, I could care less. I did what I did because I believed it was right. And I still do. One way or another, I'm still gonna shut down that fucking movie. And I don't plan on going to prison either. Is that clear enough for you?" He raised a fist and tapped it against Eve's forehead. "Am I getting through?"

Saying nothing, she pushed his hand away.

"So you don't want us to even talk with Jolly?" Charley asked.

"I don't give a shit. You can talk to the little fag all you want. Just be sure you keep your buns tight and don't bend over. Now, Eve, she can wear a microskirt and walk on all fours, and no one will notice."

Eve sighed. "I've seen the future, and I don't think it works."

"Hey, it never did." Brian seemed pleased at the thought.

Their food was served and the three of them lapsed into an uncomfortable silence, dictated mostly by Brian's intransigence. Ever since Charley first saw him at the courthouse—the first time in three years—he had been trying to get a handle on him, understand just what was going on inside his little brother's handsome head. When he last saw him, after Kim Sanders' death, Brian had looked terrible, even emaciated, despite his muscular build, presumably because he was still a heavy drug user. Now, though, he was clear-eyed, tanned, and ten or fifteen pounds heavier, all of it hard. Like Charley, he had a few gray hairs, but they in no way diminished his look of youthful strength and health.

His mind-set, though, was a different matter. As in the past, he could be charming one moment and insufferable the next. In the courtroom and later in the clerk's office, he at various times had been angry, conciliatory, sarcastic, and pleasant. Later, riding home in Charley's car, he was rude to Eve and made no mention of Charley's largesse in giving him the buyout payment early and making his entire bail. On the way, he stopped off at the bank where the check had been cleared and went in alone, whether to cash the forty-five thousand or deposit it or buy certified checks with it, Charley had no idea. And he gathered that Eve didn't know either.

After that, Brian's only concern seemed to be getting back to the motel and into the pool as fast as he could. All else was unimportant. And now there was this stone wall he had thrown up in front of them, his refusal to let anyone even *try* to save his ass. It made Charley wonder why he had bothered to come out to Colorado in the first place. It would have been so much easier just to have wired the money. And that probably was what he would have done, had it not been Eve who phoned him. Even though he had never met her, her voice for some reason had reached him, pulled him. At the moment, though, she wasn't reaching anybody. Silent, she sat there looking irritable and unhappy.

Feeling vaguely dispirited, Charley gazed out over the large room at the tables arranged in three tiered rows leading up from the curving expanse of windows. The patrons for the most part appeared to be tourists, family groups more interested in the view than in the food, which Charley found reasonably good if unreasonably overpriced. Up on the second tier, he suddenly noticed a young blond woman staring straight at him. As their eyes met, she flashed an oddly eager smile and he smiled uneasily back at her, wondering if the object of her happiness was someone behind him. But at his response, she smiled even wider, lighting up the table where she sat with an older man, a hawk-faced wiry little guy wearing a string tie and a satin cowboy shirt. Immediately the girl got to her feet and pulled the man after her, jabbering encouragement as she led him down the two stairs to the first tier. And once she was in full view and coming toward him, Charley saw that her long hair and gleaming teeth were but a small part of her equipment, that she had in fact the kind of figure seldom seen outside the gatefolds of men's magazines. Like the man with her, she was wearing cowboy boots and jeans. Only in her case the denim appeared to have been lacquered on, as did her checkered shirt.

As she reached the table, Charley pushed back his chair, preparing to get up and introduce himself, when the girl's attention suddenly focused on Brian, who till now had been sitting with his back to her.

"Hey, you're Brian Poole, right?" she said, still beaming. "We saw you on TV just this noon, and yesterday we checked out the set you totaled, me and two other girls. Boy, was that ever somethin'. My name's Belinda Einhorn and this here's my big brother Chester. He's a real cowboy. Come here from Oklahoma just to check on his baby sister, din't ya, Chester?"

By then Brian had gotten to his feet. He shook hands with both of the Einhorns and introduced Eve and Charley. And though the girl smiled warmly, Charley doubted that she even saw them, such was her excitement at meeting the notorious Brian Poole in the flesh. Charley expected Brian to bring the encounter to a close then, even if it required a touch of coolness, but his brother did no such thing. Smiling back at the girl, he let her run on to her heart's content, explaining that she had been a snow bunny in Aspen for the winter and recently had landed a job as an extra in *Miss Colorado*. Her character was supposed to be having a drink with a boyfriend in the local saloon when "the actor who plays you causes a ruckus and gets booted out the door.

"Only there ain't no more saloon for you to get booted out of!" she went on, laughing. "Not since you showed up with that bulldozer of yours!"

Brian then quietly volunteered that he was going to be at the Purple Sage that evening. "And if y'all can make it," he said, "we'd be happy to see you."

*"Can we!"* the girl gushed. "Oh, you bet we can! Wild horses couldn't keep us away! Right, Chester?"

The brother all this time had been standing slightly behind her, rocking up and down on the pointed toes of his tiny boots and grinding his fist into his hand. In his seamed and sunken cheek a muscle tightened and relaxed, like a secondary heart.

"Oh sure," he said. "You bet. Belinda and me, we'd be proud."

When they were gone, Eve gave Brian a withering look. "If y'all can make it," she mimed. "Jesus, you are some piece of work, you know that?"

Brian grinned sheepishly. "I know. I'm so ashamed I could cry."

Out the window, Charley watched the odd couple get into a shiny red pickup and drive off. In the back window there was a rack of guns.

**B**ack at the motel, there was a message for Eve to call Rick Walters. Charley followed her and Brian into their room and listened while she phoned. She got Rick immediately, but for the most part just sat there listening to what he had to say. She wrote down directions to Jolly's place, then thanked Rick and said good-bye.

Hanging up, she gave Brian a challenging look. "Jolly has agreed to see us, like right now. So the ball's in your court. What's it going to be—prison or maybe eat a little crow?"

Brian shrugged. "What good would it do? I'm not going to kiss his ass, and he's not going to let me off the hook."

Eve looked at Charley for help, and he did what he could.

"Look, I've come a pretty long way to help you, right?" he said to Brian.

"I realize that."

"And your bail wasn't peanuts, you know."

"I never said it was."

"All right. So now I want you to do this for us. And for yourself."

"Charley, it won't do any good."

"I don't care. I want you to do it."

Even then, Charley wouldn't have been surprised if Brian still refused. Finally, though, he shrugged assent.

"All right, okay," he said. "I'll go with you—just so you two can find out what these people are like. You don't deal with Jolly, you just bend over and take your medicine."

"So we'll find that out."

"You sure as hell will."

They went in Brian's pickup truck, a late-model Chevy Silverado that rattled as if he had driven it off-road all the way from California. They turned off the freeway just south of the Air Force Academy and worked their way up into the foothills, past a middle-class housing development and back into gravel road country where there were a few withered pines as well as chaparral hugging the rocky terrain. The few houses in this area were costly and modern, built almost like pueblos into the steep grade. At the top was Jolly's place, a handsome structure of glass, moss rock, and redwood, with a broad wraparound deck overlooking half of Colorado as well as a patio and a small swimming pool under construction. To get to the house they had to fork left past a lane that led down to a narrow, pine-covered shelf.

"I understand they were out scouting locations when Jolly saw this place," Eve said. "Wasn't even for sale, but he still managed to buy it, I guess in case he ever happens to be in Colorado."

"The poor bastard." Brian pulled in and parked next to a Mercedes.

A uniformed security guard came out to meet them. "You Brian Poole?" he asked.

"In the flesh."

The man asked them to stay with the truck for a few minutes. "Mr. Walters said he'd be out to brief you soon."

Brian laughed. *"Brief!* What the hell is this, a military operation? The Air Academy gonna attack, are they?"

"I'm just telling you what I was told," the man said.

Eve smiled and said there was no problem, that they would be happy to wait for Mr. Walters.

As the guard went back into the house, Charley asked what Walters' job was.

"He's one of Jolly's angels," Brian said. "Or at least that's what the crew calls them. It seems Jolly has a long history of hiring pretty young fags as his personal assistants. New movie, new angel."

"Not true anymore," Eve corrected. "Rick's been his assistant for years. Last movie he got an assistant director credit. He's really a very nice guy."

"A really very nice person," Brian said. "You'll just love him, Charley."

They had gotten out of the truck by then, and Charley was surprised at how cold the air was here in the shadow of the mountains. Above them the few remaining clouds were turning red and golden, though the city itself, lying below and to the east, was still awash in sunlight. In the outskirts a treeless plain rose gradually toward the dark green area called Black Forest, where Brian had done his demolition work. Straight north of where they stood was the Air Force Academy, also deep in shadow except for the sawtooth spires of its famed chapel, which blazed in the gloom like a row of burning pines. Even as Charley stood looking out at the academy, a line of small aircraft came crawling in from the north and began to expel bodies one by one, tiny black missiles that hurtled earthward for three or four seconds before sprouting parachutes, gaudy flowers that floated down into the mountains' shadow and finally onto the blue-gray ground.

Directly in front of them a hillside of huge sandstone boulders dropped toward the piney shelf they had seen from the road. Brian picked up a stone and hurled it down into the trees.

"Sure is nice up here," he said. "I guess it pays pretty good, slandering people, turning their lives into shit."

At that point, two men came out of the house carrying large flat leather cases and got into the Mercedes. They were wearing blue pin-striped suits and garish Hawaiian ties. As they drove off, a handsome young blond man came out onto the deck and signaled to Eve.

"He can see you now," he said. "Just you and the brother, that's all."

Eve looked over at Brian, and he shrugged with annoyance.

"Go ahead," he told her. "What difference does it make?"

"You'll be all right here?"

"Of course I'll be all right. Jesus Christ."

On their way over to the house, Eve leaned close to Charley. "Let's just forget what he said at the restaurant. Keeping him out of prison, that's what matters. So let's not hold back with Jolly."

As they started up the outside stairway, the security guard came out of the house again and took a position at the foot of the stairs, evidently to make sure that Brian didn't follow them. Waiting on the deck, Rick smiled warmly as Eve introduced him and Charley.

"God, it's cold out here!" he said, shivering. "The sun goes down and you just freeze your buns off."

He led them around the corner and through a sliding glass door into a huge room with floor-to-ceiling windows running across the entire front wall. At one end of the room, a gaunt, nut-brown man in his fifties sat at a large table dictating to a stenographer, an elderly blonde with the drum-tight, mummified kind of face created by plastic surgeons.

When he broke off, Jolly looked up at his visitors over a pair of rimless glasses. Dark, close-set eyes and a large nose and mouth gave him a sagacious, vulpine look, somewhat undone by what Brian called his slave-boy wig, but which in point of fact looked more like the mop of a cinematic mad scientist. He was wearing sandals, threadbare denim shorts, and a safari shirt hanging half open, exposing his hairy chest.

"Damian, this is Eve Sherman and Charles Poole," Rick said. "Damian Jolly, Elizabeth English, Brad Huntley."

Until that moment Charley hadn't notice the other young man sitting off to the side in a wingback chair, legs curled under him as he stroked a Siamese cat that didn't purr. Apparently another of Jolly's angels, the youth looked more like a shaven Mephistopheles, dark and mean, with a masterly sneer.

Jolly nodded but failed to say hello or that he was pleased to meet anyone. He did gesture for Eve and Charley to sit down, however, and they did so, in two of four chairs arrayed in front of the director's table-desk. Jolly took his time getting out a cigarette and lighting it with a kitchen match, which he then extinguished by waving it languidly back and forth. Through the smoke, he regarded his visitors.

"Let me see if I have this straight," he said. "You two are Brian Poole's brother and girlfriend, and you're here to see if you can get me to drop the charges against him. I'm told you have some sort of offer to make in this regard."

Charley looked at Eve, expecting her to present their ideas since she was the one who knew Rick and had contacted him. But she indicated for Charley to go ahead.

"Yes, that's right," he said. "First, though, I want to tell you that Brian is genuinely sorry for what he's done. He himself thinks of it now as a kind of prolonged temporary insanity, if there could be such a thing."

Jolly grinned. "Must be something new, uh?"

"Something going around," said the one called Brad, and Miss English tittered.

"I realize it's a contradiction," Charley went on. "An oxymoron. But it just could be right in this instance. Eve tells me that Brian hasn't been himself for some time."

"What is it you do?" Jolly asked.

"I'm a real estate broker in Chicago. The south suburbs actually."

"Come out here to save your brother's ass, did you?"

"If I can."

"Well, family ties are a good thing. I'm a strong believer in family."

"That's good to hear." Charley figured he could be as inane as the next man.

"Poole," Jolly said. "What is that, English?"

"Or Scottish."

The director grinned. "So's Jolly—English, I mean. Only thing is I ain't got one drop of limey blood. Hundred percent dago, did you know that?"

"No, I didn't."

"Well, now you do. Real name is Giolli, G-I-O-L-L-I. But my old man changed it out of shame because the family was all mobbed up, part of the Gambinos in New York. It's true, I ain't shittin' you. Most of my cousins and uncles are wiseguys, would you believe it? Always wanting to help me out too. 'Just say the word, Dominic,' that's what they call me. Yeah, sure—I say the word and someone gets smoked, I'd probably wind up in the joint right along with my goombah relatives. Good cooks, though. They got cholesterol counts you would not believe."

In response to this trove of information, Charley forced a smile, wondering whether the director was trying to threaten Brian. "Now that you mention it, you do look Italian," he said.

Jolly laughed. "No shit! You bet I do. Another dago director—just what Hollywood needed, right?"

"Afraid I don't know Hollywood."

"No, of course not. Why should you?" Jolly stubbed out his cigarette. "So let's get down to it. Just what are you offering?"

"Well, first, as I said, Brian regrets what he did. And he's prepared to make a public statement to that effect, an apology both to you and the studio."

"I hope that ain't all."

"It isn't. The main part is, well, Brian still feels that the movie—or at least the script he's read—doesn't really tell *his* story, his side of things. So our idea was that when the movie comes out, and if he still feels this way, he could make the rounds of the talk shows and discuss the movie from his perspective."

Jolly grinned again. "Are you serious?"

"Absolutely. As I understand it, when a movie opens, *any* publicity is good to have. Even controversy."

"Well, there's controversy, and then there's controversy, right? The wrong kind ain't gonna help anybody."

"He'd be talking about the movie."

Jolly looked at Rick. "What do you think? He goes around bad-mouthing the movie—you think it'd hurt us or help us?"

"It's a hard call," Rick said. "I don't know."

Jolly's other angel had no such qualms.

"Damian, the man's a psycho. He could make a public apology one day and shoot you the next. I wouldn't trust him. He belongs in a cage."

The director clucked his tongue. "Now, we don't want to be too harsh, Brad. At the same time, you do have a point." He turned back to Charley and Eve. "What was it you called it—a case of *prolonged* temporary insanity? Well, who's to say it won't continue to be prolonged? What if, when your brother finally sees the movie, he goes berserk again and starts bulldozing theaters or Christ knows what else? What do we do then?"

This time it was Eve who answered, saying that she was with Brian almost constantly and that she would guarantee he would not cause any more trouble. "He's himself again," she said. "He really is. He knows he's made a total ass of himself and that he'll have to pay a price for it. A price he'll never want to pay again."

"That makes sense," Jolly conceded. "To me anyway, and apparently to you. But then we don't go around bulldczing other people's property, do we? No, I think the only answer is to have the man himself in here, so we can judge for ourselves, see with our own eyes whether Mr. Brian Poole can be trusted to behave like a human being."

Rick apparently had known all along that Brian was to be invited in, for he was already at the door. As he went out on the deck and called down to Brian, Jolly lit another cigarette, with the same ritual as before. Eve lit up too, while Miss English sat stiffly in her chair, doodling along the edge of her steno pad. Angel Brad dumped the cat onto the floor and stood up, fondly regarding his muscular arms and flat gut. Charley absently looked about the room, a living room in normal times, but crowded now with the stuff of commerce: boxes of advertising and posters and leaning bulletin boards full of lists and drawings, one portraying the block of ersatz buildings Brian had leveled. As Charley thought about how much its rebuilding would cost, Rick came back into the room, followed by Brian and the security guard. Charley was relieved to see that Brian appeared cool and relaxed instead of combative.

The security guard moved on around Jolly's desk to take up a position facing Brian, and Charley was amazed to see the man unbutton the flap on his holster. It was so negligible a detail that Charley almost missed it, yet now he had a hard time taking his eyes off the thing, for it told him more clearly than anything else how Jolly viewed his brother.

"Well, I'm here," Brian said to the director. "So what's the deal? Am I to kiss your ass on David Letterman, or what?"

Jolly put his hands behind his head and leaned back in his chair. "As a matter of fact, that's not such a bad idea. But even then, I'd keep wondering what happens next. There I'd be, with my pants down. What do I do if you whip out a chainsaw?"

"I think I can promise you," Brian said. "No chainsaws."

"And what about bulldozing?"

"That too. No more bulldozing."

"And we'd have your word on that?"

"You've got it."

"Ah yes, the word of Brian Poole." For a time Jolly just sat there looking at Brian as if he were studying an abstract sculpture. Then, smiling crookedly, the director went on. "Your brother here seems to think you'd be amenable to doing the talk shows when the movie comes out—kind of plugging it through criticism, I guess. Tell me, is that your idea or his?"

Brian laughed softly. "Well, I can tell you it sure as hell ain't mine. I know just what your lousy, lying movie's gonna say—that Kim was a pathetic, washed-up drug fiend and I was the rotten bastard who made her that way. Am I wrong?"

Jolly smiled thinly. "So that's how you'd go about plugging the movie, uh?"

"What else? It's gonna be just another piece of shit like all your other shit, isn't it? I'd rather piss on it than plug it."

Jolly's ruddy face now was almost crimson. He looked at Charley. "This your idea of a joke, Mr. Poole?"

Seeing that Brian was already heading for the door, Charley got up too. "No, not at all," he said. "I'm sorry for wasting your time."

He and Eve then followed Brian outside. But Jolly evidently felt that the scene was not over yet. As the three of them went down the stairs, the director and Brad came charging out onto the deck.

"Fuck you, Poole!" Jolly bellowed. "You dumb fuckin' bull-dozer! You tink I do business wid a asshole psycho like you, you got shit for brains! *Fongula tutta familia,* you fuckin' asshole! You fuckin' bulldozer! It's da slammer for you!"

In his rage Jolly seemed to have forgotten how to form the *th* sound. And all the time he was yelling, he kept up a frantic sem-aphore of Italian obscenity, one moment stabbing down at them the horns of the cuckold—his pinky and index finger rising from his fist—and the next moment smacking the crook of his arm and shaking a cupped hand at them, a gesture whose precise meaning Charley never had known, other than that its sender was in a lousy mood.

As the three of them drove away, Eve gave Brian a despairing look. "Well, you sure cooked his goose, didn't you?"

Brian made no response. And Charley knew from long expe-rience that this would not be a good time to remonstrate with his brother. So he tried to make light of the incident.

"All I have to say is *fongula tutta familia,* you fucking bulldozer."

But Brian did not even smile as he sped down the winding gravel road.

# chapter three

**C**ountry and western bars were anathema to Eve. She loathed the music, she loathed the decor, and for the most part, she loathed the patrons too, Okie-Californians who tortured the language and strutted around in their cowboy duds as if they had just come in off the range instead of the late shift at the local Wal-Mart. The Purple Sage was not an exception. A huge, barnlike structure, it had a long, antique wooden bar and brass spittoons and a mechanical bull that stood neglected in an alcove. On the sawdusted dance floor a dozen or so couples moved to the energetic music of a five-piece band whose members looked to Eve suspiciously like acid rockers masquerading as country folk. Whatever their true stripe, they were so implacably loud that she was grateful for the high vaulted ceiling—actually the underside of the roof—which, with the rafters below, broke up or at least absorbed a few decibels of the din.

Still, the only way Brian and his new hick friends could make themselves heard was by shouting at each other across the Formica tabletop of the back booth Eve had insisted on, as far from the band as she could get. Though Brian was not a great fan of cowboy bars either, he had heard that the *Miss Colorado* crew had turned this one into something of a hangout, and he wanted to learn what the status of the movie was, whether the cast had left town, whether the set was being rebuilt, just what was going on. Why he wanted to know these things, Eve didn't even want to think about. It was too depressing.

Though she saw a number of movie people there—crew members mostly—Brian had no time to watch for them, not with the Einhorn siblings feeding on him so avidly. The more time Eve spent with them, the more they seemed like a loony stage mother and her tongue-tied offspring. Neither of them had changed clothes from that afternoon, nor unfortunately did their personalities show any alteration. Belinda was still unspeakably ebullient and sexy, a frightening cross between Marilyn Monroe and Rosie O'Donnell. Her enthusiasm was such that Eve halfway expected one of her straining breasts to pop a button at any moment, hopefully blinding the brother, who was so tense he looked as if he might snap a bone just sitting there, gripping his mug of beer in both hands, like a strangler.

Belinda didn't seem able to get over the fact that she was sitting in the same booth with the man who had lived with Kim Sanders—*actually lived with a superstar!* And she kept trying to pump Brian about Kim, for some reason oblivious to the fact that he had just committed a felony to protect the late superstar's privacy, as well as his own. What was Kim really like? the girl asked. Was she really such a hard case? Did she really do heroin as well as coke? Was her great hit song, *Miss Colorado,* really about herself? Was that who she really was?

Brian either ignored the girl's questions or slipped past them through misdirection, such as, "Well, who knows what anybody's really like, underneath it all?" The only question he answered honestly was about the star's last hit song—now the movie title.

"No, she was never Miss Colorado herself, just a runner-up. And her life afterwards wasn't all downhill, was it? The girl in the song is simply someone Kim made up, another country music loser. And that wasn't Kim, no matter what Hollywood seems to think."

At that point Chester managed to croak out a few words. "I liked that song. I like country music. It's the only kind, I say."

Eve imagined that Belinda knew full well why Brian had invited her and Chester to join them, simply because Brian was a man and therefore would want to get her into bed as fast as possible. Naturally the girl would want to cooperate, if for no other reason than the high she would get later on, telling her snowbunny friends all about it, how it was, fucking the man who had fucked Kim Sanders. And, lucky girl, she of course would have no idea that Brian was merely using her to humiliate Eve and offend Charley and debase himself, all in one fell swoop.

It was an old habit of his when he had failed at something, when he was really down, when he truly loathed himself. Then nothing would do but to dive right into the nearest cesspool and revel there, give those who loved him irrefutable reason to stop loving him. So Eve wasn't finding it easy, sitting across from the bounteous Belinda, trying not to be too unpleasant. After all, the girl was just doing what nature intended for her to do, doggedly persisting in her gaudy little mating dance until she eventually wound up many times a mother, fat and pregnant and plain. Eve could hardly wait.

Occasionally Eve would glance over at the front entrance to see if Charley had arrived. After dinner, he'd said he had to go back to his room to phone his wife and his son, who was an undergraduate at Northwestern Univeristy. Though Brian had given him directions to the Purple Sage, Charley intimated that he might not even show up.

"Remember, I'm old and stodgy," he'd said. "And I don't even own a pair of cowboy boots."

Eve was of two minds about his coming. On the one hand, she figured the table could certainly use his cool, wry voice, the gentle humor of an actual grownup. Then too she couldn't deny that later on it would be nice to have his shoulder to cry on. More than that, though, she simply did not want Charley to see her humiliation at his brother's hands. And it surprised her a little, how strongly she felt about this, considering that she had known the man for only a day. But then he *was* Brian's brother, and she imagined it was only natural not to want your quasi-in-laws to see you put down and humiliated.

So, later, when she finally saw him coming through the front door, she felt a pang of disappointment. At the same time, she found herself smiling at him, all the way across the room.

Instead of squeezing into the booth next to Brian, Charley scared up a chair and sat down between the two couples, figuring everyone would be more comfortable that way. He was not surprised to find Belinda Einhorn and her brother still looking like day and night. Though Chester appeared old enough to be the girl's father, he deferred to her as if he were her shy little boy. And when she smiled or laughed, it seemed almost as if she got her energy from him, drawing down on his meager wattage so she could burn all the brighter. Yet Charley knew better than to dismiss the little man out of hand, having visited his mother's Ozark relatives often enough to recognize Chester's type, the kind of man who beat the wife and kids and cooed to his hounds, the kind of man who spoke softly and carried great big guns in his pickup.

At the same time, Charley could see that Eve was not in the least impressed with the Einhorns. Though she was probably doing her best to appear sociable, smiling politely when Belinda would cut loose with laughter or some wide-eyed comment meant to be funny, Charley could see the frost in her eyes.

She was wearing jeans, boots, and a black sleeveless jersey. Her hair, thick and dark, looked a lovely mess, hanging about her face. Listening to Belinda's careless chatter, Charley wondered how the girl could be so oblivious of Eve, so unintimidated by her. And the obvious answer—that the girl was simply too thick to notice the other's coolness or even her striking beauty—somehow it didn't quite wash. Most of the time Belinda seemed content to play the sexy airhead, but every now and then a glimmer of keener intelligence would show through, like gold in a back molar.

Finally, trying to include her brother in the conversation, she said something about ranching, which resulted in Brian telling Chester about his own experiences as a greenhorn cowboy on a Texas ranch after his return from Vietnam.

"My boss was this big old Swede, probably the nicest guy I ever worked for. I remember one time he was patiently sitting on the corral rollin' cigarettes while I kept tryin' to rope this one maverick calf. Finally I got fed up and tackled the little beast. But even then I think it took me a good ten minutes to hog-tie it."

Chester looked as if he really wanted to laugh at the story but couldn't quite bring it off, the muscles in his hollowed face being too stiff for such a task. But Belinda more than made up for his failure, smiling along and laughing loudly at the end.

Charley broke in then, asking Chester about his own ranch. "Where'd you say it was—Missouri?"

"Yep, the southwest corner. Hell, if we'd a mind to, we could prackly spit on Arkansas and Oklahoma—if a body'd want to waste the spit, that is."

Talking about his ranch seemed to relax the man and for a time he became almost garrulous. The family had two whole sections of "mighty fair grassland," he said. And they were currently running almost two hundred "mama cows" on it, which meant that it had to carry almost five hundred head in the summer. His father and uncle used to run the spread, but they were both "purty crippled up" now, his daddy having been trampled by a bull while Uncle Harlan lost an arm in a hay baler.

"But the ranch, it's jest business," he said. "T'aint my real work."

"Oh, what is, then?" Eve asked.

"Politics."

Belinda looked up at the rafters. "Oh boy, here we go," she said.

Chester scowled at her. "We ain't goin' nowheres, Miss Smart-mouth. I jest told 'em what my real work is, that's all."

"Politics as in Democrat and Republican?" Brian asked.

"Naa, jest the opposite. No party at all. It's doin' away with guvmint. All guvmint. That's what I'm after."

Eve was lighting a cigarette. "Like the Libertarians?"

"No, not like them at all. They's just gabbers, that bunch. Any-ways, if yer fer real agin guvmint, ya don't organize. Ya do things fer yerself. Ya go yer own way."

Belinda laughed. "Yeah, the Chester Einhorn party."

"Politics is jest pertectin' yer propity and freedom," Chester said. "That's all it is."

"And you think one man can do all that, by himself?" Brian asked, innocence incarnate, as if he had not started out the day being charged with two felonies for doing just what Chester rec-ommended: taking the law into his own hands.

Looking down at his tiny, gnarled hands clutching the beer mug, Chester grinned slightly, a secretive, gleeful grin. "Oh, they's ways," he allowed. "They's always ways."

"Like what?" Eve asked.

The little man paused like an actor before answering, obviously relishing these moments in the spotlight. "Like guns," he said. "They's always guns."

During the silence that followed this pronouncement, Damian Jolly's assistant, Rick Walters, stopped by the table, resplendent in a Russian peasant blouse and Indian jewelry. No one introduced him to the Einhorns and he in turn totally ignored them.

"I just wanted to tell you how terribly sorry I am about this afternoon," he said. "When I invited you up to Damian's place, I thought there was a good possibility of compromise. I'm sorry how it all worked out."

Eve smiled at him. "So are we, Rick. But we appreciate your help. We really do."

Rick shook his head. "Jolly and that Italian temper of his . . . things can get out of hand pretty fast."

"Well, we don't blame you, Rick. We know none of it was your fault."

Brian looked at Eve. "Is that a fact? It sure is great to find out how *we* feel about everything."

Like a silent movie queen, Rick pressed the back of his hand to his forehead. "Oh, the noise in here, it's simply dreadful. It really is. Well, I must be off. I'll see you another time. Bye-bye."

With that, he turned and made his way through the tables and across the dance floor to the far side of the room, where he joined an elegant young couple at the bar. Leaning toward them, he said something that made them laugh out loud, though inaudibly, in the din of the Purple Sage.

Chester was looking as if he had tasted something sour. "Jest what in hell was that anyway?"

"One of the movie director's fag assistants," Brian told him.

"Ain't none of that kind out our way," the little cowboy said. "We jest don't tolerate it."

Belinda laughed. "The truth is they just don't stick around. McDonald County ain't exactly San Francisco, you know."

"And thank the Lord for that." Evidently satisfied with getting in the last word with his little sister, Chester decided to take his leave. Scooting out of the booth, he tipped his cowboy hat and shuffled backwards. "Well, it's been a real pleasure meetin' y'all," he said. "But I ain't one fer late hours. You jest git outa the habit on a ranch, ya know, gittin' up at five ever' mornin'. Anyways, I got me a real comfy room over to the Motel Six. So I'll jest leave Belinda here with y'all, and I be seein' ya, okay?"

Getting up himself, Brian shook the little man's hand and clapped him on the back and joked that he himself was one "rancher" who had never quite made it out of bed at five in the morning. Nodding solemnly, Chester turned and walked off, hunching his narrow shoulders as though against a biting winter wind.

"Well, now it's my turn," Eve said, sliding out before Brian could sit back down. "I've got a very large headache, and I was thinking you might want to give me a lift home, Charley." Smiling at Belinda, she explained why this was necessary. "Brian has to stay so he can talk business with some movie people. Isn't that right, Brian?"

"That's a fact."

Eve gave Charley a commiserating smile. "So I'm afraid you're stuck with me, Charley."

"That's okay," he said. "It's past my bedtime anyway."

"Yes, we're just going to have to leave these two in each other's capable hands. I'm sorry, but that's just the way it is."

Belinda joined in the raillery, smiling sweetly at Eve. "Well, we'll sure miss you two. We surely will."

"I know you will. But that's life."

Standing now, Charley reached down and shook Belinda's

hand. "I don't care what everybody says," he told her. "You're not that bad looking."

She laughed and bowed her head in gratitude. "Thank you, kind sir. I'll try to remember that."

Charley had to hurry to catch up with Eve, who was moving toward the front door like a cruiser through calm water. When they went on outside, the cold and the silence settled over them. Not until they reached Charley's car did either speak.

"I don't really have a headache," Eve said.

Charley smiled. "Well, that's convenient. It's not really past my bedtime."


**A**s they drove away from the Purple Sage, Eve asked Charley about his phone calls, and he told her that he hadn't been able to reach his son in Evanston, which wasn't much of a surprise. Donna, however, had been at home.

"And did she wonder why you're still here?"

"No, I told her that I had to stay one more day. I still think Brian needs a first-class lawyer, and that's what I think we should do tomorrow—line one up and make him sit down and listen to the guy. If Brian's not totally self-destructive, maybe he'll hire him. Who knows?"

"Not me, certainly."

Though Eve knew the town better than Charley did, she didn't know it well enough to suggest a nice, quiet bar where they could have a few drinks before returning to the motel. So they tried to choose one by its appearance, twice parking and going inside only to discover that the places were, respectively, too loud and too gay. Returning to the car, they continued the search. And Charley finally decided that he would wait no longer for Eve to explain what was going on between her and Brian.

"What happened?" he asked. "Did you two have a fight?"

"What makes you think that?"

"Well, cutting out this way. Leaving him there."

"With the sexy Miss Einhorn?"

"No, I didn't mean that."

"Sure, you did. But don't worry about it, Charley. It's just like I said. He wants to collar some of the movie people and find out what's happening, which could take hours. And I hated it there. I hate cowboy bars."

"So that bit of Ping-Pong between you and Belinda, that didn't mean anything?"

"Nothing at all."

They kept driving around until Eve spotted a place named Rivera's, a handsome Spanish-style tavern with potted plants bracketing the entrance and only a few cars in the parking lot.

"It looks just right," she said. "Unpopular."

And she was correct. Inside, the place proved to be quiet and nearly empty, possibly because there was no live music or juke-boxes, just the soft hum of latin Muzak. At one end of the bar there was a dark, cozy alcove with an open fire burning in a fire-place and some black vinyl love seats ranged around it, each with its own heavy oaken coffee table in front. Surprisingly, even this did not appear to be much of a drawing card, for there was only one other couple in the room, middle-aged and heavy, and so unabashedly hot for each other that Charley doubted they even knew he and Eve had entered.

When the waitress came, Eve ordered a daiquiri and Charley a double Scotch instead of vodka, since he'd had beer at the Purple Sage and didn't like to mix colors when he drank.

"It certainly isn't crowded," Eve said.

"And I can't figure why not. Myself, I've always liked drinking on my back."

Eve smiled. "It's not that bad."

But Charley wasn't sure about that. The overstuffed love seats were so soft and slanted that he had to prop his feet on the coffee table, which meant that he would either have to hold the icy Scotch continuously or unwind himself every time he wanted to pick it up and drink. Also, if they stayed long enough, he knew he could look forward to sloshing booze on himself and probably Eve as well. The fire was nice, though. And they did have a measure of privacy.

Waiting for their drinks, Charley told Eve that except for the incident at Jolly's, he had the feeling he was here on a casual visit, not the emergency mission her phone call had led him to expect.

"So far no meetings with lawyers or prosecutors or anybody else," he said. "It's all so cut-and-dried. So laid back."

Eve shrugged. "What can I say? Your brother's laid back."

"Except when he's on a bulldozer."

"Except for that, yes."

The waitress brought their drinks, and for a time they fell silent, just sat there sipping and watching the fire. And soon the amorous couple got up and left, evidently having felt inhibited by their presence.

Eve smiled. "Now we'll just have the fire to keep us warm."

Charley held up his drink. "And the alcohol—don't forget that."

"Two will be enough for me," she said. "Any more than that and I'll be a wreck tomorrow."

"Then I'd better drink fast. I was thinking more along the lines of a half dozen more."

"Charley, that's a *double,*" she said.

"Okay, then, three more."

She shook her head in mock sorrow. "I didn't figure you for a drinking man."

"Normally I'm not. I'm usually a slave to moderation. But lately, I don't know, lately it seems I don't mind getting plowed now and then. Sort of a reversion to college days. My fraternity was a famous training ground for future alcoholics."

"Maybe it's that old debil—midlife crisis."

Charley laughed softly. "I'll drink to that," he said.

Eve had taken off her shoes and was sitting almost sideways on the love seat, facing him, her feet tucked cozily under her legs. The fire crackled in her eyes and her lips were slightly parted in an expression that might have seemed hesitant and calculating in someone else, but in Eve seemed merely another aspect of her beauty.

"Tell me about your marriage," she said, hesitant no longer.

"Just like that?"

"Then tell me about Donna."

Charley couldn't see that that would be any easier, at least not for him. So, somewhat reluctantly, he told Eve that Donna was pretty and intelligent, that she was a loving wife and mother whose only fault was in being much more ambitious and competent than her husband. He had meant this last part to sound light and ironic, but Eve didn't take it that way.

"Brian told me she runs your company now."

Charley forced a smile. "Well, yes and no. It's my name on the broker's license, and I'm still president. But over time we both agreed to go our own way in the business. Donna loves selling houses—or at least managing the agents who sell the houses—and I do what I like to do."

"Which is?"

After ordering another drink, Charley briefly told Eve about his operation, not caring that he made it sound as if he were little more than a glorified carpenter. He didn't mention that the operation had earned him over one hundred thousand dollars

in profit the previous year, about a fifth as much as the brokerage itself.

That out of the way, Eve returned to his private life. "Donna,"
she said. "You still love her?"

"Of course."

"Why of course?"

Charley almost said the obvious: because she's my wife. But he
knew Eve would not have been satisfied with that, so he tried a
different approach.

"It was in our wedding vows."

"No—really," Eve said, still doggedly serious.

"Okay, then. No reason. Habit maybe."

"Do you cheat on her?"

Charley just sat there looking at her for a time, trying not to
let his anger show, even though he believed she had it coming.
"You've got no business asking that," he said finally. "But the answer is no."

"Are you mad at me?"

"No."

"Maybe if you knew why I asked," she said, her eyes suddenly
filling. "Maybe then you wouldn't be angry."

"Eve, I'm not angry."

"Of course you are."

"Then why? Why did you say it?"

Even though the tears kept coming, she continued to smile at
him. And when her face began to crumple finally, as if she were
about to cry, she fought it off, straightening up and shaking herself, like a filly twitching flies away.

"Your brother," she said. "That's why. Oh, I guess I can't really
say he cheats, since he makes no pretense of fidelity. Instead he
just throws it in your face and says live with it. Which unfortunately I do."

Charley was more puzzled than shocked. "Who do you mean? Belinda? *Tonight?*"

"Who else?"

"But that's ridiculous, Eve. She can't hold a candle to you. Why would you tolerate it? You could have any man you want. You must know that."

She shrugged indifferently. "But I love Brian. Even now, when I know not only what he's going to do but why."

Charley said nothing, waiting.

"Your brother's just not like other people. When he's like this—I mean in trouble, powerless, angry—he doesn't want love or support or sympathy. He'd never come crawling for anything. Instead he does this. He says in effect, 'Here, take a look, here's my fuck tonight.' And he dares you to go on loving him."

"And you do?"

Looking rueful and whipped, she nodded. "It's not as though I didn't expect it. In the beginning he wouldn't let us live together because he said this would happen and poison the relationship. He said he loved me more than he'd ever loved anyone, but that he could never be monogamous. Things would happen, he said. He'd be down and depressed or having a great time, and some girl would come along, some girl he would have to have. He was only being honest. In L.A., I think that's the way it is with most men, the only difference being that they're not honest about it. And that's what I told him. I said I could live with it—because I couldn't live without him."

Charley didn't know what to say. Brian after all was his brother, and he had to admit that if he looked at the matter objectively, Brian's stand was not without merit. At least he was being honest, which was more than could be said for most men, including Charley himself at the moment. He hadn't forgotten his response to Eve's question about whether he had ever cheated on Donna, for the truth was somewhat different. While he had never cheated on her in spirit, never having had an affair of the heart, he nevertheless had had a number of one-night stands during the last eight or ten years, usually when he was away from home, at a convention or the like. Though he was not proud of this, neither did it eat him up, for he believed that marriage met a woman's needs much more fully than it did a man's, in that men were more promiscuous by nature, forever frustrating their abiding lust for other women. So, over the course of a marriage, he regarded a few missteps as only natural. But they were also *private*, he believed, not the sort of thing he cared to share with anyone, certainly not with Donna, and now not with Eve either.

Still, even though he may have shared his brother's weakness, he was offended by what Eve had told him. It rubbed him the wrong way. There was just something unsavory about it, almost an element of sadism, the way it virtually institutionalized the infidelity, rubbing the woman's nose in it, making her live with it. Charley didn't like it, and he especially didn't like it if that woman happened to be someone like Eve, who he thought deserved the best.

Certainly she deserved better than this, sitting in the firelight with her lover's brother, probably wondering at that moment if Brian and his gaudy snow bunny were making love.

Charley looked down at his glass, surprised to find it empty again. "My brother's a goddamn fool," he said. "But then, I already knew that."

"He has his problems," Eve conceded. "But he's no fool."

"You couldn't prove it by me."

Since the barmaid had not appeared for some time, Charley got up, preparing to go for a refill. "You okay?" he asked, even though he could see that her glass was still almost full.

She smiled up at him. "I'm fine. And maybe you should be too. Maybe we should leave."

"I can't now. I'm angry. I'll need at least one more to cool off."

"Don't be angry on my account."

"I can't help it," he said. "I hate to see the natural order of things turned upside down."

"Meaning?"

He knew she understood, so he didn't bother to explain. "I'll be right back," he said.


The spectacle of someone sloppy drunk was so distasteful to Charley that he never completely let himself go, even at the country club or a friend's party where he could count on an invariably sober Donna to drive them home. Lately, though, he would occasionally go so far that he would have to make a conscious effort not to *appear* drunk. This was one of those times.

To make matters worse, Charley wasn't even sure why this was happening. He wasn't in a partying mood, and he certainly didn't want to make a bad impression on Eve. Yet here he was, no longer even counting the drinks he'd had. And as the evening wore on, Eve became quite talkative and seemed to want to tell him everything about her life, especially the problems she had growing up under the smothering love of a very Jewish father when she herself felt so gentile, so Irish. She also told Charley about her years in Hollywood, and he listened attentively, even sympathetically, while all the time he was thinking about other matters, such as the beguiling curve of her neck and the way her high, small breasts rose and fell with emotion as she told him this or that. And all the while, he kept drinking.

Twice he got up and made his way to the men's room, to teeter there at the urinal, full of piss and whimsy. Disdaining to wash his hands—what was so dirty about his old friend anyway?—he made his way back to Eve in the alcove, stopping on his second trip to inform a newly arrived couple that they were dead ringers for Fred and Ginger. When the man suggested he get lost, Charley happily informed him that he was already lost and wouldn't likely ever be found.

By then, Eve wanted to leave, but Charley insisted on still one more, claiming that he needed it in order to drive with "extraspecial" care. Soon, though—even before the new drink was gone—Eve simply got up and pulled him after her. And Charley found himself trailing her through the virtually empty bar. On the way, he detoured over to the bartender and warned him that he might have to hose down the couple in the corner.

"Thee gringoes," he told him, "they have no shame."

In the parking lot, Eve asked for the car keys, but Charley took himself in hand, standing straight, smiling confidently, speaking as clearly as he could.

"I'm really okay, Eve. The stuff affects my tongue more than anything else. My motor faculties are unimpaired. I'll drive us home in absolute safety. I promise."

She was standing with her back against the car, looking up at him, her expression dubious but amused.

"First, though, I'm going to need a brotherly hug," he heard himself say. And, amazed at his temerity, he took her in his arms and kissed her lightly on the forehead.

"My brother's a jerk," he said.

She gently moved out of his embrace. "You're probably right. But more to the point, are you sure you can drive?"

"Am I? Watch this." He deftly thrust the key into the lock and opened the car door.

"I'm impressed," she said, getting in.

After that little scene, which he remembered clearly, the rest of the night seemed like a crack passenger train thundering past, with only an occasional lit window. In one of them, he remembered seeing a carful of teenagers screeching past him in a rage, honking the horn and giving him the finger. Then there was a red streetlight dancing above the car, whipsawed in a suddenly roaring wind. And he saw himself trekking up a seemingly endless flight of stairs, arm in arm with his brother's lady, after which things briefly became clearer again. He remembered insisting on walking her to her room.

"And here I thought chivalry was dead," she said.

"Not by a long shot," he assured her.

At her door she thanked him. "For listening to me. For being there. For everything."

"Aw shucks, ma'm, tweren't nothin'."

She was looking at him as if he were her naughty little boy. "But tomorrow we've got to have a little talk. I need to know why a man of such moderation suddenly becomes so immoderate with me. All that Scotch, I mean."

For Charley the remark was like a foglight suddenly lit, parting the mists for a brief moment. He had been wondering that same thing. "I know," he said. "I can't figure it either. It makes no sense. I wanted you to like me."

She smiled sadly, beautifully. "But I do like you, Charley." Coming up on her toes then, she kissed him on the cheek. "In fact, I like you very much."

He smiled. "Jesus, just think if I'd been sober and charming."

"I know. It boggles the mind." She said goodnight and gently closed the door.

Charley made it back to his room and got off his pants and shoes before toppling like a felled tree into his bed, though never landing as far as he knew, never even dreaming. He had no

idea how long he slept, whether one hour or ten had passed
when he suddenly felt himself being awakened, Caesar pulled
squalling into the brutal air. Gradually he became aware that
Brian was shaking him.

"Come on, man! Get up, for Christ's sake!"

"What is it?" Charley managed. "What's wrong?"

"Just get up. We need you."

He saw that it was still dark outside, which meant that he had
been asleep for only a few hours at most. Propping himself on an
elbow, he also realized that he was still drunk. The room spun
and his gorge rose.

"Jesus, Brian, I can't. I really can't."

As he slipped back onto the pillow, Brian reached down and
pulled him up into a sitting position, steadied him, shook him.

"It's the goddamn girl," Brian said. "Belinda. She's taken too
much meth or something. We've got to get her to a hospital."

"Why me?" Charley asked. "I'm not in very good shape, little
brother, as you can see."

"It'll take two people," Brian said. "And Eve won't let me go.
The thing with Kim Sanders—you know. The cops would blame
me for this too, and the fucking media would crucify me."

"What the devil happened? What'd you do to her?"

"Nothing, man! What do you think? We had sex and I went to
sleep. Maybe she thought she was taking downers. I don't know."

"Where is she?"

"In a room I rented downstairs."

"How'd you get in here?"

Brian looked disgusted. "Who the hell cares? I got a key at the
desk, okay?"

"Whatever."

Charley stood shaking and groaning as Brian helped him put
on a sweater, jeans, loafers. Then Brian led him out onto the

walkway and downstairs, to a room at the far end. Inside, Charley peered through the open bathroom door at Eve in jeans and a pullover, trying to work with Belinda, who was sitting naked on the toilet seat. Her forehead was bleeding and there were fresh red scratches on her face and breasts and thighs. Even now, though Eve was holding her by the wrists, the girl's long-nailed fingers still raked at her body. And the words tumbled out of her, shrill and meaningless.

"Oh no, don't sleep . . . Oh, please, no, don't ever . . . No, no, I can't, I really can't . . ."

Her body quivered with tension, a condition that perversely—for Charley anyway—made her look even sexier, hard and lean instead of soft and cuddly. But it was a feeling that quickly died as his gorge rose again, this time irresistibly. Making a dive for the bathtub, he retched into it repeatedly, managing finally to bring up only a skein of vile-tasting mucus. He turned on the cold water tap and washed it down, then thrust his head into the stream long enough to feel as if he too were going down the drain. Shuddering and gasping, he got back on his feet and toweled off while Eve and Brian helped Belinda out of the bathroom and into a robe of Eve's. All the while the girl kept jabbering and jerking, as if an electric current were being fed into her body.

As Charley followed them out of the bathroom, Brian gave him a worried look. "Feel any better?" he asked. "Can you do it?"

For the first time, Charley noticed how ragged and scared Eve looked. "I'll be okay," he said, wondering just how he was going to manage it.

Eve looked at him. "Let's go then. Help me with her."

As they were leaving, Brian kept giving them instructions: that Eve should drive and Charley should hold the girl between them; that they should take the freeway south, because there was a hospital a few miles in that direction; and that Eve should do all the talking, should give the hospital a phony name and address.

"Above all, get out as fast as you can. You don't want any reporters getting to you."

Nodding impatiently, Eve hurried the girl out onto the walkway, with Charley holding on more than anything else. In the parking lot, they helped her into Brian's pickup and then got in themselves, on each side of her. As they headed for the freeway, Charley asked how the girl had hurt her forehead.

"Who knows? Ask Brian," Eve said.

"You blame him for this?"

She laughed coldly. "Who else? We weren't the ones with her. We didn't fuck her, did we?"

"No, I think I'd remember that."

Eve gave him a withering look. In between them, Belinda began to squirm and whimper. And when her hands went for her face again, Charley pulled her onto his lap and held her there, pinning her arms. At the same time a new wave of nausea hit him and he broke into a heavy sweat. He leaned his head against her shoulder and choked down the bile rising in his throat.

As they sped onto the freeway he looked out at the headlights of the oncoming cars and found them skittering sideways, multiplying. He closed his eyes and tightened his grip on the girl, grateful that he had something solid to hold onto. But she began to cry and buck against him, and suddenly she lunged toward the side and accidentally hit the passenger door handle, causing the door to pop open. Struggling to keep her from falling out, Charley shouted for Eve to pull over and stop. But Belinda went on lunging and squirming, and within a few seconds all he had a grip on was her robe, Eve's green velour, slick as grease in his sweating hands. He held on with all his strength and finally they were on the grassy shoulder of the road, bouncing along, slowing, the girl drooping further into the open doorway, like a huge green sack.

Then, just as they were pulling to a stop, she for some reason twisted in the opposite direction and unraveled herself from the robe, not unlike Cleopatra coming out of her rug, and for a moment Charley sat there with the empty, useless garment, looking down and back at the girl tumbling naked through the grass. He caught himself then and jumped out too, tripping and almost falling, not wanting to believe his eyes as he saw her dart around the back of the truck and head out across the freeway, right into the path of blazing headlights. There was a howl of car horns and skidding tires, and Charley gripped the edge of the truck bed, trying not to fall, staring past the hurtling traffic at the flash of her white legs against the darkness of the median strip. And still she ran, only now straight into the path of the cars coming from the opposite direction, these too already braking and fishtailing, adding to the terrible din.

But this time there another sound too, that of breaking glass, metal, and flesh as the lead car skidded directly into Belinda and her body did a grotesque cartwheel across the hood of the vehicle before dropping out of sight into the high grass beyond. And still more cars kept coming, horns and tires screaming as they slammed into the vehicles that were already stopped. Then Charley realized that Eve was screaming too, at him.

"Get back in! Charley! Come on!"

Sick and dazed, he did as he was told, thinking that she planned to drive across the median strip and pull up in front of the accident site, so they could more easily get the girl back into the truck and continue on to the hospital. But Eve merely swung out in front of the slowing traffic and gunned the engine, heading south, away from the accident.

"What the hell you doing?" he cried. "We've got to help her!"

Eve did not look at him. "We will. This exit ahead, I'll cross over and come back."

"It'll take too long! Come on, turn back!"

But she had already swerved onto the exit ramp, and now they roared up it at a good fifty miles an hour. At the top, she turned left and took the bridge back over the freeway. Looking down at the accident scene, Charley could feel his heart walloping his chest.

"Jesus, did you see her!" he got out. "She ran right in front of the cars! They couldn't stop!"

"Fucking idiot!" Eve said. "We were only trying to help her."

They had come to the traffic light on the other side of the freeway, but instead of getting into the turn lane, so they could enter the freeway's northbound lanes, Eve accelerated past the intersection. For a few moments, Charley did not understand what was happening, then he took hold of the steering wheel and reached over with his left foot and pushed hard on the brake pedal. Eve struggled against him for a few seconds, then gave in and pulled over to the side of the street, which was lined with gas stations and car washes and fast-food stores, a few of which were still open at this late, predawn hour. Charley roughly took her by the arm and pulled her across his body so he could slide in behind the wheel. After he had U-turned and was heading back toward the freeway, she began to cry, softly, shaking her head.

"I want to help her too, Charley," she got out. "I really do. But it's too late. Can't you see that?"

"We've got to go back."

"And do what? Make sure we incriminate Brian? Make sure he *never* gets out of prison?"

"Eve, we can't just leave her there, for Christ's sake."

"*Leave her?* Charley, there are dozens of cars there already!

And probably the police by now too! You want to explain it all to them? You want to take a breathalyzer test?"

And indeed, as he approached the entrance ramp, he could see the red-and-blue flashing lights of a police car already on the scene, apparently having driven in from the north and crossed over the median. So he drove on past the ramp and stopped the pickup on the bridge, where they could see more clearly in both directions. To the south, weaving through the stopped traffic, was the red flasher of an ambulance. Back at the accident site, a policeman on foot was directing traffic with a lighted baton, trying to keep a single line of cars moving past.

"Have you seen enough?" Eve asked. "Do we go on back to the motel, or does your sense of duty require that we go down there and ruin our lives?"

Charley put the truck in gear and started on over the freeway again, thinking that they would have to find another way back to the motel now.

"Yes, I've seen enough," he said. "And I've heard enough too."

# chapter four

Eve waited only long enough for Charley to close the door behind them before she told Brian about the accident, her voice breaking. At first, Brian looked as if he didn't believe her. He just stood there staring at her and then he looked over at Charley, apparently hoping for some sort of disclaimer: a wink, a smile, anything that might give the lie to what he'd just heard. But all Charley could do was shake his head and force out a few words of his own, no less terrible than Eve's.

"It's true, Brian. The girl popped the door open, and all I had a grip on was this goddamn thing." Still carrying the robe at that point, he tossed it onto one of the beds. "She slipped out of it somehow and took off running across the freeway. A northbound car hit her."

"Oh Jesus, no." Brian turned visibly pale. "No, this is too much."

Charley agreed. "It sure as hell is."

"Well, how is she?" Brian asked. "Did you check on her?"

Charley looked over at Eve, who had dropped into a wingback chair across the room, in front of the drapes. Since it had been her decision, he decided to let her explain it.

"It happened just this side of Fillmore. So I took the exit there and crossed back over the freeway, to get on the northbound lanes, where she'd been hit. But there was too much traffic. By the time we reached the other side, the police were already on the scene—you know how they patrol the freeway. So we came on home."

*"So you came on home."* Brian sagged onto the edge of the nearest bed.

"She could be dead, for all we know," Charley said. "And no ID, a Jane Doe."

Eve's eyes had filled. "Oh, they'll find out soon enough, won't they? I mean, who she is."

"You bet they will." Charley went between the beds and picked up the phone, a move that galvanized his brother.

Lunging across the bed, Brian depressed the cradle switch before Charley could punch in the number. "Not just yet, okay?" he said, taking the phone away, placing it back on the cradle.

Charley felt confusion more than anger. "Well, we've got to call the police, Brian," he said. "We can't just leave it this way."

Getting up, Brian put his hand on Charley's shoulder and gently guided him out from between the beds, away from the phone. "Just a little while, okay, man?" he said. "Before we call, we've got to think this thing through."

Charley looked at him in disbelief. "Think what through? I told you she didn't have any ID. The police have to know who she is. Her brother has to be told what happened."

"I know that. All I'm asking for is a little time."

"It's all going to come out in the end anyway. So why wait?"

Brian looked as if he were teetering between rage and tears. *"Why?* You want to know why, Charley? Because I didn't give the goddamn girl so much as an aspirin, that's why. Yet I'll be the one they blame, you know that, don't you? I'm the one who'll have to take the fall for it. The fucking media will see to that.

This is just too neat to pass up. They'll say it's just like with Kim Sanders—that I gave Belinda her drugs the same as Kim. And when I'm tried for the bulldozing, I won't have a leg to stand on. I'll already be Doctor Death or something like that. Something real cute like that."

Charley sat back on one of the beds, his head in his hands. He was feeling so exhausted, so hungover still, that he could barely think, let alone speak. But he knew he couldn't just leave things the way they were. "You're forgetting, Brian—Eve and I were driving the girl. We left the scene of an accident, and that's a felony. The longer we wait, the harder it will go for us."

"No way," Brian said. "As far as I'm concerned, you and Eve are totally out of the picture. All you were trying to do was help me, and I won't let you suffer because of that. So it was only me and Belinda in the pickup, not you two. I promise—you're both out of it."

Charley was not convinced. "Well, you might promise, but reality has a way of muscling in. People on the freeway must have seen us. At the very least, they saw two people—two *heads,* anyway—when we drove off and left her."

Brian gave a bleak laugh. "A naked Belinda is running across the freeway, and you think anyone was looking at the pickup?"

Charley felt as if he were in the last mile of a marathon. The task of arguing with his brother was one hill too many. Yet he kept going. "All right, let's say no one saw us and we're in the clear. Still, what the hell can you do *now,* Brian? You can't change what happened. People saw you with Belinda at the bar. Rick Whatshisname came right to the table. And then there's Chester. Little Chester knows you were with her. And if she survives . . ."

"She'll be lucky if she remembers her name, after that kind of trauma. As for Chester, he's the one I want to talk with now. I know guys like him. I've worked with them. Just give me a couple hours, Charley. Please."

"What will you say to him?"

"Just leave that to me. All you have to know is that you and Eve are out of it. I promise, man. I'm the one who got you into this mess, so let me be the one to get you out. Okay? Just a couple of hours, Charley. That's all I ask. You lie down and sleep, okay? You look like shit."

"No kidding." Looking over at Eve, Charley shrugged in defeat and exhaustion, as if they were a couple of grownups trying to deal with an impossible child. Wearily he turned back to his brother. "Okay, you've got two hours. Then I call the police."

"Fair enough," Brian said. "Now let's get you to your room."

Charley waved him off. "I'm not dead yet. I may look it, but I'm not quite there yet."

**A**n hour later Eve was feeling too exhausted to speak. She was sitting on a couch in the waiting area at one end of a long hospital corridor. Midway there was a nurses' station and beyond that, the Intensive Care Unit, to which a doctor had just escorted Chester Einhorn, hoping the little man could identify the brutally injured, comatose young woman brought in around three that morning. Near Eve, Brian stood at a tall window looking out as dawn gathered in the east, pearl gray above the hard-scrabble plain. Incredibly, he looked relaxed and thoughtful, as if he had just enjoyed a long night of restful sleep.

Back at the motel, after Charley had dragged himself off to his room, Brian had gone straight for the local phone directory. First, he called Penrose Hospital to see if they had taken in "the girl hit on the freeway."

After a momentary pause, he asked if she was alive. Then he

began to shake his head. "No, I don't know her," he said, quickly hanging up.

Then, after looking up another number, he phoned and asked if Chester Einhorn was staying there.

"Yes, I know what time it is," he said. "But this is an emergency. Please put me through."

Covering the speaker, he turned to Eve. "Motel Six. Real folksy people."

When Chester came on, Brian told him that he had just received a call from a man who wouldn't give his name. "He said that the girl I was with at the Purple Sage has been in some kind of accident and is at Penrose Hospital now." He paused a few seconds, listening, then went on. "No, I have no idea. We separated after you left. Some guy came by and invited us to a party. She wanted to go, and I didn't. She left with them, and that's the last I saw of her." Again he broke off, then finished. "Yeah, Penrose Hospital—you know where it is? Good. We'll meet you there."

After he had hung up, Eve said almost nothing. She was so taken aback, so appalled at her lover's brass-balled stupidity, that there was not much to say except the obvious. "And when the girl pulls through and tells what really happened, what then? What do you say? 'Oh, I was just kidding.' "

He had not bothered to answer. On the way to the hospital, though, he apparently had found her silence troubling.

"Just don't worry about this," he'd told her. "I know what I'm doing. But the less you know about it, the better off you'll be."

"Well, that sure gives a girl confidence," she'd said. "Nothing to worry about there."

"Just stuff that, okay?" he'd snapped. "I don't need that kind of shit right now."

"Whatever you say."

Now, down the long corridor, Eve saw Chester and the doctor

come out of the ICU. The doctor stopped at the nurses' station, but little Chester kept coming, walking as if it were a new experience for him, his arms held out from his sides slightly, his cowboy hat somehow not even swinging in his hand. As far away as he was, he still looked so relentlessly self-conscious that Eve looked away, figuring that would put him more at ease.

"Here he comes," she said.

"Yeah, I see." Brian walked across the waiting area, toward the little cowboy, who was shaking his head in sorrow and anger.

"It's her, all right," he said. "It's Belinda. And she shore is banged up. Got a fractured skull and broke legs and broke hip and internal stuff too. But the doc says she's real strong and her coma—how'd he put it?—he says it's a *shallow* one, like maybe it won't last long."

"Well, that's good news," Brian said. "It's something anyway."

Chester went on shaking his head. "Can you beat it, though—someone jest dumpin' her like that on the highway, like she was a dog or somethin'. Guess he was through with her and figured he'd jest dump her like that." He shook his head, as if in wonderment. "But he's gonna have to answer, lemme tell ya. Soon as I find out who it was, he's shore gonna have to answer."

Brian, cool as a car salesman, nodded in agreement. "I don't blame you, Chester. I'd feel the same way."

Eve, who had gotten up by now, still held back, not wanting to spook the cowboy. "It's good she's young and strong," she said. "She'll make it."

Ignoring her, Chester kept his attention focused on Brian. "The police, I guess they already took off," he said. "Doctor told me he's supposed to call them when she comes to. But I'm gonna be there first, lemme tell ya. Whoever the bastard was, I want to know first. I guess I don't need to tell ya why."

Brian nodded gravely. "You sure don't." Holding out the keys to the pickup, he turned to Eve. "Listen, why don't you go on ahead and wait for us down in the parking lot. Chester and me, we've got some business to discuss."

This was not at all like Brian, making her feel like some lowlife employee, someone to push around and ignore. Before taking the keys, she made him just stand there, holding them out like a supplicant. But instead of looking embarrassed, he gave her one of his nicer smiles, a combination of guilt and whimsy and affection. She took the keys and headed for the elevator. Chester appeared relieved to see her go.

Ten minutes later, down in the parking lot, she watched as the two men came out of the building, Brian talking earnestly, his hand on the little man's shoulder. Chester had his cowboy hat on now and there was something different even in the way he stood there for a moment, slightly bent and still, like a drawn bow about to be released. Then he walked on to his pickup, which was old, red, and gleaming, the opposite of Brian's filthy, black, new Chevy. As Chester jumped inside, Eve saw the guns racked in the truck's rear window.

Brian didn't get in with Eve until he saw the red pickup roar out of the parking lot. As he slipped in behind the wheel, he looked as if he were trying hard not to smile.

"Somebody put a burr under his saddle?" Eve asked.

Brian shrugged. "Not me, certainly."


**C**harley had not actually expected to sleep during the two hours' reprieve he had given Brian, not to mention himself. He figured he was much too exhausted, too addled, too angry to sleep. But being a cautious sort, he set the radio alarm anyway, which turned out to be a good thing, since he fell asleep immediately and kept on sleeping through the radio part of the alarm, not waking till the buzzer came on like a jackhammer in his head.

For a time he felt worse than before, drugged as well as exhausted and hungover, in no condition yet to phone the police or anyone else. In time, though, after brushing his teeth, shaving, and showering, he began to feel at least a little like himself again—except for Belinda of course, except for the burden of guilt and remorse he now carried. If only he hadn't been drunk, he kept telling himself, then none of it would have happened. She never would have popped the door, never would have slipped out of his grasp, never would have had a chance to make her mad dash across the freeway.

The only problem was, he *had been* drunk. But *why?* Why he had let himself go that far? That he still didn't know, except that it had something to do with Eve, so beautifully sad, sitting so close to him for so long, her husky voice plucking him like a guitar.

Still, he couldn't yet bring himself to pick up the phone and call the police, for the good reason that it scared the devil out of him, the prospect of being arrested, fingerprinted, and incarcerated, even if only overnight. Also he had to admit that in this instance Brian for once had made sense. In trying to take Belinda to the hospital, Charley and Eve had only been filling in for him, only doing what he should have been doing. Belinda was his mess, he'd said, and he should be the one to clean it up, a sentiment with which Charley could only agree.

But even as he was thinking along these lines, protecting himself, the pendulum would start its inevitable swing back in the other direction and he would feel scorn for his faintness of heart, worrying about his good name and creature comforts while poor Belinda lay nameless in some hospital, possibly dying. So he resolved to call within a few minutes, in fact as soon as he was dressed. But just as he as finishing, putting on a clean blue shirt, Eve knocked on the door and he let her in.

"So you're up and around," she said. "Didn't succumb after all?"

"Afraid not. Where's Brian?"

"Downstairs in the coffee shop. Claimed he was going to pass out if he didn't get some java immediately. So I'm here to collect you." She was still wearing the same clothes, the same jersey and jeans and boots. And somehow, despite all she'd been through in the last twelve hours, she looked reasonably fresh, unreasonably beautiful.

"Breakfast, huh?" Charley said.

"That's right. Food."

"Well, I'll admit I could use a few gallons of orange juice. But I thought we had some other business, you know? Belinda?"

Eve smiled slightly. "I know. But you asked where Brian was. As for Belinda, it seems your brother has taken care of everything. He phoned Chester at his motel, and we met him at the hospital. He ID'd Belinda. And whatever it is Brian told him, it sure worked. The two of them are tighter than Lewis and Clark."

"She's alive, then."

"She's in Intensive Care, in a coma. The doctors think she'll pull through, though."

"And Chester just accepts all this? He leaves his sister with Brian, she winds up half-dead in the hospital, and he doesn't have a problem with that?"

"Evidently not."

Charley held the door open for her. "It doesn't make sense," he said.

Eve shrugged. "Well, maybe Brian can explain it."

Though it was only a little after eight in the morning, the coffee shop was virtually deserted. In a row of booths that looked out on the pool, Brian was the sole occupant, leaning back in the corner of one, basking in a shaft of sunlight while he smoked a cigarette and drank his coffee.

As Charley and Eve sat down across from him, he shook his head admiringly. "Hell, Charley, you're looking almost chipper," he said.

"Chipper, my ass. You mind telling me what you said to Chester?"

"Just the obvious, that's all. Belinda and I went our separate ways. Some movie guy I don't know invited us to a party, and naturally Belinda wanted to go, being young and vital instead of a middle-aged old fuck like me. So she left, and I came on home alone."

Charley sat there staring at his brother, wondering how on earth he could look so satisfied and carefree, as if Chester wouldn't eventually learn the truth anyway, if not from Belinda, then from someone else who had seen the two of them leave together. And of course Chester would then have it in for Brian all the more, not just for what he had let happen to Belinda but also for having conned him, for having made a fool of him.

But before Charley could say any of this, the waitress served Brian's breakfast: wheatcakes, sausages, scrambled eggs, and another glass of orange juice. Charley and Eve ordered only coffee and juice. After the woman left, Eve commented on her lover's plate.

"I guess lying makes for a good appetite."

Brian smiled. "Oh, I don't think I'd call it lying, babe. Creative misinformation maybe. Say, the judicious application of creative misinformation."

"Sounds impressive," Charley said. "And when Chester finally learns the truth, he'll probably give you a lesson in the judicious application of creative gunfire."

Brian laughed. "Boy, you two are a couple of real crepe hang-ers. Aren't things bad enough without magnifying this thing with Chester? For Christ's sake, I'm out on bail for a couple of felonies, Belinda will probably never be the same, thanks to us, and fucking Damian Jolly is still going ahead with his lying movie. To me, that's sufficient bad news for the day."

"You've got a point," Eve said.

Charley did not agree. In his mind, the fact that things were already bad enough didn't make this new problem any less important. But he said nothing for a time. Outside, the pool had been opened and three preteen boys, all towheads, had begun a frenzy of diving, cannonballing, and belly flopping, trying to impress a sunbathing teenage girl in a bikini. Judging by her total indifference so far, Charley didn't think much of their chances. At the same time, he couldn't help noticing that his brother's behavior was comparably unrealistic, or at least, odd. Time and again, as Brian worked at his huge breakfast, he would start to smile for no apparent reason and then just as suddenly turn it off. Finally Charley asked him about it.

"Just what the hell's eating you?"

"Eating me?"

"Yes, what's going on?"

"I haven't the vaguest what you mean, Charley."

"You look like you ate a goddamn canary."

Brian touched the corners of his mouth. "Little yellow feathers give me away, did they?"

"Don't be cute."

Eve too had noticed. "You do seem kind of hyper this morning. Why? Because Chester bought your story?"

Brian shrugged. "I guess something like that."

"What like that?" Charley asked.

Brian didn't answer immediately. He pushed his food away and sat back, smiling an odd roguish smile made doubly odd by the fact that his eyes had filled with tears. "Christ, what a mess this thing is," he said finally. "What a stinking, unbelievable mess."

"Brian, what is it you're not telling us?" Eve said.

He burlesqued a look of consternation. "What could it be, I wonder. That I'm an asshole? No, because I'm sure you both are already aware of that." He ran his hands back through his hair, gripping his skull as if to keep it from exploding. "Even when we were kids, right, Charley? And I mean *little* kids. Remember how I could never resist a dare? Some wise guy tells us not to skate on thin ice, I had to zip on out there, right? Jump off a roof? Pick a fight with a gang of black kids? Shit, no problem. Not for crazy Brian Poole, right?"

Charley patiently sipped at his coffee. "Yeah, you were always a caution."

"We're waiting," Eve said. "What the hell has happened? What've you done now?"

He repeated her words. "Yes, what have I done now? What in God's name has the asshole done this time? Well, let me think." He frowned deeply for a few moments, then grinned in relief. "Ah yes, it comes back to me now, like a haunting refrain. But it's nothing, really. A bagatelle."

"We're waiting," Eve repeated.

"Waiting for very little, as it turns out. Really, it's no big deal. It's just that, in misinforming Chester, I guess I was a bit more specific than I indicated earlier. You might even say I didn't misdirect him—I *pointed* him."

"Pointed him where?" Eve asked. "At who?"

Charley was afraid he knew. "At Damian Jolly, right?"

Brian shot him with his finger. "Bingo! Give the man in the pink eyes a kewpie doll."

Eve didn't want to believe him. "Oh, you couldn't have, Brian. You couldn't have been that stupid."

"Afraid so," he said.

"Knowing the mess you're already in?"

"Knowing that."

Eve turned to Charley, as if she expected him to explain his brother. But he begged off.

"Don't look at me. He's the one with the answers."

"I can't even figure out *how*," she said, turning back to Brian. "How on earth could you rope a gay man like Jolly into this thing?"

"No problem. Didn't you know that the worst queers like girls too? No? Well, Chester knows it. Now he does, anyway. Beyond that, though, the story I gave Chester was basically just what I told you—that someone who saw us at the Purple Sage last night called and told me about the accident. Only difference is I gave that person a name—Jolly's angel, Rick."

Charley already had a pretty good idea what else Brian had told Chester. Nevertheless he sat there patiently listening as his brother spread it out for them.

"Yeah, it seems Rick came up to our table again after you two and Chester left, and he invited Belinda and me up to the house for one of Jolly's notorious little orgies—you know, the kind where sexy young girls like Belinda get ravaged after being pumped full of drugs and promises. Naturally I didn't want to go, but Belinda did. Trotted right off with Rick, she did."

"And Chester bought it?" Eve said. "My God, Rick came over to our table. Certainly Chester knew Rick wasn't in the market for females."

Brian was patient with her. "Well, as Chester understands it, Rick simply does what he's told. And since Damian swings both ways, sometimes Rick has to perform as a kind of roper— one of Jolly's eunuchs who go out and round up girls for the old lech. And come to think of it, I might even have mentioned where the great director's house is. Yes, I think I probably did."

"Which still doesn't tell us *why,*" Eve said.

"You mean why do it in the first place? Why sic Chester on Jolly? That ought to be obvious—to get even for yesterday. To give Jolly as much hassle as I possibly can."

"And it never occurred to you that it would all come right back on us?" Eve said. "No matter how much hassle you cause him, you cause yourself more. The police will want to know where Chester got his information, and—"

"The *police!*" Charley cut in, having finally heard all he cared to. "And *hassle!* Just what do you two think Chester Einhorn is anyway, some middle-American suburbanite who eats quiche and calls in the police when he's got a problem? Didn't you hear him last night?" Already getting up out of the booth, Charley looked at his brother with curiosity more than anger. "Those guns in his truck, what'd you think they were there for? Show?"

Brian shrugged. "What guns?"

"In his pickup," Eve said. "That's right. I saw them this morning."

Brian threw up his hands in mock amazement. "Wow, this is shocking—a country boy with a gun rack in his pickup. What's the world coming to?"

"Where was he when you last saw him?" Charley asked.

"In his truck," Eve said. "He was leaving the hospital parking lot."

"Do you know where he was going?"

"Back to his motel, I think," Brian said. "He had to phone his family about Belinda, and I think he didn't want to do it from the hospital. Pay phones scare him, I gather."

Charley drained the last of his coffee. "You sure he wasn't on his way up to Jolly's?"

Brian looked out at the pool, away from his brother's searching gaze. "Who knows? He didn't really say. But I can tell you this. If he did go up there, it wouldn't be to shoot the bastard."

"What then? Punch him out? Hundred-and-thirty pound Chester Einhorn is going up there and brawl with Jolly and his angels? Or maybe, with his great gift for language, maybe Chester would prefer to remonstrate with them. Beat them down with words. That what you think?"

"Could be," Brian said. "It's a helluva lot more likely, I'd say, than that he'd go up there with murder on his mind."

Charley knew that Brian was probably right. It was one thing to advocate reliance on firearms over government, but quite another to take your gun in hand and exact personal justice. The consequences tended to be dire. Still, there was this problem Charley had when it came to small Ozark men with guns. A problem born of experience.

"You're probably right," he said now, getting up and dropping a ten on the table. "But just to be on the safe side, I think I'll drive up there and have a look."

Brian got out his keys and tossed them to Charley. "Then you better take my truck. Remember, the road gets pretty hairy near the top."

Eve scooted out of the booth after Charley. "Well, I think I'd better go along. If we run into Rick or Jolly, I'm not sure they're ready for another tête-à-tête with one of the Poole brothers."

Brian didn't move from his corner of the booth. "Have fun," he said.

In the sixties, when Charley and Brian were still in their teens, they had spent a week or two each summer at the southwest Missouri hobby farm of their mother's sister, Aunt Sarah, and her ex–Air Force husband Randall Hoag. The Hoags' house sat on a lovely, leafy hilltop that on its easterly side looked down on the squalid farm of Smiley Moon, a part-time auctioneer, marijuana grower, and livestock thief.

In his favor, Moon had three teenage boys who each summer locked onto Charley and Brian as if they were their long-lost cousins and taught them the lore of the Ozarks: how to hunt, fish, trap, steal, and swim naked. For Charley, though, it was not the good times with the boys he remembered as much as the bad times with their peppy, wisecracking father, who liked to beat his sons with ropes, chains, cattle canes, whatever was handy. More gentle with his wife, he usually hit her only with his hand, sometimes open, sometimes not.

The one thing Smiley Moon cared for was guns. He loved to buy and steal them, and he loved to polish them and show them off. And above all, he loved to fire them. Charley would not soon forget the day Smiley came home with a new assault rifle and decided that there were just too many dogs around the place, both strays and pets. Smiling happily, wandering among his ramshackle buildings, he hunted down and killed four dogs in all, including Orville, the boys' ten-year-old border collie.

"Don't fret it," he advised. "Old dog like thet, he's better off dead, he really is."

On another occasion, driving the boys to the swimming hole, Smiley stopped the truck and shot a full-grown bald eagle out of a distant tree as if he were plinking a varmint. But his real claim to fame was that he once had shot and killed a local cattle dealer who foolishly sold him a "banger," a cow with deadly brucellosis. Since the disease could wipe out a rancher's herd—if he'd *had* a herd, which Smiley did not—and since no one really wanted to cross the defendant, the jury decided that it was a case of justifiable homicide.

So Charley had a problem when it came to small Ozark men

with guns. Evidently, though, it was a problem with its comical side, for he became aware now that Eve was looking at him and smiling, in amusement.

"What is it?" he asked. "Do I have a fly on my nose?"

"Oh, I don't know—you look so grim. Do you really expect Chester to come up here gunning for Jolly?"

"If I didn't think it was possible, I wouldn't have bothered."

Eve shrugged. *"Possible,* okay. I can buy that. But listen, if we don't see any sign of him, we just let it go, okay? No warning to Jolly. No explanations or anything like that."

"In other words, you want to keep Brian's name out of it."

"Well, sure. Don't you? If Chester hasn't done anything yet, Brian can still fix things, can't he? Just tell Chester the truth. Brian can do that at least. We'll make him do it."

Charley had his doubts. He knew from long experience his brother's gift for procrastination and dissembling. Still, he also knew he had to agree.

"You've got it," he said.

Eve smiled again. And he realized now that she was sitting as far from him as she could get, leaning back against the passenger door, her arm resting on the window sill, a cigarette burning in her hand. Whenever she dragged, she would turn her head and exhale out the window.

"You know, you don't have to do that," he said.

"I know. I've quit dozens of times."

"No, I mean blow the smoke out the window. I'm not that fragile."

"Well, that's refreshing. Most nonsmokers make you feel like a leper with AIDS."

"Is that why you're sitting way over there?"

"Only partly." She pulled her jersey blouse away from her neck and fluttered it. "Remember, I've been in these clothes since yesterday afternoon."

"Don't worry about it. You look clean and fresh. You look great."

Smiling still, she shook her head at him. "Charley, you're too much. You better be careful. I'm going to want to take you with us."

By then they were out of barren rock and chaparral and moving up into the piney area, where the homes were more expensive and isolated. And finally he saw the fork up ahead, its right lane leading down into the copse of scraggly pines while the other climbed straight up to Jolly's place, towering in the morning light, its wraparound windows reflecting the sun down upon Charley and Eve with blinding accuracy.

Just as they were driving through the fork, taking the left lane, Eve gasped audibly.

"Oh God," she said. "I think I saw something red down there, in the pines."

"His truck, you mean?"

"I don't know. It was just a glimpse. A flash."

By then, they were well past the fork and Charley decided that stopping and backing up—edging downhill through the heavy road dust—would take longer than going on up the hundred yards to Jolly's and turning around, coming back. Gunning the engine, he roared up the steep incline and pulled in at the rock-walled gate. And there he stopped. Straight ahead of him a cement-mixer truck was grinding away as workers directed a stream of wet cement down an attached sluice into a board-framed depression located next to the pool and almost directly below the wide second-floor deck of the house. As his eyes readjusted from the sun's assault, Charley saw for the first time that there were two men out on the deck, one of them Rick and the other Damian Jolly, dressed in pajamas and a silk robe. Standing there in the dry blaze of the morning sun, they were looking not at Charley or the great vista behind him but at the workers as they began now to smooth the poured cement with their long-handled bullfloats.

Charley threw open the truck's door and was starting to jump out, intending to warn the two men to get back into the house, when the director suddenly went flailing backward, a piece of his head spinning off in one direction while the rest of him fell crashing through a large picture window just as the shot rang out, followed by Eve's breathless, gulping scream. Rick meanwhile was still at the balcony railing, just beginning to crouch, looking around in horror at Jolly draped over the sill of the demolished window. Then more glass began to fall as another shot sounded, and Rick tried to vault the railing but caught his foot and fell, belly flopping into the wet cement below and scattering the workers.

By then Charley was back behind the wheel and turning the truck around while Eve kept yelling at him to do just that.

"Let's go! Let's go! Come on, let's get out of here!"

They roared out of the gate and headed back down the dirt road through their own still-unsettled dust. Charley's mouth was spitless and he could feel his heart jumping in his neck as he maintained a death grip on the steering wheel, as much to keep his hands from shaking as to hold the truck in the roadway. Next to him, Eve beat her fists against the dashboard.

"Goddamn crazy cowboy!" she cried. "Goddamn him to hell!"

Charley passed the fork without even looking toward the stand of pines in which Eve had seen the color red. And not once as he followed the twisting, plunging road down toward the city did he let himself look in the rearview mirror to find out if a red pickup truck was following them. He didn't want to see Chester Ein-horn. He didn't want to have anything more to do with Brian and his ruinous obsessions.

But even as he was thinking this, even as he tried to distance himself in his mind from what was happening, he could feel a terrible impotence growing in him, the conviction that his own wishes, his own will, simply didn't matter anymore. Much as the steeply graded road was pulling him down and down toward the city, he felt a kindred force drawing him toward a future fash-ioned not by himself or chance but by his brother.

# chapter five

When they got back to the motel, Charley and Eve found Brian stretched out on a beach towel, evidently having just completed another marathon swim. Because his eyes were closed against the sun, he didn't realize that the two of them were there until Eve spoke.

"Come on, we've got to talk. You really did it this time."

Squinting up at her, he started to say something, but she walked away, heading for their room. He looked at Charley then.

"Why? What happened?"

"We'll see you upstairs."

Brian came in his own good time, stopping on the way for a drink of water at a fountain. When he finally arrived, closing the door behind him, he repeated his question.

"Well, what's up? What's the big deal?"

Across the room, Eve shook her head and turned away, her eyes filling.

"Well?" Brian said to Charley.

"Jolly's dead," Charley told him. "Chester shot him."

At first, Brian just stood there looking at the two of them much as he had after Belinda's accident, as if he were waiting for some sign that it was all a joke, a put-on.

"You can't be serious," he said.

In his mind, Charley still kept seeing Belinda as the car hit her, and now there was Jolly doing his weird back flip, taking the bullet. And Charley found it impossible to square the wrenching violence of those images with the face before him, his brother's look of slightly amused consternation. Charley came close to hitting him, even bunching his fist and twisting slightly, planting himself. But Brian turned away, looking at Eve now.

"You're not serious," he repeated. "You can't be serious."

"It happened just as we got there," Charley told him. "Jolly was out on the deck and Chester hit him from down in the trees somewhere. First shot. Your little cowboy's quite a marksman."

"It's true, then?"

"It's true."

"You mean he did it? The little jerk actually did it?"

"That's what we mean, all right."

"I can't believe it. I just can't believe it. I mean, that he'd actually do such a thing. The man must be crazy."

Turning, Eve came straight over to him as if she too were thinking of punching him. Instead she pushed her face right up into his. "Well, he did it, all right! In fact, he fucking blew Jolly's head off! Do you understand that, Brian? Do you comprehend? Does it begin to dawn on you that this is no longer some kind of game? Jolly's head went flying right off him, like a goddamn hat or something!"

"Okay, okay." Backing away from her, Brian sat down on the edge of one of the beds. He shook his head in bewilderment. "Jesus Christ, it was just a joke. At the most, I figured Chester would go up there and hassle the little fag. Shoot out his tires or something. Nothing like this."

"Well, I'm afraid he did a little more than 'hassle' the man,"

Charley said. "About all you can do now is turn yourself in and hope for the best."

Brian looked at him in disbelief. *"Turn myself in?* For what? I didn't shoot anybody." He turned to Eve for support. "It was just a joke, for Christ's sake! Come on. Do you think I should turn myself in?"

She shook her head. "I don't know. I can't think. I'm still in shock."

"It really isn't very complicated," Charley told him. "If someone saw Chester up there, and they catch him, he'll implicate you. And if he got away, the police won't even know he's in the picture. You'll be their number one suspect. In fact, they're probably already out looking for you. Your only sensible move is to get a lawyer and surrender yourself. With luck, maybe they'll only charge you with malicious mischief."

"Instead of what?"

Charley shrugged. "I don't know—conspiracy to commit murder. Or accessory before the fact. Who knows—I'm not a lawyer."

"No? You sure as hell sound like one."

"One other thing," Charley said. "Remember what you said to us after Belinda's accident? That Eve and I were just trying to help you, and that it wasn't our fault, what happened. You said you'd make sure we weren't involved."

Getting up, Brian waved his hands as if he were shooing flies away. "Yeah, yeah, don't worry about that," he said, Eve and Charley's problems apparently not all that important at the moment.

"I'm sure we were seen up there," Charley went on. "So the police will undoubtedly want statements from us. Which means I'm going to have to get a lawyer too." The thought of all that—appearing with a lawyer and being questioned by the police, probably badgered—so filled him with anger that he suddenly snatched Brian's wet towel off the bed and sent it flying into the bathroom, where it knocked some plastic bottles off the vanity.

"Christ, what a mess," he snapped. "What a talent you have, Brian, for fucking up everyone's life. Especially your own."

Brian took umbrage. "Hey, big brother, you want to just walk out of here and fly home, be my guest. No one's begging you to hang around."

"And if I left—" Charley was about to suggest that he would want to take his forty-thousand bail money with him, but the words stuck in his throat. And he thought, Even now, Charley Poole, the proper little Boy Scout.

"If I left, what would I do for excitement?" he said, settling for sarcasm over honesty.

Brian and Eve looked at him in puzzlement, evidently thinking he was trying to be funny.

"In any case, I'm going back to my room now," he added. "I've got some calls to make." At the door he looked back at Eve. "The lawyer I get, you want him to represent you too?"

Before answering, she turned to Brian, as if she would first need his approval or forgiveness. But he had moved over to the balcony doors and was staring out at the pool, oblivious of her.

"Maybe," she said to Charley. "I'll let you know pretty soon, okay?"

Charley continued to stand there for a moment, looking at this smart, beautiful woman who seemed to have everything, yet was content to consign it all to Brian, not unlike a Hindu widow obediently throwing herself onto her late husband's funeral pyre. Charley wanted to take her by the shoulders and shake her, wake her up. Instead, nodding agreement, he left.

**B**ack in his room, Charley put in a call to Donna but was told that she was out with a client.

"A real biggie, Charley," said Rose Biaggi, who once had been his secretary. "A mansion. The client actually said that. He said he wants a mansion, no less."

"Well, that's nice, Rose, but keep after her anyway. I need to talk to her. Also get Ray Henley for me. Him or his son. I need them to recommend a lawyer out here."

"Will do, boss. But why? Are you okay? Is everything all right out there?"

"I'm fine, Rose. Just a little family matter, that's all. But keep on it till you get them, okay? I'll just be sitting here, wondering what to do with my thumb."

Rose laughed. A bawdy woman, she'd had a hard time adjusting from Charley to Donna, who ran a much tighter, more proper ship. "Well, in that case, I'd better hurry," she said. "Bye now."

In actuality, Charley was not sitting but lying back on the bed. And he was feeling sicker by the moment, his adrenaline output evidently having returned to normal. The shooting of Jolly—the fear and worry it induced—had combined with his hangover and lack of sleep to make him feel as if he had a bad case of influenza. His body ached with tension; his head pounded; his mouth and throat were parched; vomiting and diarrhea seemed just around the corner.

His anger at Brian was absolute. Brother or no, at the moment he hated the reckless bastard. And he kept telling himself that if only he had listened to Donna and stayed at home, if only he had wired Brian the final contract payment instead of flying out and playing Big Brother to the Rescue, then he wouldn't have been lying here in the beastly Goodland Motel, sick with hangover and dread; he wouldn't have acquired a new forty-thousand-dollar mortgage, nor would he have permanently assigned three-quarters of his brain to the task of woolgathering about Eve Sherman.

Donna's good sense hadn't stopped there either. *You can't help him,* she'd said. *He's been a screwup all his life.* How right she was. Only now the screwups were matters of life and death. And poor old Charley Poole would soon have to be pleading his innocence to police and prosecutors. At the thought, he shivered and felt his gorge rise, which made him wonder if he might not have the flu after all.

Picking up the remote, he turned on the television and began to surf through the channels, looking for a newscast. He figured that there probably had been a bulletin earlier, as soon as the stations learned of the incident. But now there was nothing except talk shows and soap operas and especially commercials: plump, hairless infants pushing diapers and tall, hairless black men hawking sport shoes and soft drinks while all the beautiful young women peddled everything else.

It was almost noon, though, so Charley continued to lie there and watch. And finally the local news came on, a pretty young clone of Diane Sawyer breathlessly reporting that "Damian Jolly, director of the movie *Miss Colorado,* now being filmed here in Colorado Springs, has been shot and seriously wounded at his newly purchased home above Rockrimmon." Her co-anchor, a slightly older, slightly prettier man, then took the baton and related that Jolly had suffered a head wound and was already in surgery at the hospital. His assistant, Rick Walters, trying to escape the rifle fire, had broken an arm in a leap from the balcony of the house. Appearing before reporters at the hospital, Rick said that he had a pretty good idea who had done the shooting and that he had informed the police of his suspicions, but the studio lawyers had cautioned him against saying anything more than that.

The anchorwoman then said that informed sources at the police department had identified the suspect as Brian Poole, notorious friend of the late superstar singer, Kim Sanders, on whose life Jolly's movie was based. Poole had been arrested earlier in the week for destroying the film's outdoor set at a ranch near Black Forest.

For the first time, then, Charley saw footage of Brian under arrest, looking handsome and pleasant, even amiable, as he was being led handcuffed into the county building. Next, they cut to the site of the bulldozing, showing the row of storefronts both before and after, a picturesque small-town street reduced to a pile of rubble, with the Cat dozer parked in front, like a discarded weapon. In voiceover, the anchorman explained that Brian was alleged by the same spokesman to be capable of any violence in his campaign to make the studio abandon the movie project. He was reported to have given the police a false address, and the police were said to be on the lookout for his late-model black Chevrolet pickup, which had been seen near Jolly's house just before the shooting.

As the newscast went on to other matters, Charley turned the set off. The report of Jolly being wounded didn't surprise him. As a kid, he remembered hearing the same kind of thing on TV about President Kennedy—after a large portion of his head had been shot off. And he figured this was not so much a matter of journalistic delicacy as it was simple lawyerly prudence, a reluctance to pronounce anyone dead until a medical doctor had done so. About the pickup truck, though—that made no sense at all. He and Eve had been seen not only *near* Jolly's house but *right there,* inside the front gate and at the *time* of the shooting, not just before it. But then Charley reminded himself that this wasn't the real world he had been watching, only the news at noon.

Within a few minutes the phone rang, and Donna was on the line, clearly unhappy at being pulled away even briefly from her "mansion" client. But when Charley explained things—explained them *partially* anyway—her attitude swung from impatience to shock.

"A *killing!*" she cried. "Oh my God, Charley, you've got to get out of there as fast as you can! Get away from him! He'll destroy you—I know he will!"

"Don't worry, I'm leaving as soon as I can—tonight or tomorrow morning at the latest. But first I have to go the police myself and give them a statement. I'm trying to get ahold of Ray Henley now, so he can recommend someone out here for me. I'll call you again afterwards and let you know when I'll be home."

"God, I don't know why you're so pigheaded," she said. "I told you not to go out there."

"So you did. I guess I'll never learn."

"I guess not."

"Good-bye, Donna."

When Ray Henley finally called, Charley briefed him on his predicament and what he wanted him to do. Ten minutes later a local criminal attorney phoned Charley and they made an appointment to meet at three o'clock at the county building, where they would discuss what Charley soon thereafter would be saying in his statement to the DA.

After hanging up, Charley gathered his aching body, all six ravaged feet of it, and dragged himself into the bathroom to wash up. He also washed down a couple of aspirin tablets, which in his stomach immediately turned into hot coals.

He wanted desperately to lie back down and sleep for a few hours, or at least until the meeting with the lawyer. But he knew he had to get back to Brian and keep him focused, *carry* him down to the police station if he had to. So, reluctantly, he left his room finally and went back there—only to find the door ajar and the room empty. The dresser drawers had been pulled open and all the clothes and luggage and personal items were gone. As were Brian and Eve.

**E**ve had reclined the seat so far she couldn't have seen out even if she had wanted to, which she did not, since the West always looked pretty much the same to her from thirty thousand feet: a vast tan emptiness with occasional stretches of pale lavender mountains and huge, green irrigation circles. She still had not changed clothes from the day before, was still wearing the same jeans and sleeveless jersey blouse that she had worn to the Purple Sage, and which had made her scoot as far from Charley as she could get on their way up to Jolly's in the pickup. Now, though, stretched out in the chartered jet, she hoped that she had developed at least a modicum of body odor as an appropriate little gift for her seatmate: Brian the fugitive, Brian the bugout.

At first she had refused to go, telling him that she would not be a party to such madness, helping him jump bail and add to his crimes, not to mention leaving Charley holding the bag. But Brian had trumped her, nodding sympathetically, saying that he understood and even agreed with her.

"Yeah, I guess it's high time you cut yourself loose from me. All I'm doing is dragging you down with me, and you deserve better than that. Really, baby, I understand."

And for a short time she had stood by and watched him pack, tossing and stuffing his things into their suitcases. But the thought of the two of them parting so abruptly after so long a time together was simply too much for her to handle, and she soon joined him, hurriedly packing her things right in with his. And this made her even angrier, the fact that her loyalty to him came at such a price: not only turning her into a lawbreaker but forcing her to betray Charley as well.

As they were about to leave, she asked Brian about the bail money, how on earth he could justify letting his brother suffer such a loss, and he assured her that would not happen. He said that either he would return in time, once Chester was on the hook for the shooting, or he would simply repay Charley out of the contract money.

Eve still was amazed at how smoothly Brian had handled the getaway, almost as if he had expected it to happen and had had time to prepare for it. Hiding behind dark glasses and a Chicago Bears baseball cap, he had led her down the back stairs, away from both Charley's room and the front desk. A short distance from the motel he stopped at a pay phone and arranged for a taxi to pick them up at a nearby mall. Back in the truck, he handed her his flight bag and had her take ten thousand dollars out of it, explaining that he wanted her to do all the talking and arranging from then on. He would be her backward brother, a dolt obediently tagging along.

He dropped her off, along with the luggage, just north of the main entrance to the mall. Then he parked the truck way out on the fringe of the huge parking lot and walked back to where she was, arriving only a few minutes before the taxi. Following his instructions, she had the driver take them to the airport, which was about twenty minutes away. South of the terminal, Eve went alone into the tiny office of a private air service and told the clerk that she and her brother wanted to charter a jet to Santa Barbara.

"As soon as possible," she added.

Before the clerk could answer, a man coming out of the room behind her emitted a sharp laugh and said, "How about immediately, if not sooner?"

He was chunky and middle-aged, with a florid face and an outfit that proclaimed him self-employed: khakis, a Peanuts sweatshirt, and a tan, well-crushed captain's cap. He told Eve that they'd had a cancellation that morning and had a Lear jet "all fueled and ready to go." Flying time would be two and a quarter hours and the cost would be seventy-one hundred dollars, cash or credit card. As Eve brought forth her stack of hundreds and began counting out the fare, the man laughed again, this time a touch nervously.

"Well, it's sure nice doing business with you, miss," he said. "My name's Ted Horne. I'll be your pilot."

Very soon after that they were airborne, banking and climbing above the Colorado plains before turning back and streaking west over the front range, with Pike's Peak no more than a molehill far below. And now, well on their way, Eve was discovering that even though she hated what they were doing, she was grateful for the sudden peace and quiet, the chance to lie back in the plush, cozy cylinder of the Lear jet and try to relax, maybe even sleep. But as she lay there with her eyes closed, she heard Brian twisting in his seat and then felt his breath lightly brushing her face. Opening her eyes, she found herself looking straight into his eyes not even a foot away.

"What do you want?" she snapped. "I'm trying to sleep."

He smiled ruefully. "Oh, I was just thinking—how lucky I am to have you. Or to *have had* you, I guess I should say. After all this, I imagine you'll be moving on pretty soon, don't you think?"

"That again, huh?"

"You mean back in the motel? Well, I guess it's on my mind. I guess I know I've gone too far. That I deserve to lose you."

"Well, you do put one to the test."

"I know." He paused there a moment, still smiling thoughtfully. "Charley," he went on. "You really liked him, didn't you?"

"Sure. And so should you. I really hate it, running out on him like this. Leaving him holding the bag."

"I know. I do too. I really do, babe. But I just couldn't stay. After that one night in jail—on top of the year in Mexico—I found out I just can't cut it anymore. I'd go crazy. And I honestly don't feel I deserve it. Belinda was an accident. And Chester shooting Jolly, I never even considered it a possibility. I really didn't. And as for the bulldozing, that was for good reason— you know it was. A guy shouldn't have to just accept it, those bastards taking your life and turning it into shit for all the world to see. Yet they will if I don't stop them. They're the ones who should be behind bars, not me."

Eve did not feel like discussing it all yet again. "Let me sleep, okay?"

"Sure." But he was looking at her in that special way he had, his lovely, muscular face somehow deprecating himself while romancing her at the same time, admiring her, appealing to her.

"I'll cuddle to you, okay?" he said. "I'll hold you while you sleep."

"All right. But that's all."

"Of course. What else?"

As she rolled over, he pushed up the armrests between them and moved in tightly against her, Levi's to Levi's, his arm around her, his hand cupping her right breast. Through her jersey blouse and lightweight bra she could feel her nipples hardening—until he suddenly let go of her. She felt him fussing with his jeans, probably rearranging himself. Then he came back, putting his arm around her again and pressing in tight.

"Don't be alarmed," he said. "I'm not preparing to rape you, just giving Mister Big a little more elbow room."

It had been his name for it in the beginning, a jest at his own expense. But in point of fact, it was a pretty fair moniker. In bed or elsewhere, as they set about making love, she often would slip down and inquire as to the subject's welfare. "And how is Mister Big tonight?"

At the moment, though, rest and sleep were still her priorities. And she reminded him.

"Sleep, remember?" she said.

"Of course. No problem. This is fine."

And so it was. Drifting, half-asleep, she could feel him hard against her buttocks. And she thought how delicious it would be if she did in fact fall asleep this way, with him holding her and the world so far below, out of sight, out of mind. But her nipples refused to join her in sleep, and in time she took hold of his hand and guided it under her blouse and bra, the touch of his fingers on her breasts as usual jumping like an electric current straight to her pubis. He began kissing her on the neck and nibbling her ear, and soon she turned in his embrace and the two of them began to kiss in earnest, their hands moving into the other's jeans.

As they hustled out of their clothes, Eve glanced over at the cockpit door to make sure it was drawn tight. Then she slipped down onto her knees and took him in her mouth, feeling his hands as they combed back into her hair and cupped her head, moving as she moved. Brian had brought his seat back up partially, and she knew that soon he would reach down and lift her onto his lap, his fingers digging into her buttocks while he buried his face in her breasts. And she would feel it all coming closer and closer, that time of loveliness and terror that bound her to him like a rope of pearls.

After returning to his room, Charley was at a loss for what to do. He knew he had information that the police could have used, such as the fact that Chester Einhorn was in all likelihood the killer—or at least the shooter—of Damian Jolly. Also, the police undoubtedly would have liked to know that Brian to all appearances had jumped bail and was on the run.

On the one hand, Charley knew that withholding this information even temporarily might be construed by the police or the district attorney's office as obstruction of justice. On the other, he knew it would be recklessly stupid of him to go to the police without a lawyer at his side, someone looking out for *his* interests and no one else's. So his decision was, as the cool people said, a no-brainer. He would wait till three o'clock.

Meanwhile he wanted very much to talk to someone about it all, what a lovely fix his little brother had gotten him into. He considered phoning Donna again and telling her about Brian's latest jape, but he knew that would only set her off again, at his expense as much as Brian's. That left the bed, the almost sexual appeal of getting in an hour's nap before leaving for the courthouse. But he was afraid that once he dropped off, he would sleep through Armageddon, let alone a bedside alarm. So he elected to freshen up, to shower again and put on a clean shirt and the tan Armani, the only suit he had brought with him. Though he didn't particularly like the idea, he knew that the police were prone to go easier on men who came in wearing a good suit instead of a workshirt and dirty khakis. And he wasn't Brian; he didn't *like* to stack the deck against himself.

At about two-fifteen he was getting ready to leave, just then putting on his jacket when there was a knock on the door. Thinking it might be Brian and Eve, overcome with guilt and ready to face the music, he opened the door. And there stood Chester Einhorn, carrying what appeared to be a bag of groceries. Though it crossed Charley's mind to slam the door in the little man's face, he found himself stepping aside and letting him come on in. As the door closed behind him, Chester reached into the paper sack and drew out not a loaf of bread or a can of corn but a blue-barreled pistol so huge it looked like a cannon in his hard little fist as he raised it now and pointed it at Charley.

"Where's your brother?" he asked.

Charley couldn't take his eyes off the gun. As if by magic, it had loosened his bowels and weakened his knees and sucked the air out of his lungs. He could barely speak. "I don't know. He took off, that's all I know. I drank pretty late last night and just got up. I—"

"Where'd he go?"

"If I knew I'd tell you, believe me. He just took off. Jumped bail even. I can't figure it."

Chester stood there looking up at him, eyes squinting and lipless mouth curved in the wraith of a smile. Then, abruptly, he cocked the gun—to Charley, a sound uncomfortably like that of a breaking bone. By then his hands were shaking badly.

"Seattle," he got out. "I think he went to Seattle."

"You *think?*"

"No, I'm sure. That's what he said. He's got an old friend up there. Lives aboard a boat called the *Seagull.* "

"*Seagull?* "

"Yes—plain old *Seagull.* "

"What's this fella's name?"

"I don't know. I remember Brian talking about him a few times, but I don't remember his name. Brian said they go way back, the two of them. Real buddies."

"And you're his brother. So how come you rat on him?"

Charley looked at the gun. "Why do you think?"

Chester appeared satisfied with that. "Makes sense." He uncocked the gun and motioned with it for Charley to move. "Okay, git yer stuff together. We goin' on a little trip, the two of us."

"We are?"

"Yep, we sure are."

"Seattle?"

"That's what you said, wasn't it?"

Charley was furiously trying to think of something he could do: go for the gun, jump off the balcony, pretend to faint. Only the last seemed feasible, but in the end he couldn't even bring himself to do that. He opened his suitcase and began to throw into it the few things he had bothered to unpack.

"Yessir, that brother of yers, he shore is a card," Chester said. "But we gonna find him, and he's gonna learn a thing or two, he damn well is. So hurry up, will ya?"

Charley didn't answer. But he was hurrying.

**A**n hour later Charley had reached the point where he would almost have preferred being shot by Chester rather than have to listen to one more minute of the man's nasal drone as he expounded on his dreary philosophy of life. In the beginning, though, as Charley drove Chester's bright red pickup out of Colorado Springs and headed north for Denver, he had been an avid listener to everything the little man had to say, beginning with the welcome news that Jolly hadn't been killed after all, that it was not his head but his *hairpiece* that had been blown away as the bullet apparently glanced off his skull. That glancing, however, had cracked bone and caused the director a blood clot on the brain, which had required immediate surgery.

Incredibly, Chester's greatest concern about the shooting seemed to be his aim, the fact that he had *not* blown off Jolly's head.

"I jest cain't figger it," he lamented. "That two-seventy of mine is mostly a real right-on weapon. Hell, I've hit turkey vultures with that dang rifle—and I mean when they's flyin'. You try doin' that sometime, buster, you'll find out it ain't so easy. Only way I can figger it is this dang Colorado air—itchy, lip-crackin' shit! A body cain't hardly breathe, you know that? And I jest figger that's what the trouble was up to Jolly's place. I jest bet the air was so dang thin it probly jest lifted that li'l old bullet a smidgen off dead center. Cuz I had the hairs right on him, believe you me, I did—right twixt his snotty fag eyes. Him posin' up there in his goddamn sissy robe."

Charley didn't comment on any of this, mostly out of fear that he would say the wrong thing and set Chester off, and that was not something he wanted to do. Also, Charley sensed that though the tiny cowboy's main reason for dragging him along might have been to birddog Brian, he probably needed him equally as an ear, someone to whom he could pour out his mad little heart for hours on end.

Every now and then, however, he would drop a random pearl of information, such as his casual explanation of how he had found out that Brian had lied to him—by hearing it from the one person who knew, Belinda herself, who had come out of her coma with her memory sufficiently intact to recall that she had been with Brian, not Jolly, on the night of the accident. Fortunately for Charley, she apparently had no recollection of the accident itself and had told Chester only about being with Brian in his motel room at the Goodland and innocently taking the pills he had given her—for her upset stomach, she had told Chester—this last most likely an invention on her part in order to maintain her image before her big brother as a pure and wholesome country girl debauched by a known drug fiend. Chester said he then had cautioned her not to tell the police or anyone else about Brian because he wanted to take care of that little matter himself.

"Yessir, I jest told her to lay back and not worry her purty head about anythin' 'cept gittin' on her feet again. She's got my ma and cousin Lil with her, so I jest told her to fergit all about Brian Poole cuz Chester Einhorn was gonna take care of him. And by Jesus, that's jest what I'm gonna do. My pa and uncle can handle the ranch or the dang thing can jest go to seed—I don't give a shit one way or t'other. Alls I care about is runnin' that brother of yers to ground and havin' him suck on this for a while." At which point he waggled the three fifty-seven magnum in Charley's face. "Let him get a real good taste of it—that's all I want."

Then he chuckled and shook his head fondly, like an old man gossiping on a park bench. "That old Brian, though, you gotta hand it to him, you know that? He's really some piece of work, he is. What a card! Gettin' me to do his dirty work like he done, and damn near makin' me like it too. He's some kinda charmer, all right. Hell, old Brian, he could charm the birds right down outa the trees if he'd a mind to, and that's a fack."

"So why not drop all this?" Charley suggested. "Jolly wasn't killed. And Brian didn't call the law in on you. He just split. You're in the clear."

Chester snorted and shook his head, as if Charley were something of a card himself. "What do you take me for? Some candy-ass city fool? Don't you think I got enough smarts to figger out that if the law gits to Brian afore I do, he's gonna sing—and I don't mean sing 'Miss Colorado' neither. The ballad of Chester Einhorn, that's what he's gonna sing. And you know it same as me. So there ain't gonna be no droppin' nothin', not now and not never."

It surprised Charley that he could adjust so quickly to a situation that should have been a scene on television or in the movies rather than a slice of his own life. Here he was, competently driving on while this wiry little cowboy waved a cannon in his face and prattled on in the very lingo of showbiz: "singing" to the police and "taking care" of Brian and giving him "a real good taste" of a gun barrel. But the lingo in no way tempered Charley's anxiety and fear. Chester may have had the dialogue all wrong, but Charley still knew the little man was for real, in fact was probably the very worst—and commonest—of America's bad dreams: another lunatic with a loaded gun.

With this in mind, Charley wouldn't let himself relax for a second. He knew with every breath he took that his life was on the line and that his survival might well depend on just how patient and calm he could be, and how *ready,* when his moment came. So he waited. And he listened.

"You best be sure about Seattle," Chester warned him. "Cuz that's where we goin', all right. And if old Brian turns up on the moon, then *that*'s where we goin'. Cuz justice is all that counts in this world, Charley, and they's only one way to git it. You go out and take it, that's how. Court justice and all that horse manure ain't fer people like me, it's fer lawyers and judges and big business honchos, that's who. It ain't nothin' but a guvmint subidy fer 'em, jest like welfare and food stamps is fer niggers. No different. No sir, if yer a workin' stiff and you want you some justice, you gotta go git it fer yerself. You git you some guns and learn how to use 'em, and then you can think about gittin' you some justice. Cuz there ain't no other way, and that's a fack."

They were descending from the higher ground south of Denver down into the city, which appeared to have been erected in the middle of a lake, a rusty yellow layer of smog that stretched far out into the prairieland to the east. Listening as Chester droned on, Charley thought how nice it would have been to push the little cowboy overboard, right into the yellow lake. Sweets for the sweet.

Much of the time Chester didn't bother to hold the gun on

Charley, or for that matter even to keep it in his hand. Sometimes he would casually lay it down on the dashboard in front of him, either because he enjoyed playing cat and mouse or because the thing was heavy and he judged Charley wasn't fool enough to struggle over a loaded gun while zipping along the freeway. Still, holding the gun or not, the little cowboy kept his eye on Charley. Most of the time he sat leaning back against the passenger door, his boots barely touching the floor as he chewed contentedly on a match and squinted over at his captive, his seamed and sunken face looking almost happy for a change, almost relaxed, as if the two of them were driving farther and farther from that biting cold wind he was always hunched against.

"Anyways," he said, "I bet ya been wonderin' how come my politics is like they is. I bet ya been wonderin' what in hell happened to old Chester. Well, I'll jest tell ya. I don't s'pose I mentioned it before, but it was my great granddaddy who got our place, back after the Civil War. He traded fer it with some dumb Cherokee, gave him two beat-up horses and a barrel of rotgut for all twelve hunnert acres. And we've had the place ever since. My granddaddies and my pa and uncle—and now me and Belinda— us Einhorns, we been livin' and dyin' there for over a hunnert years. And it's a real nice little ranch, it really is. Only problem is this crick we got. It cuts across our north quarter and it's got these rock cliffs and all that kinda purty shit that turns city folk on. Anyways they come on over from Tulsa to picnic there or skinnydip or what the hell have ya. And they tear up the fences and leave their garbage and they shit all over the place. So my pa and me, we useta jest git our guns and run 'em off. Shoot over their heads and such. Give 'em a scare. You know."

At that point he shook his head in rueful disbelief, a philosopher still amazed at the world's perfidiousness.

"Then one day the goddamn sheriff waltzes in and tells us the guvmint declared the crick a 'scenic waterway' or some fool thing, and we had to fence it off so's our cattle wouldn't dirty it up. Meantime the public had the right to come in and do whatever fool thing they wanted—on *our land,* mind you—and we couldn't do one dang thing about it. Well, my ma, she writes the guvner and our congressman and senators and everybody but the goddamn dogcatcher. But of course it don't do one damn bit of good. The guvmint one day jest tells ya ya don't really own what's been yers fer a hunnert years. So what in hell is a body to do? Change who ya vote fer? Change yer political party? Call up radio talk shows and piss and moan about it?"

Chester laughed at the absurdity of the idea. He snorted and shook his head. "Not this cowboy, no sirree. Instead, what I did was *undeclare* our li'l crick a 'scenic waterway.' I jest git out my guns jest like before, only I don't show myself this time. And I don't shoot above no heads either. I blast Thermos jugs and shoot beer bottles right outa their grubby mitts, and I part their fag hair and shoot their fuckin' dogs too. And when the sheriff comes roarin' out afterwards, I'm jest settin' there on the porch swing drinkin' a beer, innocent as a lamb. They couldn't prove nothin'. Some weekends they'd send out a deputy to guard the fuckin' trespassers, but soon as he'd leave, I'd jest start in again. And finally they wasn't no more trespassers. And we had our crick back." At that point he actually lifted the gun to his lips and kissed it. "That's what I mean by a party of one. Me and this li'l baby, that's all the political party I need."

Heading west out of Denver, Charley followed the interstate, four smooth lanes of blacktop snaking through the mountains, often in well-lit tunnels. Soon, just past Idaho Springs, Chester grunted and motioned for Charley to turn off the freeway, onto a two-lane highway running north. On this road, they drove past a couple of turnouts, places where tourists could park and take in the spectacular scenery. And eventually Charley saw a turnout without a single car or tourist, and he judged that the stone parapet bordering it was low enough so the door of Chester's high-riding truck could swing open above it. It crossed his mind that he was probably being fatally reckless, that in a few seconds he would be gambling with his life. Even then, he could not stop himself.

Braking and turning in, he looked over at his captor. "I've got to piss," he said. "Either outside or here in the truck. Which will it be?"

Chester took hold of the magnum and brought it to rest on his lap, pointed at Charley. "Okay," he said. "Jest don't think you can git out and run. Jest shake the dew off your pecker and git back in, you got that?"

Nodding meekly, Charley opened the door above the parapet and started to get out. But even as he placed his left foot down onto the wide stone surface, he swung his right hand backwards in a vicious arc and chopped the wiry cowboy in his Adam's apple. Then he seized him by the front of his denim jacket and, yanking him out of the driver's door, tossed him like a sack of garbage over the parapet and down the side of the mountain.

Shocked by what he had done, Charley just stood there and watched as Chester plunged down the steep grade, frantically reaching for an occasional bush or scrub pine and fighting to get on his feet but falling again and tumbling, sliding, ultimately coming to rest about two hundred feet down, with the gun, incredibly, still in his hand. Without quite knowing why, Charley was relieved to see him move slightly, already struggling to sit up. And finally the little cowboy craned his neck and looked back up the mountain.

Charley waved to him. Then he got into the truck and drove off, heading back toward Denver.

# chapter six

Sex with Brian almost always left Eve feeling good afterwards, sated and loved and fulfilled. And usually she was able to carry those feelings with her into sleep, like an armful of flowers. But not this time. This time, even as she and Brian parted and began to pull their clothes back on, Eve felt as if she'd fallen out of a cozy bed into a pool of ice water.

"Well, that was fun," she said. "A couple of desperadoes pretending everything's cool."

Brian laughed. *"Desperadoes?* Oh, come on, babe, it's not that bad."

"No? Well, I'm just a tyro at all this, never having been a fugitive before."

"And you're not now. Maybe I am—but you're not."

"That's reassuring coming from the only Californian who's not a lawyer."

But Brian refused to be baited. Continuing with his impression of a secret agent—as Eve considered it—he calmly told her that he wanted her to go forward and tell the pilot that they wished to change their destination to the Burbank airport.

"Why?" she asked.

"In case they're on to us. Santa Barbara was just a red herring.

We actually go there, we'll probably find a welcoming committee waiting for us."

"What do I tell the pilot?"

Brian frowned. "Oh, let me think. Why not just tell him we've changed our minds, that the meeting we were going to hold in Santa Barbara, now we want to postpone it? Something like that."

"I'd feel better if I had a bath."

"A little sticky, are we?"

She mimicked his smug smile, and he laughed. As she got up and moved past him, he smacked her on the bottom.

"Still world class," he said.

"Will it look world class in stripes?"

"They don't wear stripes anymore. Orange jumpsuits now. You'll look positively fetching."

"Thanks. That's all I needed to hear." With that, she opened the cockpit door and went inside.

At the airport, Brian again assumed the role of Eve's dim-witted brother, tagging along after her in his Chicago Bears cap and sunglasses, leaving it to her to find a skycap and wave down a taxi. Following the instructions he had given her on the plane, she told the cabbie that they wanted to go to Hollywood, to some reasonably priced motel there, and he took them to the new Ramada Inn just off the Hollywood Freeway. Eve paid the cabbie and registered for their room, paying cash for two days in advance, while Brian used the lobby pay phone to call "an old friend."

Not until they were in their room and Eve was hurriedly stripping for a shower did she learn the identity of that friend: Stephanie Hodges, a rich old lover of Brian's, the woman he had turned to after Kim Sanders' death, the woman who had hidden him from the media during that unhappy time. Though Eve didn't much care for the idea of staying with one of Brian's old flames, she didn't make a fuss about it, mostly because she was so eager to get into the shower and take root there.

"Her daughter's coming for us," Brian said. "So don't take too long."

Eve didn't bother to answer, thinking at first that she would take as long as she damn well pleased. But there were things she had to know, questions she wanted answered before the girl arrived. So within a few minutes she was out of the shower, dried, and dressing, this time in black stone-washed Levis and a man's peppermint striped shirt.

"Brian, we have to talk," she said.

"So talk."

"I want you to listen."

"I'm listening."

"All right, then." She found herself suddenly so tense she was short of breath. "Until I get some answers, I'm not going any further. I'm not going to Stephanie's with you."

"Okay—answers about what?"

*"About what?"* Faced with his maddening aplomb, she was trying hard not to lose her temper. "Well, just what the hell do you think? I have to know how far you plan to take this whole thing. I mean, are you going to continue trying to sabotage the movie? And do you plan on being a fugitive for good, and if so, have you somehow got it into your head that I'll just go along like a good little girl? A good little moron? Is that what you think?"

Brian looked genuinely puzzled. "Jesus, I don't know," he said. "I haven't really thought about all that. I'm just rolling with the punches, you know? Just taking things one day at a time."

For Eve, that was answer enough, all the reason she needed to abandon ship as soon as possible. "And not worrying all that much about me, it seems. Well okay, Brian. So be it. You go on alone with the girl when she comes. I'm pulling out. And I'm going to keep the money and give it back to Charley, to cover the bail he put up."

Brian sat down on the bed. "Just like that, huh?"

"Yes, just like that. You try to stop me and I'll scream for the police."

"Jesus Christ, Eve, have I ever touched you in anger?" He was shaking his head, in confusion or disbelief. "You want to cut out, fine, you're free to go. I told you I expected it. It only makes sense."

"I'm glad you agree."

"I just don't see why you'd expect me to have things all planned out. I thought we'd just go up to Stephanie's for a few days and see which way the wind is blowing, find out what the studio's going to do about the movie. Then I'll have a better idea what to do."

"Then you agree with me about the money?"

"Sure. I already told you that. I just wanted to wait until Charley put the police onto Chester for the shooting, that's all."

"How will you get by?" she asked.

"Forget the money," he said. "The question is, how do I get by without you?"

Eve stood there looking down at him still sitting on the bed, his hands folded in his lap, his long legs thrown out, the bent, rueful, affectionate smile just beginning to form, the deep blue eyes as guileless as a child's. And once again he had her. She already knew that. He had seduced her just as surely as on the jet.

"Oh, all right," she said. "A couple of days up at Stephanie's, and then we come down and face the music, okay?"

"Except if there's any music to be faced, I'm the one who'll do it, not you."

Getting up then, he took her in his arms and kissed her on the forehead and the nose and finally on the mouth, slowly and tenderly, barely touching her lips, a loving kiss, uncomplicated by sex or passion. And this was something about him that she always found surprising, that as masculine as he was—as unsubtle and insensitive as he often seemed to be—he nevertheless invariably knew just which button of hers to push, and when to push it.

"Just a few more days, all right then, honey?" he said. "I need you. I need to know you're there."

Nodding, she hugged him and turned her head, trying to hide the tears in her eyes.

Terry Hodges came for them in a beat-up old Travel-All station wagon that looked almost brand new on the inside, even though the car itself was almost as old as the girl, who was a skinny teenager with a boy's haircut, baggy jeans, and a sleeveless Raiders sweatshirt. When Brian had let her into the motel room, responding to her virtually inaudible knock, she had seemed almost too shy to speak. And her hangdog, apologetic look gave Eve a pretty good idea what Stephanie herself would be like: another aging Sunset Boulevard prima donna, with all the mothering instincts of a shark.

The girl was a competent driver, though, and soon they had reached Mulholland Drive, the strip of road winding along the top of the hill-sized San Gabriel Mountains, which divided the major part of the city from the San Fernando Valley. Eve of course had been on the road many times before, usually at night and in the company of men who wanted to park and show her its famous nocturnal vista of sparkling lights while running their hands up her thighs. Her ex-husband Richard had also taken her there, to show her the "handling characteristics" of his new Mercedes sedan. True to form, he never once had gone over the speed limit, an example of the mind-set that made her father recommend him so highly to her as husband material.

This day, like that one, was hot and still and so smoggy that the skyscrapers in downtown L.A. appeared to be floating in air. Though Brian had opened the front door of the wagon for Eve, she had declined, taking a backseat instead, figuring that the girl already knew Brian and that they would have things to talk about. Since then, however, it had become apparent to Eve that a good deal of the girl's shyness was probably due to Brian himself, either because of his newfound fame or simply because he was what he was: her mother's handsome ex-boyfriend. Brian tried repeatedly to make conversation with her, but each time she would mumble something and retreat into herself, blushing deeply.

Finally she slowed the car and turned onto a gravel lane that ran along a spur of the mountain.

"We're just up ahead," she said.

At the end of the lane, after passing two other houses, they came to a Spanish-style home sitting behind a tan stucco wall half-hidden by chaparral, which covered the hillsides, tinder waiting for the spark of fall. Driving on through the an open wrought-iron gate, they parked in a graveled area in front of the house, which at first looked small to Eve. But as she and Brian got out their luggage and followed Terry down a brick outside stairway, she saw that the place was considerably larger, with an L-shaped daylight basement floor running under the main part of the house and continuing at a right angle to it. Inside the angle there was a brick patio with umbrella tables and chairs scattered between a swimming pool and the low stucco parapet that edged the entire property.

On a chaise under one of the umbrellas a bleached-blond

woman in chartreuse lounging pajamas lay stretched out like a corpse, one listless hand holding a cigarette, the other a half-full champagne glass. As Brian and Eve reached the patio, the woman put down the glass and struggled to get to her feet, almost falling in the process. Eve was happy to see that though Stephanie undoubtedly had been quite attractive in her day, she was now a total mess, with sagging breasts, flabby hips, and skin so sun-damaged she could have passed for a Navajo matriarch. Smiling broadly, she held her arms out wide enough to gather them all in.

"Brian, darling!" she cried. "You naughty boy!"

"Stephanie," he said.

Standing with Terry, Eve watched as the two of them embraced.

**O**nce Charley was back on the interstate, he turned on the truck's hazard lights and drove well over the speed limit, hoping to attract the attention of any police cars lying in wait along the road. But none appeared. At Golden, a Denver suburb, he turned off and soon found a police station, where he wasted over twenty minutes trying to penetrate the thick head of a burly policewoman whose only concern seemed to be in demonstrating that she had bigger balls and a fouler mouth than any man in the place. Fortunately, a detective overheard what Charley was telling her, and things began to happen. Middle-aged and professorial, the detective whisked Charley away from the Amazon and into the captain's office. Within minutes, calls had gone out to the FBI, the state police, and the police in Colorado Springs. Also, in private, Charley was able to phone the lawyer he had hired to represent him. After explaining why he hadn't shown up at the courthouse, he told the man not to bother to drive up to Denver, that with the FBI now involved in the case, he saw no alternative except to tell them everything in exact detail. The lawyer advised him against such a course of action but said he would comply with Charley's wishes, if for no other reason than that he was already so busy he didn't know if he was coming or going.

A short time later Charley found himself in a squad car with the detective and the chief, leading a caravan of state police cars back to the turnout where he had thrown Chester down the mountain. When they got there, however, there was no sign of the little cowboy, and the state troopers were unable to decide whether he had climbed back up and hitched a ride or set out across the rugged, piney terrain on foot. Farther up the road there was a more gentle slope down the mountain, and a half-dozen troopers descended it and fanned out, looking for some sign of the fugitive. Others drove on ahead, hoping to find him standing by the side of the road, thumbing his way. The officer in charge radioed in for bloodhounds, but was told that it would be at least two hours before the dogs could be on the job.

Meanwhile seven FBI agents in three cars arrived on the scene and quietly took charge of both cases: the manhunt for Brian as well as for Chester. Charley overheard one of the agents telling the Golden detective that Brian and his girlfriend had flown to Santa Barbara, which made Brian's case a federal one now, having crossed state lines to avoid prosecution.

Two of the FBI agents introduced themselves to Charley and said that they would be taking him back to Denver, for debriefing. Their names were Dickinson and Ramos, and they were nothing at all like Hollywood stereotypes of federal agents: humorless Anglos with blond hair and all the charm of Gestapo agents. These two were, respectively, black and Latino, tall and short, lean and fat, but comfortably alike in their attitude of weary cynicism. If they were excited at the prospect of working on the Brian Poole case, with its showbiz cachet, neither man showed it. Rather, they picked at each other like a biracial Laurel and Hardy, almost as if it were their duty to keep Charley amused all the way back to Denver.

Once there, however, seated around a cheap table in an ugly room of the federal building, the two got down to business. While Ramos took notes, Dickinson operated the tape recorder, telling it the time and date, the case they were working on, and who was present in the room. Then he spoke to Charley.

"Okay, Mr. Poole, why don't you just lay it out for us, from start to finish. Then we'll ask a few questions, okay?"

"Fair enough."

Charley took his time, not wanting to overlook anything. Starting with Eve's phone call the previous Sunday morning, he took the agents through the two days since then almost hour by hour. And in the telling he found it difficult to believe that it was in fact only two days that had passed, and not a week. He recounted everything exactly as he remembered it, shaving the truth slightly only when it came to Belinda's accident, knowing that was where he and Eve were most vulnerable, for having left the scene of an accident.

"Eve wanted to get to the girl just as much as I did. But it didn't occur to her to cross the median strip—"It's against the law," she told me later. So she drove on to the next exit, which was just up ahead. We crossed over the freeway and tried to take the entrance ramp heading north, toward the accident. But a police car was already on the scene—both lanes were blocked—and cars were stopped on the ramp too. We couldn't get to the girl. So Eve decided to drive back to the motel and get Brian, and I thought the three of us would then drive to the hospital and contact the police. But Brian said no. He said the girl was his responsibility, that he had been with her when she overdosed or whatever it was, and that he and Eve would go to the hospital alone. He said there was no reason for me to get involved. With that, I went back to my own room and crashed. You'll remember that I'd had quite a lot to drink, certainly more than I'm used to. I was wasted."

That was the tone of much of his statement, presenting himself warts-and-all for the agents, not wanting to come across as some sort of fraternal white knight on a mission of mercy to his no-good brother, only to find himself dragged into the mud with him.

Ramos was keenly interested in the fact that Charley not only had put up Brian's bail but also had given him almost forty-five thousand dollars besides. Charley explained it a second time.

"As for the bail, I never even thought about losing it. I mean, I thought that Brian wanted his day in court. I thought that was what the bulldozing was all about, to give him a forum to present his case against the movie. And I figured he'd repay the bondsman's commission out of the forty-five thousand I'd given him, which, as I explained, was simply the final payment on my buyout of his half of my parents' estate: the family business, the family home."

Ramos wagged his head. "I dunno, that's still a real lot of bread, you know? I got a brother who's a priest, and I wouldn't loan him a dime."

"What dime is that, I wonder," Dickinson said, smiling crookedly, turning to Charley. "Man's got six kids—you believe that? Only Catholic in America who still uses the rhythm method."

Ramos grinned. "*Pelvic* rhythm, that's my problem. I got too much."

"Well, you may think so, but everyone knows it's us African American people of color who've got all the rhythm."

Charley gathered from their patter that they did not consider him much in the way of competition for the Ten Most Wanted list, which came as a relief. Finally the agents wanted him to go over again what he'd told them about Chester and where he might be headed. And this time Charley stressed even more the unlikelihood of there being a *Seagull* in Seattle. He told them that the boat and the name were merely scraps of memory he had from a letter and photograph he'd received from Brian back in the seventies: Brian and a couple of his hippy buddies standing and sitting on the stern of a yacht with the name painted below. And it might not even have been the *Seagull*, Charley said now. It could have been something entirely different, and the boat itself might even have been moored in Vancouver, not Seattle. He said he had just tossed the idea out to Chester, like throwing him a bone, hoping he would take it and run—and leave Charley behind.

"Anyway, I can't believe he's still on the way to Seattle, with so little to go on, just the name of a boat. I figure he's doubled back by now. I figure he's headed for home."

Dickinson concurred. "Yeah, you're probably right. He's probably planning to hide out in his barn or a shed, something like that. Anyway, revenge is a dish best served cold—heard that on TV the other night."

Ramos snorted. "Who wants a cold dish anyway? I like 'em hot, man."

Dickinson looked at Charley and shook his head, as if in sad acknowledgment that there was no hope for his partner.

Later, after getting a room at the downtown Marriott hotel, Charley phoned Donna and reluctantly told her about his latest Brian-related adventure, being kidnapped by Chester. And when he told her that he still wasn't quite ready to fly home, she lost her temper before he could explain.

"I can't believe you, Charley! What in God's name is wrong with you? Are you totally crazy? Do you want to get yourself killed? Don't you like it here anymore? Don't you love me at all?"

And she became even angrier when he told her about Brian's bail, that it was he who had put up the forty thousand as a first mortgage on the Sumter place, which she knew he had recently purchased.

"*And you lost it?*" she cried. "He cuts out and leaves you forty thousand in the hole? You actually trusted that maniac to—"

"Donna," he broke in, "that's why I'm not coming home yet. If I can find him before the authorities do, and if I can get him to return voluntarily, we might be able to get the money back. And if not, then I'll just take back the contract payment. We'll come out okay."

Donna was not convinced. "My God, what a hopeless dreamer you are! You actually think you can find your asshole brother before the FBI does? Just what have you been smoking? This new girl of Brian's, what is she, a drug dealer too? Is that what's happened? Did they get you onto crack or something?"

Charley groaned. "Oh come on, get real. With your help, I might just be able to find Brian."

"*My help?*"

"You know the Brian file we've got at home, all those old cards and letters from way back, the stuff my mother and I saved? I want you to get it out and fax it to me here at the hotel."

"And what good will that do?"

"The FBI already knows he and his girl flew to Santa Barbara, but I don't think he'll stay there. I figure he'll drive down to L.A. and impose on one of his old friends to take him in, someone he's stayed with in the past, like one of his old stuntman buddies, someone like that. When he wrote home, he sometimes included a return address. So fax the envelopes too, all right?"

She didn't answer. "Have you talked to Jason?"

"I tried Sunday, I think it was. But he wasn't in."

"If *he* asked you to come home, I bet you'd do it."

"Don't talk like that, okay? It's stupid. Tell me, if someone just stiffed the agency for forty grand, wouldn't you try to get it back?"

"Not if I might get shot doing it."

"Chester, you mean? Donna, he's not after me—he's after Brian."

"Well, I hope he finds him."

"I know you don't mean that."

"Don't I?"

"No, you don't."

Before she could argue the point, he went on and gave her the hotel guests' fax number and explained that she would have to phone him before sending, so he could clear the time with the desk.

"Yes, yes, I know all that," she said. "I'll fax you a lot of ancient cards and envelopes, addresses of people who are probably dead now or who move every six months. And then you'll go out to L.A. and look them up and say, 'Hey, you wouldn't have happened to see my wacko little brother lately, would you? And if not, then how about a needle in the old haystack? Maybe you've seen one of those."

"I'll wait for your call," Charley said. Then he hung up.

In the evening, after going over the faxes a third time, Charley had to admit that Donna's sarcasm had been on target. Trying to find his brother this way, with these few faded names and addresses, would indeed be like hunting for a needle in a haystack. The one fax that intrigued him was of the photo of Brian and two of hippy buddies lounging on the stern of an old wooden yacht with its name painted below in black and gold: *Seagal.* It surprised him that he had come so close to remembering the name, not that it amounted to anything, a twenty-year-old photo taken on a boat that long since had probably rotted away and sunk. If anything, the photo underscored the futility of his plan. Still, he knew that he was going ahead with it. And he was afraid he knew why—because he had to do everything he could to see her again soon, so he could stand her right in front of him and make her look him in the eye and explain just how a person got to the point where other people became so casually disposable, mere *things* you could use and toss, like a pen or a Kleenex.

She had phoned him, and he had come. She had asked for money, and he had brought it. He had freed her lover and entertained her, comforted her, while that lover cheated on her. And there had been something more between them too, not love perhaps, but something special, something beyond a budding friendship. He had seen it in her eyes. Or at least he thought he had.

Yet here he was, a fool with empty pockets and empty dreams. As for the money, he wasn't about to let them get away with that either, toss it away like something else they no longer needed. Forty thousand dollars was almost as much as he took out of his little construction company in salary every six months. So it was not negligible, not to him anyway. But from long experience he knew how his brother's mind worked. And he had no doubt that Brian, seeing how prosperous Charley and Donna had become, had naturally concluded that they had screwed him out of his just inheritance somewhere along the line. Not for a second would it occur to him that their prosperity was due to twenty years of hard work, building up the agency and expanding into a second business. As far as Brian was concerned, the forty-thousand bail was probably his by right, to do with as he saw fit.

But Eve had to know better. And that was what rankled in Charley's mind, that she had gone along with Brian so easily, apparently fully content to be his willing cohort in thievery. And in doing so, she had totally violated Charley's high opinion of her, which angered him probably more than anything else.

It was after nine o'clock, and he was standing at his hotel window, looking out at the mountains. Having seen front range sunsets before, he was not greatly surprised at the beauty of this one, though he suspected that the Denver smog had added to its luster, intensifying the broad sea of indigo flowing above the mountain peaks, its far shore shot with streaks of vermillion and gold. He wondered if Eve and Brian were still out there in the sunshine, searching, or whether they already had found refuge, some other sucker to use and throw away.

At ten o'clock he realized that he was still much too exhausted and addled to sleep, so he went up to the restaurant bar on the hotel's top floor, a comfortably dark room with tall windows looking to the west and north. He took a corner booth and ordered garlic-sauteed prawns and cheese toast, along with an Absolut martini that in time was followed by two more, the last a double. Feeling better with each one, he went back to his room and phoned Donna, even though it was after midnight in Flossmoor.

"Did I wake you?" he asked.

"What do you think? With a business to run and a husband who's off somewhere playing cops and robbers with psychos?"

"Donna, I'm safe and snug here in Denver."

"But you're still going out to L.A.?"

"For forty thousand bucks—you bet. And remember—the psycho cowboy's out of the picture. I sent him to Seattle."

"So now you've just got your psycho brother to worry about."

Charley sighed. "Donna, I didn't call to fight. I just wanted to tell you—remind you—that I do care about my home—and you—and I do want to get back there as soon as I can."

"You called to say you 'care' about me?" She made it sound like an insult.

"Oh, come on, Donna, I love you. You know that."

"Do I?"

"You should."

"All right, then, you love me," she said. "So can I get back to trying to fall asleep now?"

"Sure. Have at it."

"Goodnight, then."

"Yeah, goodnight."

After he'd hung up, Charley lay there in bed thinking about the conversation he'd just had and how dispiriting it was, how dispiriting they all seemed to be lately, even with three martinis humming in his blood. He didn't know what the answer was: whether he should never phone Donna late, never phone her after drinking, or simply never phone her at all.

He slept poorly that night, anxious for morning, when he would check out of the hotel and get on his way to California.

# chapter seven

**E**ve could not believe she was standing still for such treatment, accepting it almost as her due. It was late afternoon and she was alone in the twins' room upstairs, supposedly lying down and resting before dinner. Instead she found herself pacing and smoking in front of the doors to the balcony, which looked down not only on the pool and patio but a good part of Los Angeles as well.

At the moment Brian was in the pool doing his passable impression of Mark Spitz, zipping from one end to the other, turning and pushing off underwater, taking a breath about once every lap. The Hodges, mother and daughter, were his audience. Terry, still in jeans and a sweatshirt, was standing back in the shadows, her pale eyes unblinking and her mouth slightly parted in an expression of almost reverential awe as she watched Brian stroking smoothly through the water. Stephanie meanwhile looked both proprietary and pleased, as if a horse she'd bought was having a good afternoon workout. She was once again sitting in the shade of an umbrella table, still wearing lounging pajamas and holding a lit Marlboro in one hand and a glass of champagne in the other, like the dual components of her life-support system.

Disgusted, Eve turned away from the doors only to face the walls of the room, which were festooned with *Playboy* centerfolds, school pennants, and posters of Metallica and other rock bands. The twins, as Brian had explained, were Stephanie's by her second husband, a studio lawyer to whom she had granted custody in exchange for clear title to the house. The boys were now at Stanford Law, and though they hadn't visited their mother in years, she still kept their room exactly as it had been a decade earlier, a place for teenage boys—and now for Eve.

When Brian had carried her bags upstairs for her, helping her settle into the room, he had tried to explain things, saying that he thought she should have been able to understand Stephanie's feelings, not wanting to put him and Eve together in the same room, sleeping together *in her house,* where he and Stephanie once had been lovers.

"Of a sort," he'd added. "I mean, nothing like us. I mean, there just wasn't much choice, you know? She let me stay here—kept the goddamn reporters off my back—so I just kind of went along. But it was no big deal, believe me. She was a lot like now, in no shape to do much of anything but drink and talk. And that's all she wants from me now, to stay up and gab all night with her. That's why she wants me in the room next to hers, for convenience, that's all. She runs down at about dawn and then sleeps till one or two, and then manages to get up only with Terry's help. The poor kid."

Eve gave him a wry look. "Maybe the poor kid could use a bit of your time too."

"Well, she needs something, all right. Stephanie works her like a coolie. Not just the cooking and cleaning, but the shopping too. Stephanie claims she has agoraphobia and can't leave the place."

"I'm not surprised."

Brian mistakenly read that as a sign of sympathy and acquiescence. Taking her by the shoulders, he moved as though to embrace her. But she pulled back. He frowned in consternation.

"Anyway, just a little patience, okay, babe? A couple of days and we'll be on our way. And at night don't think that because I'm down there with her alone that anything's happening. All you have to do is sneak downstairs and listen. All you'll hear is Stephanie running on about her miserable life, that's all. If I touch her, it'll only be to give her one of her precious massages. Nothing else."

Smiling slightly, Eve shook her head. "Well, that sure is a relief to hear. I just can't wait to get up every few minutes and sneak downstairs to make sure you're not fucking the lady."

Brian looked crestfallen. "Aw, come on, baby, give me a break. Can't you see I've got enough other shit to deal with right now? Jesus Christ."

"You'd better leave," she said. "I think I hear our hostess calling."

At the door, Brian had turned and looked back at her. "And fuck you too," he'd said.

So now here she was, in her *assigned* room, alone with her twin beds and rock stars and acres of silicone breasts. Lying down, she lit another cigarette and thought again about leaving on her own, how she would go about it. Just call a cab, pick up her things and the money—and leave? Could it be that simple? Soon, though, her mind began to wander and she found herself thinking again about Charley, wondering where he was, what he thought of her now, running off the way she had, leaving him holding the bag, all without a word of apology or explanation, to all appearances every bit as selfish and thoughtless as his little brother. And the worst of it was that she could never explain. It was too late for that. There was simply no way she could ever make him understand how it had happened, how torn she had been, having to decide so quickly between him and Brian, between decency and love. Well, the least she could do was make sure he got his money back. And she would, she vowed. One way or another, she would see to it.

Still, that in no way eased her feelings of shame and remorse. It continued to surprise her, how deeply she resented the idea that Charley probably thought of her now as his brother's perfect little soulmate, just another selfish, heartless jerk. "But I'm not like that!" she wanted to cry out. "I'm not like that at all."

Having smoked her cigarette down almost to the filter, she looked about for an ashtray. Seeing none close by, she flipped the cigarette out through the balcony doors, hoping it would clear the bougainvillea below and drop into the pool, maybe right in front of Mr. Spitz himself.

Terry came and got her at five-fifty, saying that Stephanie wanted everyone in the game room for the six o'clock news, followed by *Hard Copy,* the tabloid show, both of which had been following Brian's story.

"She's been taping them," Terry said, then looked away in unexplained embarrassment. "We both think it's really great, what Brian's done. I mean trying to shut down the movie like he has. We know he didn't shoot Jolly."

Eve said nothing.

The game room was situated next to the living room, near the front of the house. There was a handsome old pool table, a Wurlitzer, and a large leather sectional sofa arranged about the fireplace, with a television and a VCR off to the side. Brian and Stephanie were sitting together, facing the TV, Brian in chinos and a USC sweatshirt and Stephanie in her same pajamas, a lit cigarette in one hand and the other resting on an end table, her fingers fondling the stem of her champagne glass.

"Well, it's about time you came down," she said to Eve. "That long a beauty sleep, you certainly don't need it, you know."

Eve smiled coolly. "You should have told me."

"Anyway, you want to keep up with your fella's exploits, don't you?"

"Not particularly." Sitting, Eve too lit a cigarette.

Brian explained. "To her, they're not exploits, they're crimes."

"Oh, come on," Stephanie scoffed. "I can't believe she feels that way."

*She,* Eve thought. It was as if she weren't even there. "Crimes against himself," she said, and immediately wanted to kick herself for going along with them, letting them set the rules of engagement.

"How against himself?" Terry asked.

"Because he's the one hiding out. Because he's the one headed for prison."

Stephanie laughed. "Well, nothing like standing by your man, I always say."

"And I always say, fuck off."

"Hey, come on, you two," Brian said. "Let's just cool it, okay? And it's news time anyway. Let's see what lies the bastards are spreading tonight."

For the next five or six minutes the networks kept Stephanie busy, switching from one to another, looking for Brian's story. But to that point there wasn't any coverage, and this seemed almost more than she could bear.

"Goddamn pissant liberals!" she complained. "In a couple minutes they'll all run some phony story about some ghetto school where the fuckin' minorities are supposed to be doing just fine. But the real news, like Brian's cause, they just totally ignore it! What assholes!"

She had barely finished her tirade when Dan Rather came back on, sweaterless now that it was summer. "This morning," he reported, "motion picture director Damian Jolly was seriously wounded by rifle fire while standing on the deck of his house in Colorado Springs. The immediate suspect in the shooting is this man, Hollywood hanger-on Brian Poole, who was arrested last Saturday night for bulldozing the outdoor set of *Miss Colorado,* the movie Jolly has been filming. The movie reportedly is based on the life of the late country music star, Kim Sanders. Four years ago, while in the company of Poole, the singer died of a drug overdose in Colorado Springs. Out on bail, Poole is reported to have fled to California in the company of his present girlfriend, Eve Sherman."

As Rather covered the story, there were brief intercuts of Jolly before the shooting, then wounded and being wheeled from his house on a gurney, then of Brian being brough to jail, followed by shots of the bulldozed set and finally a still photo of Eve.

"Wow, from the lips of Dan Rather, no less!" Stephanie cried. "You're famous, kiddo, and for a lot longer than fifteen minutes, I'll bet."

Brian grimaced. "Infamous, you mean. And that hanger-on bullshit—is that what we call stuntmen these days? And what I can't figure is why they're not onto little Chester yet. What the hell is Charley doing? He knows the truth."

"Maybe he's just getting even," Eve said. "Can you blame him?"

"Yes, I can blame him! Jesus Christ, I could be charged with attempted murder."

Stephanie meanwhile was busy flipping back and forth between the other networks, looking for more of the story. And finally she found it on ABC too, where the substitute anchor

merely mentioned the shooting before turning the story over to
a reporter in Colorado, an earnest young black man who covered the same material as Rather had, adding nothing.

Later, though, on the tabloid show *Hard Copy,* their reporter
Diane Dillon was characteristically scooping the competition.
Already in Colorado Springs, the stylish young brunette was
standing outside Penrose Hospital, with Pike's Peak rising sceni-
cally in the background. First, she reported the details of Jolly's
wound: a glancing shot off his skull, cracking it and causing a
blood clot on the brain. The surgeons had opened the skull and
removed the clot, an apparently simple operation that nevertheless had left Jolly in intensive care, heavily sedated. Dillon
then went on to her scoop.

"From sources close to the FBI, I've learned that Brian Poole
might not have been the shooter after all. Reportedly there is another man—a cowboy, I was told—who was either paid to do the
shooting by Poole or did it for reasons of his own. Whether the
FBI already has this man in custody, I don't know. But I assume
we'll learn more by tomorrow."

Brian smiled with relief. "Way to go, *Hard Copy!*"

"More like, way to go, Charley," Eve said.

"Whatever, I'll take it. Better than the thin gruel CBS had to
offer."

"True. I especially liked that part about you traveling with your
girlfriend Eve Sherman. Sort of like Bonnie and Clyde. My life-
long ambition."

Little Terry evidently thought her hero wasn't getting the respect he deserved. "Well, it wouldn't bother me any. I mean,
considering what Brian's trying to do. I'd think any woman
would be proud to be with him."

Stephanie laughed, briefly moving her champagne glass away
from her lips. "That's my girl," she said.

Eve bit her tongue. She was after all Stephanie's guest and would soon be eating Terry's cooking. If they didn't quite see the whole picture, so be it, she thought. She knew from experience that they were not the first females to be taken in by Brian Poole.

After dinner the three adults sat outside under oil-fed Hawaiian torches, with the electric grid of Los Angeles spread out below, as tidy as a dream of Baron Haussmann. The sunset had already faded behind the next rise, deepening the darkness in the canyon below, where Eve could hear a lone coyote yipping. With her champagne glass still firmly in hand, Stephanie was waxing enthusiastic about the subject apparently closest to her heart: her loathing of "Upper Mehico, grease trap of the Pacific," as she called California.

"There are so many beaners on welfare now—them and their yellow brethren—that they've drove property taxes simply out of sight. Imagine, someone like me, who actually owns the roof over her head—and I mean owns it free and clear—and taxes are so high I can't even afford to stay here anymore. Poor Terry has to do all the work herself—the house, the pool, the yard, you name it—and I'm still going down the toilet."

"Maybe you ought to rent out a few rooms," Brian said.

"Oh sure. To who? Some would-be actress or agent who'd always be promising to pay me *next* month? Or stealing me blind. No thank you."

"So what are you going to do?"

"What can I do? I'm one of the new property-poor. I'd be better off broke. Then I could live it up on welfare. I could have Jane Fonda take care of me."

In order not to miss a second of Brian's newfound fame,

Stephanie had brought a portable TV out to the patio with them. She had placed it on an umbrella table and kept working with it until she got a news broadcast. CNN, with the sound barely audible. Brian immediately lunged for the set and turned up the sound, for there on the screen was Charley, coming out of what appeared to be a high-rise hotel in a large city—Denver, Eve imagined. As reporters thrust their mikes at him, along with a dozen simultaneously shouted questions, he stopped and raised a protecting hand, smiling uncomfortably, as if he were being mobbed by a crowd of raucous children. When the reporters finally quieted down, Charley spoke.

"As you may know, I came out to Colorado from my home in Illinois to help my brother, mostly just to get him out of jail. And I can tell you he had nothing to do with the shooting of Damian Jolly. He was swimming in a motel pool in Colorado Springs at the time. So why'd he run? I don't know. Simple panic maybe. And there's one other thing I want to say. The woman traveling with him—his girlfriend, Eve Sherman—I can tell you definitely that she's not involved in any of this, and that includes his vendetta against the movie company. She's simply traveling with Brian, and from what I could see, trying to get him to stop the vendetta. She shouldn't be considered his partner in any of this. More his victim, I'd say."

The reporters let loose with another torrent of questions and Charley waited patiently for a break. Giving up, he started moving through them toward a waiting taxi.

"Home," he told one of the reporters. "I'm just going home."

The reporter came on then and told the viewer what the viewer had just seen and heard. Brian turned down the sound.

"Well, that sure ought to help," Stephanie said. "With the shooting charge anyway."

"Yeah, but why no mention of Chester Einhorn—I don't get

it," Brian said, giving Eve a sardonic look. "But then I got the feeling I'm not the one he's really concerned about."

Eve let that pass.

"Nice-looking man, your brother," Stephanie observed. "Though of course not as yummy as you."

Brian licked a finger and ran it over his eyebrow. "Well, of courth not. Leth not be ridiculouth."

Eve stood up and stretched. "My God, I feel like I've been sitting forever." She looked at Brian. "I'm going for a walk down the road. You want to come?"

He frowned. "Jesus, I'd like to, but I'm afraid that if a car came along I'd pull a Quayle—the old bunny-in-the-headlights routine."

Eve stared at him, wondering if he was serious. "Up here?" she said. "And on a cul-de-sac at that?"

Brian shrugged. "Just call me cautious."

"That'll be a first."

As Eve turned to go, Stephanie offered a word of caution. "You better be careful. This is cougar country. And coyotes too."

Eve smiled back at them. "That's all right. I'll enjoy the company."

Brian laughed. "Ouch!" he said.

To reach the gate, Eve had to walk along the inside of the stucco wall that bordered the property, a wall whose visible height varied from five feet at the front of the house to only a foot or so along the patio perimeter, though it undoubtedly was much higher at that downhill point, the major part of it being out of sight. Leaving the pool area, Eve went past the garage and headed out through the open gate, which was bracketed with burning coachlights.

On the way to Mulholland Drive, she passed the two other

houses that shared the lane. Built on stilts, they both looked as if Brian and Charley could have pushed them down into the canyon without breaking a sweat. As she walked, she kept thinking about Charley's radio interview, how he had gone so far out of his way to speak up for her, and it made her feel even worse than before, more ashamed than ever. She slaps him in the face, and what does he do? He turns the other cheek. What a lousy, unmodern, un-American thing to do, she thought, a man behaving like that, like some kind of plaster saint just to put people in your debt, just to shame them and make them feel two feet tall.

And just to make them cry, she added now, looking through tears at Stephanie's gate, the orange-glowing coach lights. She wiped her eyes and blew her nose, and vowed again that the next morning she would begin to set things right. She would get Charley's money and call a cab, and if anyone tried to stop her— well, they just weren't going to. That's all there was to it.

**B**ack at the patio, Brian and Stephanie were right where she'd left them, anchored to their redwood lounge chairs, Brian lying back with his hands laced under his curly head, Stephanie sitting more erect, holding firmly onto her glass of champagne, which seemed to be the only beverage she stocked.

"See any cougars?" she asked.

Eve smiled. "Just their eyes glowing in the dark."

"Well, that's good. I figure we don't need any more excitement around here. I think Brian has provided elegant sufficiency for one day." Chuckling at the felicity of her words, Stephanie drained her glass and immediately started to refill it. "This is probably the most excitement we've had in Tinseltown since O.J. was practicing his golf swing."

Brian thanked her for the comparison, and she laughed happily. Swinging her cigarette hand wide, she gestured toward Hollywood and Beverly Hills.

"Why, I bet they ain't talking about anything else down there except you, kiddo. Especially the brass at Wide World Studios. I'll bet right now them bastards are padlocking their doors and shaking in their Gucci combat boots."

"Fat chance," Brian said. "They're too busy collecting bad art."

Stephanie laughed again. "Oh, you think so, do you?"

This cryptic exchange puzzled Eve, but she didn't care enough to ask about it. Though she still had a drink—her own glass of champagne—she barely touched it, contenting herself instead with just sitting there and smoking, saying nothing. But her hostess more than made up for her silence and abstemiousness, continuing to pour down her off-brand bubbly as she prattled on, slurring her words and giggling and sometimes misplacing an elbow, almost toppling out of her chair.

"I just bet you can't figure me as a starlet," she said to Eve. "But I was one, all right. Fact, I was some looker, lemme tell you. Skin like peaches and cream, and boobs out to here. Only trouble was, I kept fucking the wrong producers. Sy Wineglass! Now, who the hell ever heard of Sy Wineglass? What does he get me into? *Attack of the Lizard People!* Great stuff like that. I didn't really give a damn, though. The flicks may have been lousy, but I looked great up there on the screen, fifty feet of primo tits and ass." She sucked down some more champagne, then lifted her glass as if she were toasting some unseen crowd. "So what happened, right? That's what you're thinking, right, Eve? Well, I'll just tell you—nothing happened except that I was a true California girl, that's all. Why, I bet I spent half my goddamn life laying out in the sun in a fucking bikini. Probably soaked up a couple billion volts of ultraviolet by now. And probably smoked a couple billion cigarettes too. And then, this stuff—" She waggled her glass, spilling some of the champagne onto the front of her jogging suit, which she had changed into before coming outside. "It all contributes, believe me. So here I am, Stephanie Hodges, forty-eight-year-old starlet with seventy-eight-year-old skin. And in these hills there's probably fifty thousand just like me. We ought to form a union and sue somebody, right? Maybe Sy Wineglass, huh?"

Again she laughed. Eve, however, did not share her hilarity. There was something about her story, its eerie similarity to Eve's own stint in Hollywood, that made her feel uncomfortable. But, trying hard to put things in perspective, she reminded herself that at least she'd never had a boob job, nor ever screwed a Sy Wineglass. And—thanks to being of a different generation— never routinely baked for hours in the sun. Still, there were the beach movies and the caveman epic, her own glorious fifty feet of tits and ass. It made her feel almost sympathetic toward Stephanie. But it didn't make her like her.

While Stephanie had been running on, Eve at one point had glanced absently up at the house and caught sight of Terry in her bedroom, lying in the dark with her head propped on a pillow on the window sill. Eve had crooked her finger at the girl, inviting her down, but her only response was to slip out of sight, like a turtle drawing back into its shell.

And now Stephanie was getting up, squirming forward in the chair and reaching out for a Brian's hand. On her feet finally, she tipped up the champagne bottle to make sure it was empty before abandoning it.

"Well, I'm gonna turn in. And you, mister," she said to Brian, "I'm gonna need a real primo massage tonight. So bring them big strong mitts of yours and drop by, you hear?"

"Your wish is his command," Eve said.

Stephanie laughed. "Don't I wish!" Then, waving indifferently to her guests, she teetered toward the house.

When she was gone, Eve and Brian sat there for a time saying nothing, as if neither could think of a way to break through the wall that had formed between them these last days. It was Eve who spoke finally, but only to add to the wall.

"Shouldn't you be reporting for duty? You and those 'big strong mitts' of yours."

"Give it up, okay? What choice to I have?"

"You have plenty."

"Like what—calling the FBI and saying here I am, take me?"

Eve shrugged. "Isn't that what it comes down to in the end?"

"Well, this ain't the end. Not yet anyway."

"I was afraid of that."

"Patience, Eve, that's all I ask. A couple of days. Can't you manage that?"

She looked at him without expression. "We'll see."

"Right." Without even kissing her goodnight, he started for the house then, along the way plucking a beachball out of the pool and kicking it hard in Eve's direction. The ball sailed over her head and fell harmlessly into the canyon below.

Alone finally, Eve remained there on the patio for a time gazing out over the parapet at the vast grid of streetlights converging somewhere beyond her sight. And she found it oddly pleasurable, looking down upon an entire metropolis, a place where millions suffered and exulted, slept and raged, in icy silence. The city looked so tidy in fact that she could imagine a space ship slipping in over the mountains and immediately hurrying off, its alien crew thoroughly intimidated by the rigidly geometric pattern of light, an obvious symbol of a highly advanced people, disciplined, unemotional, probably puritanical.

# chapter eight

**B**y noon of the next day Charley had contacted only one of the four names on his list, friends with whom Brian had stayed during his checkered career in Hollywood. Charley had no doubt that over the years his brother had stayed with many others too, girlfriends most likely, but these four were the only ones from whose dwellings he had written home and included a return address. In a fifth note, a postcard actually, he had mentioned that he was all right, in fact was very comfortably ensconced up on Mulholland Drive, but he hadn't included any name or address, an understandable omission considering that that had been during the period after Kim Sanders' death.

The first name on the list—the person Charley had just checked out—was Sally Tan, a studio makeup artist who lived in the San Fernando Valley on one of a hundred identical streets lined with small L-shaped ranchhouses so numbingly alike Charley couldn't imagine how drunks ever found their way home. Sally Tan's house, however, had a redwood exterior, which gave it a certain cachet in the midst of its pastel-stucco neighbors. It was also handsomely landscaped and well kept, which for some reason made Charley feel temporarily optimistic—until Sally Tan herself came to the door. A small, pretty Asian, she nervously edged out onto the porch instead of inviting Charley in. And instead of speaking, she hissed. Her "turd hosbin" was asleep inside and Brian was eight, nine year ago and she had nothing to do "wid all dis bad bizness" and anyway her hosbin would kill her if she woke him.

"So you go now," she'd said. "You leave. Good-bye now."

With that, she had sidled back into the house and left Charley standing there like a rejected encyclopedia salesman. Back in his car, he checked the map again and judged the second address to be about five miles west, in the Northridge area, also in the Valley. When he got there, however, it wasn't a house he found but a shopping center, and not a very new one at that.

The drive from Northridge to Venice, where the third person on the list supposedly lived—and where Brian's condo was—took Charley almost an hour, which made him grateful that his rented Thunderbird had a decent air conditioner. Though he knew it beggared belief, the freeways seemed even more jammed than they had been on his last visit to L.A. a decade earlier, when he, Donna, and Jason had spent ten days touring the California coast, from San Francisco to San Diego. It was a vacation Charley did not remember with fondness. Jason had been relentlessly sulky and Donna had been tireless, dragging the two of them to every tourist site on the map. Charley had endured it stoically, knowing that it would be not only his first touring vacation but also his last.

Before trying the third name on the list, he drove slowly past Brian's condo and wasn't surprised to see that it was under surveillance by two shirtsleeved cops sitting in an unmarked car three doors down, baking in the scant shade of an almost leafless tree. It was the canal part of Venice, a wasteland of row bungalows and duplexes facing narrow, concrete-lined streams laid out like the irrigation rows in a cornfield. The trees bordering the canals were so few and so dessicated Charley surmised that it was either the salt air or the local ethos—a pharmacological bohemia—that was killing them.

The address of the third person on the list, Waldo Trask, led Charley to a tire repair shop located only a few blocks from the ocean. Charley surmised that there was a loft or apartment above, so he went up the side stairs and rang the bell. Inside, he could hear a radio or stereo playing a Melissa Etheridge song loud enough to be heard over the tire shop's power wrench, whose recurrent howl virtually shook the building. In time, the door opened and a lean, perspiring woman with spiky dark hair and cold eyes stood looking down at Charley two stairs below. She was wearing Speedo trunks and a heavy sweatshirt that proclaimed her politics: I'm a Fucking Queer.

"Yeah?" she said.

"I'm looking for Waldo Trask."

"He ain't here."

"When do you expect him?"

"I don't. An hour, maybe two. Why? What's your business?"

"It's with him."

"Oh really?" She didn't like that very much. "Well, like I said, he ain't here." With that, she slammed the door in Charley's face.

"I can believe it," Charley muttered, reflecting on her sweatshirt's slogan as he went back down the stairs.

Having at least an hour to kill, he left the car where it was and walked over to Venice's famed ocean walk, another of the tourist spots Donna had insisted that the three of them experience. Located between the beach and an eclectic assortment of buildings—houses, cottages, businesses—the ocean walk was a broad, mile-long blacktop that appeared to be home to a permanent population of eccentrics, exhibitionists, and lost souls of every stripe. Indeed, it seemed almost as if the tide along that stretch of coastline ran the wrong way, washing up the flotsam of the country, not the sea.

As before, there were the usual drunks and bodybuilders and mimes, these last a breed that Charley felt deserved public flogging whenever and wherever they appeared. Fortunately there were also the sexy young Rollerbladers in bikinis, happily zipping along, leaving in their wake an epidemic of unrequited lust. Despite these representatives of the past, however, Charley could see that the ocean walk had changed considerably, and for the worse. Unlike before, there were now countless beggars and homeless families and lost children cadging cigarettes, food, change, whatever they could get. An easy touch, Charley was soon out of change, as well as dollars and fives, so he made his way back to the car and went looking for a McDonald's.

Ninety minutes after he'd had the door slammed in his face, he was back at Trask's. And this time it was not the mild-mannered lesbian who answered the door but a huge black man with a shaved head, an eyepatch, a missing ear, and a stainless steel clamp where his right hand should have been. Judging by the way he moved, Charley figured that his right leg was prosthetic as well.

Charley introduced himself, and the man shook his hand, his left hand.

"Waldo Trask," he said. "Come on in."

Charley followed him across the loft to a living room area: a sofa and chairs ranged around a large screen TV near the front windows. There was also a workout area with Nautilus equipment, treadmills, and a punching bag, as well as a kitchen area, a curtained-off bedroom, and an artist's studio, a place where someone had painted expressionistic pictures of very muscular women striking threatening poses. Charley didn't have to wonder who the painter was, though she was not in evidence at the moment.

Without asking, Trask got two cans of beer out of the refrigerator and gave one to Charley.

"I know what you're thinking," he said. "Stuntman must be be a real dangerous profession."

Charley smiled slightly. "The thought did cross my mind."

Sitting, Trask lifted his false leg and dropped it heavily onto an ottoman. "The joke is none of it happened as a stuntman—just riding home on my Harley. This semi appears out of nowhere, and I take the bike down, hoping to slide on under. Only at that same moment the fuckin driver slams on the brakes and swerves to miss me. As a result, I catch nine of his eighteen wheels. That was my last stunt, believe me."

"Does Brian know about this?"

Trask shook his massive head. "I don't think so. We been out of touch these last few years."

"When I see him again I'll tell him."

Trask made no response to that. And for a time he just sat there like a great mound of flesh. Undoubtedly a large, muscular man to begin with, he was now well over three hundred pounds, much of it fat.

"I take it this is about what Brian's done," he said. "All that shit on TV."

"That's right. I want to find him before the police do. I want him to give himself up. It'll go easier on him if he does."

Trask shook his head. "Well, like I said, we ain't been in touch for years. But Brian Poole, man, I'd do anything I could to help him. Five, six years ago I was scraping bottom—all the booze and coke I could glom onto—and he took me in, no questions asked. I owe him."

"Can you think of any other place he might be staying? Maybe some old girlfriend's?"

"What if he don't wanna turn himself in?"

"Then I just walk. I go home."

Again Trask was silent for a time. Finally, grinning, he shook his head once more. "Old Brian—I remember one of the last times I saw him. I'd been on a job in New York, and he'd invited me down to Tennessee, where he was living then with Kim Sanders, on her so-called farm. Place had gold faucets, for Christ's sake. Anyway, Kim Sanders—man, what a piece of work that gal was. While I'm there, her source comes callin', and Brian kicks him out. Well, Kim comes unglued, and they have this big fuckin' brawl. Practically destroy the house. Brian tells her he's cuttin' out with me. So what does she do? She gets a rifle and sticks the barrel in her mouth. 'You go,' she croaks, 'and I'll do it. I really will.' So what does Brian do? He turns to me and says 'Ain't love grand?' Well, that gets her to laughin' so hard she's chippin' her teeth on the gun barrel. And the first thing you know, she's jumpin' into his arms, with her legs wrapped around him, and he's carryin' her off to the bedroom. I didn't see them again for a good three hours."

"That sounds like Brian, all right," Charley said, smiling. Still, he didn't want to be sidetracked into reminiscence and story-telling with Trask. "But listen, any name that comes to mind—some place he might be—I'd really appreciate it if you'd give me a call." He got up and handed Trask a card from his hotel.

"Bel Air Hotel, huh?" Trask said. "You must be a tycoon, Charley."

"No, I just got lost, that's all."

"And you really think it'd go better for him—turnin' his-self in?"

"That's why I'm here. He's my brother."

Trask smiled. "He ain't heavy, he's my brother, huh?"

"That's about it."

"Well, I'm sorry, man. I just don't know where he might be. We been out of touch too long."

"That's all right. I understand. And thanks for the beer."

On the way out, Charley saw Trask's roommate looking at him from behind the bedroom curtain. He wondered if she hated all men, or just him.

Sometime during the night, while Eve was asleep and dreaming, he came to her. She was dreaming that she was out on Stephanie's road again and that there was a cougar down in the chaparral, moving parallel to her, its eyes a brighter orange than that burning in the coach lights up ahead. And suddenly Charley was there too, gently taking her hand as he walked along between her and the cougar.

"Don't worry about mountain lions," he said. "Their eyes are worse than their bite."

Though she had smiled at him, she found herself wondering if she had ever experienced this before: humor in a dream. And then she realized that she was waking, that her covers had been been pulled back and a body as naked as her own was cuddling in against her, hard and smooth, its breath redolent of champagne and cigarettes.

"Jesus, I'm sorry about today, baby," he said. "I just had to see you. I had to hold you. Really. I need you, honey."

Fully awake now, Eve was aware of Brian's right arm slipping under her shoulders, pulling her toward him. He had moved his left leg across her pelvis and legs, and she could feel his cock already hard against her hip.

"I'm sorry to wake you," he went on. "And don't worry, I didn't come for sex. I just needed to hold you, babe. I needed to feel you in my arms."

He was already kissing her lightly on the forehead and the eyes and cheek, and now he moved to her mouth, gently, just brushing her lips with his own. But as she didn't resist, he kissed her more deeply, though without pushing his tongue into her. With his free hand, he caressed her breasts and then circled her other shoulder, so that she soon found herself lying in the sinewy bracelet of his arms, with his body more on top of her now, his erection flat against her pelvic bone.

She was aware that once again he was pushing all the right buttons, doing just what she wanted him to do, giving her just what she needed. Going to sleep, she had felt lost and alone, a twenty-nine-year-old woman, unmarried and childless, not even sure of her lover. And she had longed for just what she she had now, the feeling of being at the very center of her universe, locked in Brian's arms, covered by his sleek body, listening to his loving words. Her one fear was that she might start to cry, because her tension all day had been so great and its release now so sudden. She hated that about herself, the weakness of the female, the need to be held and protected and loved, hated it so much that she could feel herself trembling from the effort not to give in to it.

In the end, though, she could not hold back her tears. And Brian felt them too, tasted them.

"Aw, baby, I'm so goddamn sorry," he said. "I love you so much."

Normally that would have been it, the key to the floodgate, and she would have begun sobbing. And she dearly wanted to do so now, to feel the delicious joy of total surrender. But her pride would not let her, and she continued to lie there in his arms, her eyes streaming as he went on kissing and caressing her, telling her how sorry he was about everything and how much he loved her. And in time, as her tears ebbed but his erection did not, she moved down in the bed just far enough so that he was between her legs, virtually unable to keep from entering her.

"Hey, I didn't come for this," he said. "Really, honey."

"I believe you. But what the devil, huh?"

Though his face was burrowed into her cheek and hair, she could feel him smile.

"Right. What the devil?"

In the morning Eve decided to postpone leaving Stephanie's, at least for another day. And she couldn't help suspecting that that might have been the reason for Brian's night visit, because he had sensed her growing anger and resentment and moved to end it, throwing her a few bones of tenderness and caring. In talk-show psychobabble, she figured she had become both his victim and his ennabler, allowing him to be the bastard he seemed increasingly inclined to want to be.

This morning, however, no one could have accused him of anything but the best behavior. From the twins' bedroom Eve had been watching him down in the pool, patiently trying to teach a fearful Terry how to swim while Mama looked on from her shaded lounge, both hands firmly locked onto her life support system. This day Stephanie had forsaken her lounging pajamas for white culottes and an awning-stripe blouse, not a happy choice, since her lower legs looked like bags of grapes.

Though Eve thought it odd that a healthy eighteen-year-old would have to be taught to swim in her own backyard pool, she of course didn't plan on saying anything about it. Rather, she decided to join the two of them down in the pool. Unfortunately she hadn't been able to find her favorite swimsuit—a one-piece black faille—and instead had to make do with a skimpy monstrosity Brian and bought for her at a Victoria's Secret shop, a white bikini that covered little else besides her nipples and crotch. Though she didn't care much for either of the Hodges, bloated Stephanie or the boardlike Terry, she took no pleasure in showing them up, waltzing out to the pool finally, almost as naked as her namesake.

"God in Heaven!" Stephanie bawled. "The news helicopters see you in that, they'll land right on top of us."

Eve made a face. "The joys of travel. It's the only thing I could find—one of Brian's little inspirations."

"It's okay by me. But I think you're going to make Terry blush."

"Oh, come on. You two must sunbathe naked up here all the time."

Stephanie laughed. "Not bloody likely. Not anymore, not with my skin. And Terry's as modest as a nun."

"I see she's learning to swim."

In the pool, the girl was dog-paddling furiously, supported by Brian's hands under her belly.

"Well, let's hope so. If she can learn from anybody, it'd be Brian. If he told her she could fly, I think she'd jump right off the wall here and start flapping her arms."

"Her Svengali, huh?"

"No, her *hero*'s more like it."

Eve made no response to that. After testing the water with her foot, she balanced on the pool's edge and made an adequate little dive into the deep end. She swam the length of the pool three times, then got out and lay facedown on a beach towel, feeling that if she was going to burn anything, it might as well be her fanny. As usual, the sun acted on her like a narcotic and she soon fell asleep. When she woke, she found herself quite alone, the other three apparently having gone back into the house. Worried that she already might have acquired a touch of sunburn, she moved into Stephanie's shaded chair and lit a cigarette. Through her sunglasses she saw Terry looking down at her from her room, caught her for just a second before the girl dove out of sight. And she saw Brian and Stephanie talking heatedly about something in Stephanie's room. Then, a little later, through the same patio door, she saw Brian looking at a magazine while Stephanie hovered next to him, grinning and shaking her head in amusement.

Later still, Brian came out and sat down next to Eve. "Did you have a good sleep?" he asked.

"You might have woken me up, you know. I could've burned."

Brian ran his hand along her thigh. "I don't know—you look okay to me."

"Wrong side," Eve said. "Incidentally, what was all that quacking about inside? You and your mistress."

"Hostess, remember?"

"Whatever."

"Nothing important."

"Naturally."

A short time later Brian went back into the house, then reappeared a few minutes later carrying a large white telescope and tripod, which he set up near the parapet, pointed down at Bel Air. He spent some time looking into it and adjusting it, and soon Stephanie came out and peered through the viewer and adjusted it some more. Then, announcing that she was going to lie down a while, she went back inside. Eve lit another cigarette and lay there smoking as long as her curiosity permitted. Then she got up and went over to where Brian was.

"What're you looking at?" she asked. "Naked ladies? Fellas? What?"

"Just messing around." Brian patted her on the bottom. "Speaking of naked ladies."

Eve slapped his hand away but continued to stand there, wanting a look. Brian was slow to respond. Finally, almost peevishly, he stepped aside.

"Well, all right, have a look," he said. "Be my guest."

"If you insist." Smiling in puzzlement, she put her eye against the viewer, which was situated at a right angle to the body of the telescope. But all she saw was real estate, a large Bel Air house on an acre or so, walled in, very private and luxurious.

"Stephanie's showing me the houses of the stars," Brian explained. "That one's Tom Selleck's place. When he's in town."

"Fascinating," Eve said. "I didn't realize you were a fan. Or that he was an art lover."

"You mean those sculptures outside? Yeah, I guess he is."

"And even a totem pole."

Brian took hold of the end of the telescope and moved it a few inches, which had the effect of pulling the viewer from Eve. "There's a lot more to see down there than one stupid house," he declared. "The Capitol Record building, for instance. On a clear day you can see the young executives jumping out of windows."

Eve swung the telescope back towards Brian. "Here, you take it—I didn't realize it was private property."

He forced a laugh. "What the devil you talking about? You want to look, look."

"Later," Eve said. "Before I burn to a crisp, I've got to get out of this classy suit you bought me."

As she headed for the house, Brian got in the last word. "Hey, it shows off your finer qualities."


**B**y the time Charley got back to his hotel, he was not feeling very optimistic about his rescue mission to California. The way things were going, it seemed a safe bet that he wasn't going to rescue much of anything: not Brian, not Eve, and not his money either. But thanks to Dan Courtney, he at leat had a nice hotel to come home to.

Courtney was one of a dozen or so rich Chicago lawyers who lived in Flossmoor and belonged to the country club. Not having the best of marriages, Courtney and his wife made it a point to have the best of everything else. They loved to travel almost as much as they loved coming home and telling anyone who would listen about the places they had visited: just which restaurants and hotels and spas were the very best. In L.A., he told Charley, one simply had to stay at the Bel Air Hotel. So at the airport, when the taxi driver asked an exhausted Charley his destination, nothing else came to mind.

"The Bel Air," he said, like any other millionaire movie producer. Still, he was not unhappy with his choice. Located up a small canyon off Sunset Boulevard, it looked like a group of beautiful old Mediterranean villas set amidst an arboretum. Charley could just imagine how the Courtneys, taking it all in, had immediately set about composing paeans for the folks back home, all the untraveled yokels at Flossmoor's Nineteenth Hole.

Though Charley's room was one of the less expensive, at three hundred a night, it was so beautifully furnished he almost hated to see it wasted on him. For as usual, his first moves were to kick off his shoes, stretch out on the bed, and turn on the television, which had been carefully hidden in a cherry-wood armoire. Absently he surfed through the channels, barely noticing what was on, still unable to get his mind off what he'd learned from the last name on the list.

The address was in Ojai, a small artsy-horsey town located in the mountains about seventy miles northwest of Los Angeles. Since it was a rural address, just a road name and a box number, it had taken him almost as long to find the place as it did to drive up from L.A. Even then he almost missed it: a run-down five-acre horse ranch squeezed in between two scrabbly hills. The return address on Brian's letter home had said only c/o Bannister, so Charley wasn't sure whether he was looking for a man or a woman. Whichever, it was a man who appeared, coming out of a small metal barn as Charley drove in and parked. The man appeared to be in his late fifties or sixties, bent and wiry, with a stubble of white beard on his dour face.

"I'm looking for Bannister," Charley said.

"Well, you found him. What can I do for you?"

Charley told him his business, and Bannister looked even more dour. He lit a cigarette and kept staring intently at the ground, as if eye contact would have cost him dearly.

"So you want to know if Brian Poole is here?"

"Or if you've heard from him. Anything you might know."

"You want to get to him before the police, huh?"

"That's right."

"Sort of save him from himself?"

"Something like that."

Still not looking at Charley, Bannister smiled crookedly, as if in pain. "Well, mister, you sure have wasted your time. Oh, your brother stayed here all right, a long time ago. And lemme tell ya, if all I had to do was spit to save his life, I wouldn't do it."

Charley didn't know what to say to that. "Hard feelings, huh?"

"Yeah, you sure could say that. We figured him and our Joan was engaged, you know? Gonna be married. It was, oh, ten or twelve years ago. Yeah, we even let them sleep together, in her room, just like they was already married. And Joanie, our beautiful Joanie, she couldn't of been happier. She really loved the guy. And he even took her home to Illinois—you probably met her then."

"Thanksgiving?"

"Yeah, that's right. Around Thanksgiving."

And Charley did remember the beautiful young blonde that Brian had brought home with him, the girl he referred to as Harpo, because she was so shy and quiet.

Bannister lifted his gaze now, pale blue eyes that seemed to burn like gas flames. "Then one day your brother, he just up and disappears. And Joanie finds he's got a new girl, someone else to use and throw away."

"Well, I guess you were right—I seem to have wasted my time." Charley started to turn away, wanting to get out of there as soon as he could. But Bannister's words held him.

"For us, though, it didn't end there. No sir. Joanie just couldn't accept it. A one-man woman, I guess. Anyway, from then on for her it was just booze and drugs, ODs and rehabs. Till finally it got to the point where her mom and me, we just almost didn't care no more. Then one night the L.A. police phoned us. Joanie'd overdosed again. Only this time she never woke up."

"I'm very sorry. As you say, she was a beautiful girl. A nice girl."

"But not nice enough or beautiful enough for your brother, was she?"

Charley didn't even try to answer that. He shook his head in commiseration, then got back into his car and drove away.

Lying on top of his bed in the hotel, Charley reflected that it was not yet six o'clock on the first day of his quest, and he was already finished. There were no more names on the list, no more places to go. Nevertheless he didn't feel inclined as yet to fold up his tent and head for home. That undoubtedly was what he should have done, but he simply wasn't ready yet for such a total defeat. So instead of watching the news on TV and then cleaning up for a Courtney-like evening at the hotel—drinks in the mahogany-

paneled bar and dinner later in the celebrated French restaurant—he slipped into a sportcoat and headed for the open sewer
of downtown Hollywood, thinking he might just as easily stum-
ble into Brian and Eve there as anywhere else.

He left his car in an attended parking lot and set out on foot,
walking up Hollywood Boulevard toward Sunset. Though it was
still daylight, he couldn't actually see the sun, just an area of
greater brightness in the heavy, smoggy air. There was no breeze,
but the countless cars whizzing past kept the dirt and waste paper
moving constantly, right along with the tourists, who Charley
imagined were feeling as uneasy as he was at finding themselves
on foot amidst what appeared to be one huge perambulating sex
bazaar. The pimps and whores came in all colors and costumes,
most of them painted children, brazen as riot cops. And they
were thoroughly modern too, sporting not just dreadlocks and
rainbow beehives but also the latest in technical support: beep-
ers and cell phones and probably laptops in their pimpmobiles,
which were not pink Cadillacs anymore but dark green and black
BMW sedans.

Charley thought of going to a bar and developing a mild buzz
before dinner, but decided it was still too early. So he began
checking the theaters as he walked along, thinking he might
take in a movie before dinner, preferably something not about
space wars or time travel or the burdens of teenage virginity. Not
that he actually wanted to *watch* a film—he had too much on his
mind for that—but he did want to sit in quiet solitude, without
having squads of prepubescent criminals fighting popcorn wars
all about him.

Leaving Hollywood Boulevard, he came back on Sunset for a
few blocks, about to give up when he spotted a small porno theater on a side street. And this surprised him. He had thought
that VCRs had put all such theaters out of business long before,

yet here one lived on, like an artifact of another age. Figuring that it at least would be dark and quiet inside, he went on in.

Charley had no problem admitting that he enjoyed pornography, all those sexy young women who seemed to like giving head even more than the men liked getting it. From experience, though, he knew that ten or fifteen minutes after he took his seat in the theater his eyes and brain would glaze over and he would watch the rest of the film much as he might sit on the beach and observe the surf rolling in, with the same pleasant feeling of uninvolvement and abstraction. At the moment, however, he found himself entirely caught up with what was happening on the screen, where a beauteous girl named China was doing her thing on a rug of animal pelts with a man and a teenage girl. As his interest mounted, he wondered why the supposedly imaginative sex entrepreneurs of Southern California had never thought to introduce midget prostitutes to patrol the theater aisles, blowing dirty old men like himself for twenty or thirty dollars a shot. He speculated that the entrepreneurs might have feared that the midgets' tiny feet could have stuck to the floor, or that if they had fallen, they might never have gotten up again, would have been caught in the primordial sludge forever, like the mastodons in the nearby La Brea Tar Pits.

**H**ours later, in a Sunset Boulevard cocktail lounge, Charley sat nursing his third vodka tonic as a boxing match was playing on the television set behind the bar. The lounge was the kind he preferred, small and dark and devoid of chic, having no stained-glass windows or antique wooden bar or sawdust on the floor, nothing that might pull in the yuppie crowd. Of the seven men at the bar, Charley judged that he was the youngest by a good ten years. There were a couple of Chicanos, an African American, and the rest Mediterranean ethnics of one kind or another. They were drinking beer or boilermakers, and they wore polo shirts and dark polyester trousers with bladelike creases. There was also an Asian woman sitting alone at the end of the bar and three young hookers in a back booth, evidently taking a breather from their labors. Every so often their brassy laughter would ring out, and some of the men would turn and look at them with disapproval.

In the mirror behind the bar, Charley's gaze occasionally connected with the almond-shaped eyes of the Asian woman, who would then smile warmly at him. She had long, upswept black hair and the delicate features of a Thai or Vietnamese. Much of the time she seemed on the verge of smiling, which gave her a look of amused sophistication largely undone by her taste in clothes: skintight purple velour slacks and a green sateen blouse topped off with pound of junk jewelry. Charley would have figured her a prostitute had she been younger, or conversely, if she had *looked* older, more used up.

In any event, before long the bartender brought him a fresh drink "compliments of the dragon lady," and since this was a first in his life—a woman unknown to him buying him a drink in public—Charley felt he couldn't simply smile at her in the mirror and leave it at that. And anyway, the woman interested him. So he picked up his new drink and moved down the bar, taking the stool next to hers. In heavily accented English she told him that her name was Mary Lee and that she had bought him the drink because he looked so troubled and she wanted him to know that he had at least one friend in the world. He asked her why the bartender called her the dragon lady, and she said she often wondered the same thing, which made him laugh, which in turn brought a lovely smile to her face. They went on drinking and talking, and Charley learned that she was a movie theater cashier on her day off, that her family had been wiped out in Vietnam, and that she had been in America for twenty years and had divorced the marine sergeant who had married her and brought her over.

Later, Charley took her down the street to a steakhouse, where they had dinner and brandies. Afterwards, he walked her to her apartment, and when she invited him in, he declined.

"Why?" she asked. "You don't tink I'm sexy?"

"Oh no, I think you're very sexy. It's just that my life is pretty complicated right now."

"You spend anudder hour wit me, dat make your life more complicated?"

"I'm afraid so."

She looked at him with open disgust. "You know what? I tink you a fag. I tink you a dirty fag."

"Well, you're wrong," he said. "Anyway, thanks for the drink."

As he turned away, she repeated her charge, loud enough for a couple across the street to stop and look. He kept on walking.


**W**hen he got back to the hotel, there was a note for him to phone Waldo Trask. After dialing the number on the note, he waited through six rings before anyone answered. It was the lesbian.

"Yeah? Teddy here."

Charley asked for Trask. Without responding, the woman left the phone. Finally Trask came on.

"After you left, I started thinking," he said. "And it finally came to me, the name up on Mulholland. It's Stephanie Hodges. I don't know her exact address, but I can give you directions. You want to try it?"

"You bet I do," Charley said.

# chapter nine

Charley did not arrive at Stephanie's until ten in the morning. He had just driven through the open gate and parked when the front door of the house flew open and Eve came running out, only to stop dead when she saw who it was. Recovering immediately, she smiled and came over to the car as he got out.

"Charley!" she said. "God, I'm glad you're here."

Confused by then, Charley just stood there with his hands hanging at his sides as she gave him a gingerly kiss on the cheek.

"I thought you were Brian," she said.

"I'm sorry to disappoint you."

"Oh, you haven't—really. But I can't imagine you're very happy to see me again. How on earth did you find us?"

"Dumb luck, mostly. You say Brian isn't here?"

It was if he'd jerked her awake. Suddenly she looked fearful and worried. "No, he certainly isn't. And I'm afraid he's gone off the deep end again, Charley. When I heard your car, I thought maybe he'd changed his mind and come back."

"From where? Why? What's he done?"

She shook her head despondently, her eyes suddenly moist. "Oh, it's crazy. I'm not even sure. I just got up. Come on in. Stephanie—the lady of the house—she's in a state of shock. Her daughter Terry, who's only eighteen—Brian took her with him. And they took both cars for some reason."

Charley followed her into the house. She was wearing a black T-shirt and khaki shorts and did indeed look as if she'd just gotten out of bed. Her hair was a mess, a lush, dark brown tangle, and she wore no lipstick or eyeliner. Still, she somehow managed to look as beautiful as ever.

"Stephanie's downstairs and at the other end," she said, leading the way though the house, which was typical California Spanish, but older than most, Charley judged, better built than the contemporary staple-gun variety.

As they walked, Eve looked back at him. "What really pisses me is that I was planning to leave today," she said. "I was going to take the money you gave him and send it back. But now you'll never know. You'll never be sure."

"I'll take your word for it."

Again she looked back, this time with a rueful smile. "I imagine you would."

"About Brian," he said. "What he's up to? Tell me what you know."

"Well, the people making the movie about Kim Sanders—Wide World Studios—the studio head lives in Bel Air. With a telescope, you can see his house from here. Stephanie says he's got a world-class art collection and that right now Brian's on his way there to destroy it."

Charley groaned. "Jesus. Won't he ever quit?"

"I'm afraid not."

Charley followed Eve down a hallway that ran past a small study and a bedroom with glass doors on the other side, through which he could see a patio and swimming pool. At the end of the hallway, they entered a large bedroom that looked, like its king-size bed, unmade, lived in. An unhealthy-looking woman with blond hair sat sprawled in an easy chair, dabbing at her swollen eyes with a wadded handkerchief. On the lamp table next to her there was an open champagne bottle, an empty glass, cigarettes, and an ashtray.

Eve introduced Charley to her and the woman nodded vaguely, as if she weren't quite sure what was going on.

"My baby," she said. "The son of a bitch has taken my baby with him, and she's gonna wind up in prison right along with him."

"You sure about what he's doing?" Charley asked. "The art collection?"

Stephanie nodded. "I heard them leave about a half hour ago. And when I got up, I found this under my door." She handed Charley a sheet of lined yellow paper.

Unfolding it, he read:

*Stephanie,*
*Please don't worry about me. It has to be done, what we're doing. I'm in Brian's hands, so I'll be all right. I know I will. If all goes well, we'll be home soon.*

*Love,*
*Terry*

Charley looked at Eve. "You seen this yet?"

She took the note from him. "No, I'm afraid not."

"I meant to show it to you," Stephanie told her. "Really, I was going to—I just don't know what I'm doing. I'm so scared. My baby's gonna wind up in prison because of him—I just know she will."

Charley pulled a coffee table around and sat down in front of her. "Stephanie, listen, maybe we can stop him. Maybe it's not too late."

"I wish I could believe that." She reached for the champagne bottle, then set it back down. Her hands were shaking noticeably.

Eve meanwhile had read Terry's note. "Why would he take her with him? I don't get it?"

"Maybe he needed both cars," Charley said. "But first, Stephanie, how do you know where he's headed? I mean, this guy's art collection?"

"I guess in a way I'm to blame," she said, reaching down and picking up a newspaper supplement. "For some reason I save all these *Calendars,* the magazine section of the Sunday *Times.* A month ago they ran this story on Kevin Greenwalt, the new president at Wide World Studios." She opened the supplement and showed them the article. "His old man was a mogul at Universal. He's the one who started the collection. And now the kid carries on with it. Some of the paintings are really valuable. And I guess Brian figures that since they're out to ruin his reputation, it's only fair to ruin something of theirs. Get even, you know? Send them a message."

"Greenwalt's place—it's the one the telescope's trained on, isn't it?" Eve said.

Stephanie nodded. "I was kidding with Brian about it only yesterday. I never dreamed he'd just go right ahead and do it." Unsuccessfully, she tried to snap her fingers. "Just like that."

Though Charley wondered what telescope they were talking about, he didn't take the time to find out. "Do you have any guns here?" he asked. "Do you know if Brian took any with him?"

Stephanie shrugged. "There's my second husband's gun case in the game room. But I don't know if Brian took any. I didn't think to look."

Charley got up. "We'll look on the way out. And maybe you better come along," he said. "If we do intercept them, you're the best bet to talk your daughter out of it."

"Oh no, I can't go with you. I just can't." Dropping the magazine, Stephanie held up her hands for them to see. "Look how shaky I am. I can't do anything. I really can't."

"It's up to you." Charley picked up the magazine and started for the door. "We'll do what we can."

Eve led him to the game room, where he saw that the glass case had been left open, with a key in it. Two of the rack spaces were empty.

"Oh Christ," he said. "I don't like the looks of this. I can't believe he'd take guns. What's he on—drugs again?"

Eve shook her head. "Not that I know. Come on, let's hurry."

She led the way out onto the patio and up the outdoor stairs, the two of them running by now. Seconds later they were in Charley's car, roaring down the cul-de-sac to Mulholland Drive, where Eve told him to turn left. Considering what might lay ahead, for himself as well as for Eve, Charley thought the weather at least could have cooperated, served up yet another typical Southern California summer day, clear and warm, with a touch of the sea in the air. But this was a Midwest day, already in the nineties, only dry as hemp, with a Santa Ana blowing in from the desert, replacing the smog with sand and dust. There was a distant wail of fire engines, and to the west, beyond the next rise, a column of smoke angled out to sea.

"Turn left again at Beverly Glen," Eve said. "It goes straight down to Bel Air. It's probably four or five miles to the house."

"You think it'll be hard to find?"

"Afraid so. The streets are all about twenty feet long and have chic little names, not numbers. It's all very woodsy and countrified.

"Great."

Eve looked over at him. "You mind telling me what we're going to do? What we *can* do?"

"I've got no idea. Try to intercept him. Try to talk some sense into him. And if we can't—I don't know—kidnap the girl and call the police on him."

"You think we should do that?"

"It's high time somebody did something, wouldn't you say?"

Instead of answering, Eve lit a cigarette. "I just can't believe he'd go this far," she said. "And the cunning bastard, he knew enough not to let me in on it. He knew I wouldn't go along."

"This Terry, what's she like?"

"Timid and introverted. Plain. Worships Brian."

"Enough to go this far? To risk jail?"

"So it seems."

"What kind of cars do they have?" Charley asked.

"An old nine-eleven Porsche and an even older station wagon—the big kind for pulling trailers. Like a truck."

"A Travel-All?"

"Yes, that's it."

As Charley turned onto Beverly Glen and headed down toward Bel Air, he asked Eve to glance through the *Calendar* article and give him the gist of it. So for a short time they drove in silence as she pored over the story. Then she summarized: "Well, as you saw, there's this nice big picture of Greenwalt and his wife in front of a Jackson Pollock—Jesus, what that must be worth! The wife is a Bryn Mawr graduate in fine arts and, quote, 'one of Hollywood's rising young hostesses.' The basic part of the collection—and the valuable part—are all abstract expressionists like Pollock and de Kooning and so on. And then he's got a lot of rising young turks too, names you never heard of, like Willis, Hensen, Andrews . . ."

"Never heard of any of them."

"No kidding."

"Does the article say anything about the physical layout of the place? The security system?"

The paintings are all in what was once a 'grand room' or ballroom. And Greenwalt isn't worried about thieves, it says. The gallery, as he calls it, is fireproof and burglarproof and most of the paintings are too huge to carry. The sculptures in the outdoor sculpture garden are so humongous you'd need a crane to move them, according to Greenwalt."

"Anything about the household staff?"

"Not a word."

"How about the studio and his movie work? Anything about *Miss Colorado?*"

Eve shook her head. "Only that he puts in a twelve-hour day and the studio has six films in various stages of production. And that Greenwalt believes he has, quote, 'the right formula for reversing the studio's precipitous decline over the past few years.' "

She put down the magazine and looked over at Charley. "Tell me—is your mouth dry?"

"Like chalk."

"Good. I was afraid I was coming down with something."

**O**nce they got on Bel Air Road, they had to backtrack up Brown Canyon, looking for Alana Lane. As Eve said, the area was indeed woodsy and numberless, with hidden little streets shooting off like tendrils from Bel Air, which was a narrow blacktop corkscrewing up the canyon past rustic wood fences and rows of giant eucalyptus trees that stood naked, their bark hanging in genteel tatters. There also were pepper trees and conifers of every kind, and palms too, farther back, closer to the houses, some of which were dark and wooden, not the almost uniform Spanish stucco that reigned in Beverly Hills.

Charley was beginning to wonder if they were lost—just as they came upon Alana Lane, a tendril curving down toward Beverly Glen Boulevard, but dead-ending just this side of it. At the end of the short, curving street there was a stucco wall enclosing Greenwalt's estate. Inside, on the highest ground, was the house, huge and white, with an orange tile roof. Though the wrought-iron front gate was standing open, Charley pulled up to it and stopped.

Eve looked at him with frightened eyes. "What now? Just what the hell do we do?"

"We go in," he said.

"And then what?"

"Christ knows."

Throwing the car back into gear, Charley headed up the hill to a point where the driveway forked, the right lane leading to the front entrance while the left went around to the rear of the house. Continuing on the left lane, they passed Greenwalt's "sculpture garden," a reflecting pool surrounded by objects that looked as if they had been placed there by a gang of practical jokers. There was an actual electric chair sitting on a slab of concrete; there was a standing twelve-foot-high wooden cigar with sly, painted eyes and flippers for arms; there was a polished steel doughnut the size of an earthmover tire; and finally, weirdest of all, a black-painted shed that looked suspiciously like a ten-hole outhouse.

Charley smiled grimly. "Well, he hasn't struck here yet. Too bad."

"There's the Travel-All," Eve said.

Pulling in next to it, Charley was disappointed to find it empty. He had hoped that the girl would be in it, waiting, a "wheelman." Then he could have either cajoled her or forced her into his car and had Eve drive her home, getting them both out of harm's way and leaving him free to go inside and deal with Brian alone. He knew he didn't have much chance of talking him out of his folly, but he could try at least. And failing that, he could always hit him in the head with a baseball bat, as he'd done when they were kids—by accident, hitting the catcher instead of the ball. More likely, he would simply pick up a phone and call the police.

"You better stay here," he said to Eve, who was already out of the car.

"No, I better not," she said.

"Right."

Going around a high hedge, they entered the backyard, which contained a large swimming pool and cabana as well as a tennis court. At the near end of the pool there were so many umbrella tables and other pieces of outdoor furniture that the place had the look of a hotel—an *empty* hotel. There was no one, anywhere.

But there was a back door—standing open. Charley's legs suddenly felt like sandbags.

"I'm gonna pee in my pants," Eve whispered.

"Then stay behind me."

Though she gave him a wry look, she did slip behind him as they crept inside, into a rear hallway with utility rooms on one side and a huge kitchen on the other. At the end of the hallway a skinny young woman cradling a shotgun sat back in an oak kitchen chair, facing a closed door.

"Jesus Christ, Terry!" Eve said to her. "Have you gone completely mad?"

The girl looked walleyed with terror, but that didn't keep her from swinging the gun onto them.

"Brian!" she called. "Brian, we've got visitors!"

"I'm Brian's brother," Charley told her. "It's not too late. Why don't you drop the gun and go home with Eve."

The girl looked even more terrified. *"Brian!"* she called.

Charley glanced at the door she was guarding. "Who's inside?"

"Who do you think?" she said. "The servants. The slaves."

"I want a word with my brother." Ignoring the gun, he moved past her, following the hallway as it widened, circling the base of a curving stairway and leading around to the foyer, which was marble-floored and elegant, with an ornate fountain in the center: a pair of cuddling bronze cherubim pouring water from a pitcher in an endless stream. On each side of the foyer there was a wide doorway, one leading into a large, beautifully decorated living room and the other into the gallery, which apeared to be about sixty feet by thirty, a brilliantly lighted room with dozens of huge nonobjective paintings lining the walls and a row of sculptures—mostly "assemblages" and "found objects"—running down the center.

Going on into the gallery, Charley saw Brian moving feverishly along the wall of paintings with a can of aerosol paint, spraying on each of them a single huge, sweeping letter in metallic Day Glo pink.

THIS IS SHIT, he wrote, and moved on to the next row of paintings, yelling at Charley as he worked.

"Get your ass out of here, man! This is none of your fucking business!"

"Is it Terry's?"

"Ask *her!*"

By now Eve had come into the gallery too, and she appeared mesmerized by the scene before them, Brian's great, gaudy letters imposing at least a semblance of order and meaning on what otherwise seemed at best a riot of color: a Jackson Pollock that looked as if it once had served as the floor of a pigeon coop; a de Kooning that could have been a self-portrait by an inebriated Charles Manson; a Motherwell that looked like an extreme close-up of a giant crushed crow, a monumental oozing of blackness. And there were others: a piece of awning ten feet square;

a green carrot on a field of vomit; a door doodled by an idiot; and one painting that appeared to be nothing but a frame. Almost all of them by now bore Brian's huge, slashing letters, which finally added up to a second message, the one that had brought him here:

### NO MISS COLO FILM

Finished, he tossed the spray-paint can into one of the assemblages and ran past Charley and Eve into the foyer and down the hall, where he got the shotgun from Terry. He told her to go out to the wagon and wait for him. Then, charging back into the gallery, he yelled again at Charley and Eve.

"Will you two get the fuck out of here! What do you think you're gonna do, *stop* me, for Christ's sake?"

It was a reasonable question, and Charley might have laughed at himself—at the ridiculous futility of his mission—if he hadn't been so angry and scared. He took Eve by the arm.

"He makes sense. Come on, let's go!"

But she pulled her arm free. "No, wait."

And she stood her ground at the gallery doorway, watching in utter fascination as Brian raised the shotgun and pointed it at the sole artwork in the huge room that didn't appear to belong there: one of the new latex trompe l'oeil sculptures, a sitting nude so totally lifelike it had not only painted-on skin and eyes but real hair, real eyelashes, real nails. And at the moment it looked for all the world like a real person about to be killed in cold blood. Then the shot rang out and the thing exploded in a shower of plastic and hair and other junk, all of it shockingly bloodless. Moving backwards then, toward the doorway, Brian pumped four more shots into the gallery, these into paintings he had already defaced.

Charley took Eve by the arm again, half shoving her ahead of him, and this time she made no resistance, running on toward the back entrance, unaware that Charley had stopped at the door Terry had guarded, to see what condition her prisoners were in. Opening it just a crack, not ready yet to be seen and later identified, he made out one man and three women, all Asians, sitting in the dark on the floor of a large pantry, their arms, feet, and mouths duct-taped.

Satisfied that they would be all right, Charley followed the others outside, running most of the way. He jumped into the car and turned the ignition key—only to hear the starter continuing to grind, as the engine flooded. And for an eternal fifty or sixty seconds he and Eve could do nothing but sit there and wait for the thing to clear.

Meanwhile, with Terry sitting next to him, Brian backed the Travel-All around and headed for the sculpture garden. In his initial charge, he felled the towering cigar and then proceeded across the shallow reflecting pool and totaled the king-size black outhouse, carrying bits and pieces of it with him as he circled on the golf-green lawn, ripping and gouging it until the station wagon was in position for a second run at the sculptures. And this time he tore up the electric chair and smashed into the huge stainless steel doughnut, which caved in the front of the wagon at the same instant it broke loose from its base and started rolling downhill, gathering speed as it went, finally crashing through the estate wall and wobbling a bit before continuing downhill, heading through the brush for Beverly Glen Boulevard.

Charley tried the ignition again, and this time the engine fired, almost drowning out Eve, who was pleading with him to get moving.

"Come on, Charley! Come on, for God's sake!"

Heading down the driveway, Charley had to slow down because of the Travel-All ahead, limping along, spouting steam from its damaged radiator. But once they reached the street, the narrow, curving Alana Lane, Charley floored the accelerator and they went shooting past the wagon.

"Shouldn't we wait for them?" Eve asked. "What if they don't make it?"

Charley glanced over at her. "How could they not? God still looks out for children and idiots, doesn't he?"

"Then why isn't he looking out for us?" she asked.

The last thing Charley wanted to do was go straight back to Stephanie's and wait there for the triumphant return of Brian and his new sidekick. He would have preferred cruising into Hollywood and finding a quiet little bar where he and Eve could have spent the afternoon with some cool vodka tonics. But she rightly pointed out that his car and license place might have been seen by a neighbor of Greenwalt's or someone passing through the area, so he headed back up Beverly Glen toward Mulholland. And almost immediately they came upon an accident scene: a white Rolls Royce sitting askew in the middle of the road, its rear half squashed flat and its doors and hood gaping open, as if the vehicle were bellowing in pain. Beyond the wreck, a narrow path of vegetative blight led straight up the lawn of a luxurious hillside home to the engine of destruction itself: Greenwalt's silver doughnut, lying on its side in the grass, looking not unlike one of the worn-out tractor tires farm women painted white and put to use as planters. All it lacked was a hub of daisies.

After punching through Greenwalt's wall, the doughnut evidently had continued hurtling downhill until it reached bottom in the backseat of the Rolls, then bounced on across the road and started uphill. Miraculously, no one seemed to have been hurt. The car's apparent occupants—a runtish, sunbaked bald man and a well-preserved blonde, both in tennis whites—were outside the car, the man whooping and hollering at anyone who would listen while the woman merely stood by the side of the road, calmly smoking a cigarette. Other cars had stopped and their drivers had gotten out to gawk, but as yet no police were on the scene. So Charley simply drove around it all and kept going.

When they arrived at Stephanie's, taking the side stairs down to the patio, she came out of the game room carrying a bottle of champagne and almost fell over one of the pool chairs. Charley caught her and helped her back inside.

"Terry's all right," he assured her. "They should be home soon, mission accomplished."

Stephanie's mouth fell open. "Then, he did it? He *actually* did it?"

"Oh, you bet he did," Charley said. "He was in rare form. Hollywood will never be the same."

"We got there too late to do anything but watch," Eve told her.

"And Terry helped?" Suddenly Stephanie had the look of a stage mother, her terror of a few moments before giving way to pride.

"I'm afraid so," Charley said. "She was his accomplice in every sense of the word. He even had her toting a shotgun."

At that, Stephanie had to feel her way down into a chair. "Oh no. Please, tell me the truth."

"That *is* the truth. But there's no reason to panic. Chances are, she'll be pulling in here any second now. Home free."

"You think so?"

No, Charley did not think so, at least not the *home free* part. Until now, he really hadn't given it much thought, why Brian and Terry had taken both cars. But the more he considered it now, the more he became convinced that Brian had taken the Porsche along with them as their *getaway* car. Which meant they probably had left it somewhere near Greenwalt's, some out-of-the-way place where they could later abandon the Travel-All, transfer to the Porsche, and take off—but for where? Charley had no idea, except that it would not likely be Stephanie's, since the police would surely find the Travel-All before the day was out, and it in turn—its license plate, pink slip, whatever—would soon lead them to Stephanie's.

Charley turned to Eve. "Where's your room? I think we ought to check Brian's stuff."

Eve gave him a look of wide-eyed innocence. "Well, we'll have to go to *Brian's* room for that, won't we, Stephanie?"

"Brian's room?" Charley asked.

"Yes, we were assigned different quarters," Eve said, smiling sweetly now. "Why? You think he's taken off?"

"Could be why they took the Porsche along."

"It sure could." Eve led him out of the game room and down the same hallway, this time stopping at the bedroom next to Stephanie's. "Yes, Stephanie just insisted on having him to herself," she said. "But only for conversation, she claimed. And of course massages. The lady do like her massages."

Charley didn't know what to say to that, so he said nothing, just stood there watching as Eve quickly went through the room, checking the closet and the drawers and the adjoining bathroom.

"You're right, he's not coming back," she said. "Some of his stuff is here. But the important things, like his razor and swim trunks and the flight bag with your money in it—they're missing."

"Beautiful," Charley said.

"So what do we do now?"

"Well, it would be pretty stupid to hang around here and wait for the police. So why don't you hurry up and pack, and I'll take you wherever you want to go."

"I'm all for that," Eve said. "The only problem is *where*. My parents' place and the condo are probably both staked out."

"I've got a room at the Bel Air Hotel," Charley told her. "I'll be flying home tonight, but you could stay there. I could pay a week or so in advance."

She smiled quizzically. "You'd do that? You'd put me up at the Bel Air after the way we bugged out on you?"

"I figure that wasn't your idea."

"It wasn't. But still—" She shook her head. "All right, I'll go, but not to the Bel Air. I just thought of a place that won't cost a cent."

"Good."

Starting out of the room, she looked back at him. "I'll be ready in a minute."

**W**hile Eve was upstairs getting her things together, Charley went back to the game room and told Stephanie that they were leaving. He also said that he believed there was a good chance that Brian and Terry would not be coming back very soon, because they had taken both cars and Brian's things were missing. This was not something Stephanie wanted to hear.

"You're crazy!" she cried. "You don't know what you're talking about! If you knew my Terry, you'd never say such a thing. She'd never leave me in the lurch like this, without even a car. I can't get around. And I can't keep up this big house all alone—she knows that!"

"I hope you're right," Charley said. Then he went on, trying to advise her what to do in the event the police did come to the house before Terry and Brian returned. He suggested that she keep her story simple, that she admit she had taken Brian in but hadn't known he was wanted by the FBI and the police.

"Tell them you don't read the papers or watch the news on TV. They can't prove any different. And tell them Eve left right after she and Brian arrived. There's no sense involving her in this new thing. She didn't even know about it."

Toward the end, Charley could see that Stephanie wasn't listening to him, in fact was straining to see around him. Fingering the remote, she turned up the sound on the TV.

"Move over!" she cried. "It's on now! The noon news is on!"

Just then Eve came into the room, quietly setting down her luggage. Charley sat back against the arm of the sofa. On the TV, the news anchorman had just paused to glance at a late bulletin a young woman had handed him. Now he returned his steely gaze to the camera.

"We'll report on the fires in a moment. But this just in—another development in the *Miss Colorado* case. Channel Seven has just learned that fugitive Brian Poole, boyfriend of the late Kim Sanders, has been identified as the man who less than an hour ago broke into and vandalized the Bel Air mansion of Kevin Greenwalt. Greenwalt is a noted art collector and head of Wide World Studios, which is producing *Miss Colorado,* based on Kim Sanders' life. The Beverly Hills police report that the suspect, along with a young female accomplice, gained access to the Greenwalt mansion and, after forcing the servants to disarm the security system, proceeded to vandalize one of the most valuable modern art collections in America. Here's Donna Chan, on the scene."

The picture cut to a striking young Asian woman in Greenwalt's house, standing with the man himself at the entrance to the gallery, with the defaced paintings in the background.

"Thank you, Paul. I'm here in the art gallery of the Greenwalt home with Kevin Greenwalt. Sir, can you give us any sort of estimate of damages caused by the suspect?"

Greenwalt, staring into the studio, kept shaking his head in disbelief. "Well, you can see for yourself," he mourned. "The damage is almost total. It's incalculable. The man is simply insane. Look at the message he leaves us: No Miss Colorado film. And where does he scrawl it? On a Franz Kline, for God's sake! On a Motherwell! I just can't believe it!"

"Me either," Charley said, waiting to hear something he didn't know, such as whether the police were looking for the station wagon or the Porsche, or his own rented car for that matter. But the newscast moved on to the brushfires, and Charley went over to Eve and picked up two of her three bags.

"Well, I guess we'll be on our way," he said to Stephanie.

In response, she waggled her hand as if she were shooing away flies. "Yes, go on, leave. My Terry will be back soon enough. I'm not worried."

"Good," Eve said, picking up the other case. Following Charley, she went out onto the patio and together they hurried up the stairs to where Charley's car was parked.

"Where are we headed?" he asked.

She smiled at him. "How about Santa Barbara?"

# chapter ten

**B**efore driving up to Santa Barbara, Charley first had to go back to his hotel to check out. On the way, Eve explained that though she couldn't stay at her parents' home, figuring that it, like Brian's condo, would be under surveillance, there was also her widowed aunt's place in Carpenteria, near Santa Barbara.

"And it'll be empty," she told him. "Aunt Maureen went along with my parents to Ireland. They'll be gone another two weeks."

"Does Brian know about the place?"

"Sure, but he wouldn't go there. I probably told him about their vacation in Ireland, but he never listens. As far as he knows, Aunt Maureen is at home. And anyway, he wouldn't be able to get in even if he wanted to. You have to know the security code."

"Which you do?"

"Which I do."

"Fine. I'll drop you there, and then go on to the airport."

Eve smiled at him. "Home to Illinois, uh?"

"Might as well. Brian could be anywhere, right? So I guess my bird-dogging days are over."

When they reached the hotel, Eve said that she would wait in the car for him, but he explained that he would be a while because he had some telephone calls to make and suggested that she might prefer to wait out by the swimming pool or in the bar.

"Looking like this?" she said. "They'd probably put a mop in my hand and tell me to get to work."

"Of course," Charley said. "Eve Sherman, the typical American washerwoman."

She joined him outside the car. "You just haven't been in town long enough, Charley. Half the drudges here expect to be stars one day."

"If I can't find you when I get back, I'll know you've been discovered."

"Finally!" She was smiling as they parted.

In his room, Charley tried to phone Donna at her office, but was told by Rose Biaggi, his old secretary, that Donna had driven up to Evanston to see Jason, their son. Charley asked if anything was wrong.

"Only that you aren't here, boss. We keep seeing your brother on network TV, and I think Donna expects to see you on it soon too, as his victim or something."

"I hope you disabused her of that notion."

"Oh sure, me telling Donna what to think."

"Tell her I'll phone her at home tonight."

"Will do."

Calling Denver next, Charley was able to get Agent Ramos on the phone almost immediately. He told him where he was and why, and Ramos made a clucking sound, as if he were shaming one of his six children.

"You told us you were going back to Illinois," he said.

"I changed my mind."

"Well, I guess so."

"Somehow forty thousand dollars seemed worth it," Charley said. "I guess I just lost my head."

"I hear you, Charley. It's just when an important party in a case like this says he's gonna be at such-and-such a place and then changes his mind, we want to hear about it."

"That's why I'm calling now."

"Well, I guess we'll just have learn to live with that, huh?"

"It's up to you."

"Right. Now, about your brother. I take it you ain't found him yet."

"No."

"So you weren't in on that little art gallery caper, then?"

"That's right."

"I kind of figured that." Ramos, who apparently had plenty of time on his hands, then began to ruminate on the "gallery caper," allowing as how Brian's taste in art was pretty much like Ramos' own. "Fact is, I think your brother improved on some of them paintings, you know? Which don't mean, however, that we ain't still after his ass. "

"No, I'm sure you are. More than ever."

"That's a fact."

Charley then told Ramos that he would be flying home that evening and that if the FBI needed him for anything, he would be happy to cooperate.

"That's good to hear," the agent said.

"You've got my Illinois address and phone number."

"Yessir, right here in front of me."

Minutes later, packing his few things, Charley couldn't help feeling that though Brian might have been on the FBI's Most Wanted list, the agents themselves were not exactly consumed by the need to bring him to justice. They evidently considered him something of a flake, a dilettante, a harmless miscreant when compared with the usual run of monsters they normally dealt with.

After checking out and and tipping the bellboy at his car, Charley went looking for Eve and found her at the pool, a large blue oval surrounded by lounge chairs and umbrella tables set amidst exotic palms and flowering trees. In the shade of one, Eve lay back with her eyes closed and her lips slightly parted, as if she were about to whisper a secret. Charley hated to disturb her.

"You ready to go?" he asked.

She smiled at him. "No, I've decided to take you up on your first offer and stay here a couple of weeks."

"Too bad," he said. "I've already checked out."


**O**nce in the car, with the windows up and the air conditioner purring, Charley asked Eve about Brian—where he might be headed, what his plans might be—but she said she had no idea. The Greenwalt incident apparently had been a spur-of-the-moment thing, she said, like almost everything else Brian ever did. So she could only assume that his plans now would continue to be spontaneous and impulsive.

"I wonder if he's skipped town," Charley said.

"Well, he's certainly got enough friends around. When they retire, movie people often head north—Oregon, Washington, Idaho."

"And you think some of them would take him in?"

"Especially the stuntmen. They're mostly a bunch of outlaws anyway. Or at least they like to think they are."

Following Eve's directions, Charley drove north to the Ventura freeway, then headed west toward Santa Barbara, which was about ninety miles away, at the eastern end of what Eve called the south coast. As Charley expected, the freeway was a roaring river of cars, a good portion of them Japanese. For many miles, Charley debated with himself whether he should even bother to state the obvious to Eve. Finally, he went ahead anyway.

"You know the FBI's after you too," he said.

That made her shudder. "Don't remind me."

"What do you plan to do?"

"For now, nothing. Lay low. Let them come to me. I haven't really done anything but tag along with Brian."

"That's what I told them."

Eve smiled at him. "I know. We saw you on TV. And I thought, there he is, trying to save our butts—after we left him hanging."

Charley smiled too. "Funny, that's kind of the way I saw it."

Eve laughed. "Big surprise!"

"Would you mind a bit of advice?"

"Of course not."

"Let me contact the feds for you. And if they sound reasonable, you get a lawyer and turn yourself in."

Eve nodded solemnly. "I know you're right. And I'm sure that's what I'll do finally—but not quite yet. I need a few days—don't ask me why."

"I don't have to. I think it's sort of like going to the dentist. Easy to put off."

"It sure is," she said.

She asked if he would mind her smoking a cigarette, and he heard himself say, "Of course not," even though he would just as soon have had her throw up on the dashboard. However, he did ease the electric windows partially down, hers as well as his.

"The phone calls you made at the hotel," she said, "was one of them to the FBI?"

"Yeah. I wanted to let them know where I was and that I'll be flying home tonight." Smiling slightly, Charley looked over at her. "They asked about the Greenwalt thing, whether I was involved."

"You didn't tell them we were there, did you?"

"It must have slipped my mind."

Eve shook her head in amazement. "God, what a scene that was. I'll never forget it."

"Neither will Greenwalt—or at least the aftermath."

Taking a last drag on her cigarette, she stubbed it out in the ashtray and left it there, stinking. And Charley thought how preposterous it was that a smart, stylish woman like Eve could be so oblivious to such a gross act. But then he had been there himself. Until six years ago, he too had been a smoker. He too had had a stone dead nose.

"You called your wife too?" Eve asked, not looking at him, her expression casual, indifferent.

"Yes, but I couldn't reach her. I'll try later. By then maybe I'll know what flight I'll be on and can tell her when I'll be home."

"Does she know about the bail money?"

"Afraid so."

"Then she must have a real high opinion of me, right?"

"Higher than she does of Brian, I'd say."

"Which is not saying much, I take it."

"Eve, she doesn't know you. She's never even met you."

"Lucky lady."

Charley looked over at her. "Oh, I don't think I'd call her so lucky."

He had intended it as a polite cliché, a counter to Eve's denigration of herself. But once said, the words seemed to hang ominously between them, freighted with an entirely other meaning. Eve made no response, however, in fact did not even look over at him, so he couldn't tell what construction she had put on them. Reclining her seat a few inches farther, she lay back and stared out the passenger window, which she had closed again. And for the most part, that was how the trip proceeded, with the two of them locked into an uneasy, almost electric silence.

Not until they reached Ventura was Charley able to see the ocean. Beyond that point the freeway snaked west, squeezed in between the sea and the mountains. And finally it skirted Carpenteria, a small seaside town located five or six miles down the coast from Santa Barbara. Just past the town, Eve told Charley to turn onto a side road, which soon curved north, climbing into the foothills between lemon groves that gave the salty air a fine, clean edge, therapy for L.A. sinuses. Higher up, there were more side roads with houses on them, expensive, modern dwellings with unrestricted views of the sea. And the house of Eve's aunt was no exception, a small, well-built Spanish-type affair sitting on two acres of lemon trees, with a stunning view of the ocean from almost all its windows and especially from its terrazzo deck, at one end of which was a sunken, empty hot tub.

As Eve had promised, getting in proved no problem. After plucking the front door key from under a flower pot, she went inside and punched in the code that disarmed the security system.

"How the devil do you remember the number?" Charley asked.

She smiled impishly. "Easy. It's my birthday: four, eight, sixty-seven. Aunt Maureen and I used to be very close." She was moving about, opening windows and doors, letting in the lemony air.

"Christ, what a view," Charley said, standing at the open doors to the deck.

Eve smiled. "Whenever I come here, I can't get enough of it— for about five minutes. Then I want to see people again, or their cars and boats—something human, you know? An empty ocean is just that."

Charley continued to look at it, vast and blue, sparkling under an equally vast, blue sky. "I don't know," he said. "It looks pretty damn nice to me."

"Just wait five minutes."

"Actually there's plenty of action out there. Only it's out of sight, under the surface."

"But it isn't human action."

"You know what the tree-huggers and PAWS people would say to that? Thank God, it isn't."

"Right. But I'm not one of them."

"You want humans. You want real blood-and-sweat action."

She struck a self-mocking pose. "You bet."

"Somebody like Brian," Charley said.

"She made a face, wrinkling her nose in deliberation. "No, not like him. Not right now. He's too . . . what?"

"Reckless? Single-minded?"

"No—wacko."

They laughed at that, but not very easily in the end, as if they both worried that they might have offended the other. Eve turned and headed for the kitchen, pausing at the doorway to look back at him.

"Listen, I don't know when you plan on leaving, but Aunt Maureen really has a terrific larder—a freezer absolutely chock-full of anything and everything. And I would really like to make us dinner. I mean it, I *really* would. It's been so long since I've even boiled an egg."

"You poor thing," Charley said.

"I'll tell you what, you find out when you're leaving, and maybe try to get as late a flight as you can, and I'll try to get the food on the table in plenty of time. Okay?"

Charley smiled. "This is one of those offers a guy can't refuse, right?"

"Right."

**B**efore Charley was able to reach Donna, he had learned that there were no nonstop flights from Santa Barbara to Chicago and that it was already too late for him to catch the last nonstop out of LAX to Chicago, a United flight leaving at six P.M. He made reservations for the next day, then tried again to reach Donna, this time succeeding.

He was in Aunt Maureen's sewing room, which offered the only real privacy downstairs. So he was able to speak freely, omitting the sort of information that he knew would only anger Donna all the more, such as the fact that he was temporarily alone with Eve. Instead he told her that he was calling from a pay phone and had just left the FBI offices in L.A., having phoned them after hearing about Brian's Bel Air escapade. They then had asked him to come in, which he had, in the process losing the whole afternoon.

"And you were right," he said. "I didn't find a trace of Brian until it was too late. And I've got no idea where he is now."

"Big surprise," Donna said.

"Right. So I'm coming home." He told her that the last nonstop to Chicago was already booked up, so he was going to have to get a room out by the airport and fly home in the morning, which meant of course that he wouldn't be getting in until late afternoon, Central Time. His car was still at the O'Hare parking lot, and he mentioned now that he hoped it would start.

"After all this time," he added.

"And whose fault is that?" she said.

"Mine, Donna. All mine. Tell me, how's Jason?"

"Mystified, like his mother. Just before I left him, we heard the news about Brian and the art gallery. And Jason asked me why on earth you're still out there. I guess he feels a reasonable man would want to put as much distance as he could between himself and his psycho brother."

"I'll be home tomorrow afternoon," Charley said. "Late afternoon."

"I'll believe it when I see it."

"Good-bye, Donna. Take care."

"I always do," she said. "Unlike some people I could name."

After hanging up, Charley took a deep breath and went back into the kitchen, where Eve was hard at work, with an apron covering her T-shirt and shorts. He saw that she had got out bottles of vodka and tonic, and had made drinks for them. He picked his up and took a deep draught of it.

"This hits the spot," he said. "Thanks."

"Later, though, at dinner, it's martinis," she said. "Okay?"

"You twisted my arm."

"And how are things at home?" she asked, busying herself, not looking at him.

Charley smiled ruefully. "I guess they could be better. Donna wonders what I'm doing out here."

Eve looked incredulous. "Well, what about the money? Doesn't she think it would be a good idea to get back what you lost, paying his bail?"

"I don't think she believes that's going to happen. With good reason, I might add."

"You came close, though. If you'd caught him at Stephanie's, you could have got it back—what he hasn't already spent, anyway."

"You think he would have parted with it peaceably?"

"That I don't know."

"Well, it wouldn't have mattered. Peaceably or otherwise, I would've taken it home with me."

Eve looked over at him, evidently surprised by his tone. "Yes, I think you would have," she said.

"Incidentally, it's too late for me to catch a plane out tonight. After dinner, you point me to a cheap motel, all right?"

She gave him a look of mock disgust. "Don't be ridiculous. There's plenty of room here. With three bedrooms, I think we ought to be able to manage."

Charley wanted to say that though *she* undoubtedly would manage quite well, it might not be all that easy for him.

Instead he shrugged in agreement. "If you insist, okay. This is another one of those mafia offers, right?"

"Right, the kind you can't refuse." Smiling, she took him lightly by the elbow and ushered him toward the doorway to the dining room and beyond. "So why don't you go out on the deck and enjoy my aunt's five-minute view. I've got important work to do."

Charley smiled. "Ah, those are the words every man loves to hear."

"I don't doubt it, shiftless creatures that you are."

"But cunning—you'll have to admit that."

"The devil, I will."

Carrying his drink, Charley did just as Eve suggested, going out onto the deck and sitting back on a lounge chair. In front of him, Aunt Maureen's terraced lawn dropped down to a grove of lemon trees small enough that he could easily see over them. Even though it was later now, the sea and sky appeared brighter as the sun descended off to the right, beyond Santa Barbara and a long white sickle of beach. By any reasonable standard, he knew that he should have been feeling pretty good, waiting there for dinner in this lovely setting, stretched out with a drink in his hand and the California coast spread out before him. But in point of fact he was feeling intensely uneasy, and he was afraid he knew the reason: the prospect of spending the night there alone with Eve. Not that he thought he would make a play for her or that she would respond favorably even if he did; he was reasonably certain that neither of those things would happen, even when night fell and the two of them might be less than sober. Still it worried him, just the thought of spending a long evening with her, and later trying to sleep in a bedroom near hers, probably with only a wall between them.

He knew how he already felt about her, how often he thought about her, how much he wanted her. And he worried that this pleasant evening and night spent together in the lemon-scented air would only set the hook deeper in him. He could already see himself taking off in the morning, a walking basket case, nose pressed to the jet's window, to see if he could locate the little house in the lemon grove, where he'd left behind a sizable portion of his heart.

He vowed now not to let that happen. He would marshal his defenses and steel himself against her. After all, he was not some schoolboy who went around wearing his heart on his sleeve. He was a grown man with a wife and a son. He had a life a half continent away, and the lovely Eve Sherman was simply no part of it. Yet even as he sat there constructing his defenses, sipping at his drink and gazing out at the sea, what he really saw was Eve lying by the Bel Air pool and sitting next to him in the car and moving about the kitchen in her aunt's apron, her hair a curly, lovely mess.

So when she came out and got him for dinner, he felt addled and clumsy, wanting to behave with a certain cool correctness, yet at the same time totally unable to stifle the pleasure, even the happiness, he felt at being with her, looking at her, listening to her. And the meal didn't help much either, for she had made one of his favorites: stuffed pork chops, scalloped potatoes, applesauce, and peas. And she had set out everything he needed to make a pair of straight-up Absolut martinis.

"I'm sorry about the wine cellar," she said. "There isn't any. Aunt Maureen's allergic to the stuff, so her guests get to abstain right along with her."

"No problem," Charley told her. "When it comes to wine, I'm a great connoisseur of colas."

"And which do you like best?"

At the moment, he had his martini in hand. "This one," he said, which made Eve laugh, a rich easy laugh that because of her beautiful mouth—all those perfect teeth—became something one saw as much as heard.

Before coming out to get him, she had combed her hair and put on a bone-white summer dress that accented her light tan. And she smelled good too, all of which pretty much routed Charley's determination to keep his defenses up. Instead he found himself more than content just to sit there and eat and drink and make light conversation with her, hopefully funny enough so he could see more of her laughter.

Inevitably, though, the conversation got around to Brian, and for the rest of dinner there wasn't much to laugh about. Eve asked him about the charges against Brian, apparently assuming that because Charley had been questioned by the FBI, he would have a pretty good idea what his brother faced. But he explained that the agents tended to ask a lot more questions than they answered. Nevertheless he told her what little he knew, most of it having to do with Brian's crimes in Colorado.

"The new stuff," he said, "the Greenwalt thing and running away with Terry—I just don't know. But putting a gun on the servants and locking them up, that's assault and probably kidnapping too—I'm not sure. In any case, if and when he's caught, I honestly can't imagine he'll get off with less than twenty years."

"*Twenty years?*"

"Eve, it's just a guess. I'm not a lawyer. I don't know any more about these things than you do."

"But twenty years, Charley! Some killers don't even get that, do they?"

"He almost got Jolly killed."

"Only because that Chester was a wacko. It wasn't what Brian intended."

Charley took down about a third of his martini. "You're probably right," he said. "But even if it were twenty, there's early parole and time off, things like that."

She gave him a rueful smile. "Oh, let's not talk about that anymore, okay?"

He wanted to remind her that he wasn't the one who had brought up the subject, but he didn't. "I'm with you," he said.

"You know, there's all this furor over what he's done," she said. "But nobody seems to care *why*. The networks and the pundits, they couldn't care less about his motives."

"That's usually the case, isn't it?"

"Maybe so. But still . . ."

Eve went on then, telling Charley more about Brian and Kim Sanders, how much he had cared for her and even fought for her. In a story oddly similar to the one Waldo Trask had told Charley, Eve explained how bad the situation had become at the country singer's posh farm outside Nashville. As Kim's career waned and her need for narcotics steadily increased, Brian had tried to keep the drug peddlers away, even to the point of beating up on one who came right to their door. The man swore out a complaint against him, and Brian spent almost a week in jail before Kim sobered up enough to find out where he was and get him out.

"And finally I guess he just gave up," Eve said. "Kim dragged him off to her cabin near Colorado Springs, not far from where she was born. And for the next six months I guess all she did was drink and listen to her records and shoot up with heroin and whatever else she could get. Brian told me he went for long walks and did a little grass and coke. And since he couldn't stop her from using, he sometimes had to go out himself and find the stuff for her. He said the night she died—the night she overdosed—it was just like most other nights, the two of them lying together on a mattress in front of the fireplace and listening to music and sleeping off and on. But in the morning, when he finally awoke, she was already cold. He had no idea when she'd died. So he called an ambulance and the police, and when they asked him where he was when she died, he simply told the truth."

"And then the feeding frenzy began," Charley said.

"Right. The media all over the place, sticking their mikes in his face. And from then on, he's been this lowlife pusher who slept while his ladylove, the great superstar, died beside him."

Thinking Eve looked close to tears, Charley reached over and put his hand on her arm. "I don't think very many people feel that way anymore."

"No, now he's the *wacko* lowlife who . . ."

Unable to finish, she started to get up, probably headed for the bathroom to cry. But Charley moved faster, getting up at almost the same instant and holding her there for a few moments before she gave in and sank back down.

"I know how you feel," he said. "I realize you love him, Eve. But this meal's just too fine to waste. We can talk about Brian later, okay?"

Smiling sadly, her eyes moist, she nodded as he sat down again too. "And maybe not even then," she said.


Later they took their drinks out onto the deck and watched the last streaks of sunset following the sun into the sea. Charley commented that the place smelled even better now than it had earlier, and Eve explained that as the breeze lessened, the bushes and trees around the house—hibiscus and jacaranda and bougainvillea—got their chance to show off.

"It doesn't sound much like Flossmoor," Charley said.

"What do you grow there?"

"Oak trees mostly," he said, which made her laugh.

"The truth is, though, it's very beautiful. In fact, that's one of the things I miss out here, the great old trees, the oak forests. Flossmoor seems more, I don't know, more like America."

Eve pretended to be offended. "It wouldn't if Norman Rockwell had lived here."

Charley laughed. "You've got a point."

She went over and turned off the hot tub, which had been filling since they'd come outside.

"The tub's ready," she announced. "Now, if we only had some swimsuits."

"We don't?"

"No, I checked Aunt Maureen's room. No guest suits, just her own, which could serve as a tent. So I guess we'll just have to go with our underwear."

"Boxer shorts?" Charley said. "You sure you're ready for that?"

She laughed. "Indeed I am!"

Charley had already brought out glasses and a pitcher of martinis, and Eve now placed three candles around the tub and lit them, candles that she said were guaranteed to keep the mosquitoes away. Charley turned away from her as he got out of his clothes, all except his shorts, and he pretended no great interest in Eve as she slipped out of her dress now and edged down into the tub, her taut, lovely body naked except for a lacy white bra and panties.

The two of them slipped all the way down into the water, with only their heads visible, facing each other about six feet apart, both smiling as the hot, churning water caressed their flesh.

"It's kind of like that beer commercial," Charley said. "It just doesn't get any better than this."

Eve laughed. "I'll second that."

Pushing back and upwards, Charley poured their drinks and reached out to give one to Eve.

"Not yet," she said, her head still the only part of her above water. "There's one thing I want to say first, while I'm still sober. You know what you said inside, about knowing that I loved Brian?"

Charley nodded.

"Well, I just wanted you to know I'm not sure about that anymore. Lately it seems that my feelings for him are more sadness and anger, you know? I mean, it hurts me to see the state he's in. And I get angry too, at the things he's doing. But love? I just don't know anymore, Charley. Okay?"

Charley wasn't sure what to say to that. Setting her drink close to her, he nodded sympathetically. "Of course, Eve. And being his brother, I think I know where you're coming from."

"I'm sure you do." Suddenly then she smiled, happily, beautifully. "There! That's over. Now we can soak."

"Right."

She took a sip of her martini and set it back down. In the position the two of them were in, half reclining, their bodies tended to rise in the water, and as a result, their legs kept touching.

"There is one other fly in the ointment," she said now. "Underwear. *Clothes!* In a hot tub, they just don't feel right, at least not to me. So I was wondering, if I were to suggest we dispense with them, would it be possible for you not to think I was coming on to you?"

"Of course."

"Why 'of course'?"

"I don't know. Because of Brian, for one thing."

"What else?"

"Because if that's what you said, so be it. I believe you."

Eve shook her head, almost in wonderment. "Charley, you're

something special, you know that? I don't think I've ever known a man like you before."

"You poor kid."

"No, honest."

"It's my shorts, right?"

She laughed. "No, I mean the fact that you can be such a straight-arrow one minute—such an innocent—and the next, funny and sophisticated. And you're so easygoing on the outside . . ."

"And on the inside, what? Paranoid schizophrenic?"

"No, easygoing."

"You found me out."

"Well, what about it? *Au naturel?*"

"Why not?" Putting down his drink, Charley slipped out of his shorts and tossed them onto the deck just as Eve began to remove her bra and briefs, all done underwater. In her case, though, she didn't toss them onto the deck so much as *set* them there, which caused her to come up out of the water for a second or two, exposing her breasts in the process.

Naked now, unencumbered, she and Charley settled back, content to loll there in the burbling water, with the candles burning about them and the sky beyond the lemon trees slowly darkening, becoming almost the inky color of the sea, where a scattering of oil-drilling platforms winked on and off, red and green. Their legs continued to touch every now and then, and Charley helplessly felt his cock swelling. Afraid she might see him through the water, he sat back farther and took his drink in hand, wanting to drain it almost as much as he wanted her not to notice his tension. So he sipped at it slowly, saying nothing, unable to take his eyes off hers, unable to read what he saw there.

Oddly, Eve suddenly was looking almost grave, as if she had remembered something unpleasant or pressing. And she too seemed to have nothing to say. It was as if, in becoming nude, they had rendered themselves mute. Occasionally she seemed to forget about the natural buoyancy of her body, and her breasts would rise briefly out of the water, two perfect little islands, pink at the crest. And Charley continued to wonder if she could see his erection through the water. Rattled, he poured himself another martini and gestured to freshen hers, but again she declined.

"No, I'm fine," she said.

Charley settled back then, somewhat puzzled by the intensity of her gaze. As he watched her, the corners of her mouth curled upwards in the hint of a smile, one of irony or reflection.

"It's funny," she said, "being here like this. Doesn't it make you kind of regret that we're not more like Brian? I mean, him and his meaningless one-night stands."

Not quite knowing what to say to that, Charley heard himself going off on a tangent, practically babbling. "I've got this weird phobia about phrases like that—I mean, one-night stand. I mean, it might have been hip at one time, but now it's just a cliche. Like 'on the rocks'. I sometimes order Scotch and ice, and the waiter invariably looks dumbfounded for a moment, then says, 'Oh, you mean *on the rocks.'* I'm tempted to bring in a real rock one day and drop it on his foot and say, 'Now, *that* is a rock. What I want is ice.' "

By then, Eve was smiling at him as if he were a child. "Charley, I think you're evading my question," she said.

Nodding in defeat, he set his drink down. "Yeah, I suppose you're right. I guess I just didn't want to admit that I lied to you in Colorado about my faithfulness. The fact is, over the last ten years or so I've done my share of cheating too—away from home, at conventions and the like, one-night affairs every bit as meaningless as Brian's. And worse in a way, because I don't like to admit to them."

"You're ashamed of them?"

Charley started to say 'Of course,' another lie, but caught himself in time. "No, not really. I can't truly say I think it's wrong or evil. I mean, all our married lives, men fight against the desire for other women. We look at all the beautiful girls—all the beautiful women—and we eat our hearts out, while our wives seem to have pretty much what they want—the home and the kids and, on occasion, us. So I guess I rationalize. I tell myself that an occasional dalliance far from home—what does it hurt? When I return home, things don't change. Everything's still pretty much just like it was before, not bliss maybe, but not misery either."

Eve shook her head. "That's a pretty sad story, Charley."

"Is it? Yes, I suppose so. But I wanted you to hear the truth, Eve. And please don't think I'm telling you this in order to make things happen between us here tonight. I'm glad you're true to Brian. But even if you weren't, nothing would happen between us."

"Why? Because of Brian?"

"That too."

"What else?"

Charley didn't answer immediately. He knew he had been backed into some some sort of ultimate corner where there could be no more facile twists and turns, no more evasions. And he regretted it, because he knew the truth would put an end to the whole lovely evening as well as to his own stupid, hopeless dreams and send her running for the nearest exit. When he spoke finally, his voice was matter-of-fact, even cold.

"I think you know the reason, Eve. I'd never want it to be a one-time thing. I'd never want it to end."

As before, her head seemed disembodied, floating on the roiling water, the beautiful face and abundant hair, the large green eyes looking almost orange in the candlelight. But suddenly the eyes were glistening and the head was moving toward him and rising, followed by her shoulders and breasts and arms coming up out of the water, the arms reaching for him.

"That's just how I feel, Charley," she said.

**A**fter making love in the hot tub—actually more *out* of the tub than in it, as passionate as they both were—the two of them went upstairs to Aunt Maureen's bedroom and continued to make love off and on through much of the night. Charley was amazed that he still had it in him, this sudden surge of youthful virility, but he had no doubt as to its source: the lovely, wondrous creature beside him, and under him, and on him.

The California night played its part too, warm but dry, with a light breeze moving the gossamer curtains and a half-moon dimly lighting the room as well as the lovers' bodies. Charley was not sure when he fell asleep, but he suspected that it was three o'clock or later, for he slept till almost eleven the next morning. Eve was already out of bed, showered and bathrobed, preparing just the sort of breakfast they both needed, or at least wanted: pancakes, bacon, eggs, the works.

Later she found a cache of champagne, a half-dozen bottles of Mumm's her aunt must have been saving for a special occasion.

"One just like this," Eve said. "She must have known you were coming."

They laughed at the double entendre, unintentional though it had been. And they did tap into the champagne, but lightly, the two of them not needing much in the way of stimulation. They spent most of that day in bed or in the hot tub, with occasional forays into the kitchen for sustenance. And when they weren't dozing or making love, they talked. They talked about their lives, but only partially, at Eve's insistence omitting any mention of Brian.

"Just for now," she said. "I know he's your brother, and he's been my life for three years, but I don't want him intruding now, okay?"

Charley frowned. "Aw, gee, I was hoping we could just lie up here and talk about him full time."

Eve gave him a push, as if she were trying to knock him out of bed. "Smartass," she said.

"I know."

"Charley, I'm serious about this."

"I'm sorry," he said. "Of course I agree. I don't want to talk about or even think about anyone who ever touched you before."

She smiled at that. "The possessive type, uh?"

"You bet. You're mine now. I own you. I can do with you as I choose. And right now I choose this." He lightly bit her below the navel and moved upwards, still biting and kissing, going from one breast to the other.

She laughed contentedly and pulled him higher, bringing his mouth to hers. And then they grew quiet, as it all began to build again, their own private phoenix rising from the ashes of its last immolation.

Late that afternoon they drove down to Carpenteria to buy fresh fruit and vegetables, along with other food items that Aunt Maureen kept in her huge freezer but which Eve wanted fresh. Afraid that someone might recognize her, she had put on dark glasses and covered her head with a scarf, and even then she didn't go into the store herself but sent Charley, with a list. Inside, checking it as he filled the cart, he felt like a little boy. A very happy little boy.

The next day the two of them ventured down the coast to Santa Barbara and not unexpectedly found it heavily infested with tourists, its exotic tree-lined streets and handsome Spanish buildings overflowing with Northerners and Easterners, many standing in line just to get a table at a sidewalk cafe or to enter one of the city's picturesque shopping courtyards. Eve again had covered her hair and put on the darkest glasses she could find. Still, she did go along with Charley into a couple of shops, where he bought some needed clothes: underwear, shirts, slacks, a jacket, and tennis shoes, deck shoes actually, since he wouldn't have been found dead in a good modern sports shoe, the Nike and Reebok stuff, with all their stripes and whorls and glitz. Later, he and Eve went walking barefoot along one of the city's splendid beaches, though it too was overrun with visiting humanity.

That night, after a steak dinner and more hot-tubbing and lovemaking, Charley lay awake while Eve slept beside him. It was a warm night again and the moon had finally made its appearance, a little lower and slimmer, but still bright enough to fill the room with a soft blue light. Eve was lying on her side, facing away from Charley, with a sheet covering her almost to her shoulders.

For a time, resting on his elbow, he lay there looking at her, at the dark hair carelessly spread across the white pillow and at the line running from her shoulder down to her slim waist before rising again, steeply, into the thrilling swell of her hip, which in turn flowed down into her plump, yet hard, buttocks. And it occurred to him that if he had handed God a work order for a mate, she would have been a twin of Eve, this new friend of his, this woman, this beautiful creature he now loved.

He was so lost in the moment, so lost in her, that he suddenly found himself reaching over and gently peeling the sheet off her, so he could look at her without anything in between. He knew he should have been thinking of other things, such as Donna, his home, his life in Flossmoor. How on earth could he square all that with this? With Eve? And then there was Brian. Given all that, he had no illusions that what lay ahead for him and Eve would be anything like sweetness and light. For that matter, he had no way of knowing how deep Eve's feelings for him were. Possibly all this was merely a matter of opportunity, of time and place, of lemon trees and the sea.

But none of that made any difference. In truth, he was happy and even grateful to be in the predicament he was in. For the first time in years, he felt *alive*.

In time, embarrassed by what he had done, he carefully pulled the sheet up over her again. But even then he compensated for his loss by moving in tightly against her, putting his arm around her waist and gently cupping her breast in his hand. And he whispered, too softly for her to hear.

"Sleep, my love."


**L**ate the next afternoon the telephone rang, signaling the end of their idyll together. At first, the two of them just stood there and looked at each other, Charley to see if she was going to pick up the phone and Eve evidently to see if he thought she should.

"It could be about my father," she said. "He's not in the best of health."

"Then you better answer."

She did so, softly saying "Hello," then listening for a few moments, during which she mouthed the caller's name to Charley: "Brian." Then she went on.

"How'd you know I'd be here? . . . What's wrong with her? . . . Brian, she's eighteen. If she doesn't want to go home, what could *we* do? . . . 'We' is Charley. He's here with me." She turned to Charley then. "He wants to talk with you."

Charley took the phone. "It's me," he said.

"Taking care of my girl, huh?"

Charley ignored that. "Where are you?"

"Seattle. That's all I can say on the phone. But I do need to see you and Eve A.S.A.P. I've got to figure out what to do—I mean, like how to turn myself in. Where and when. Stuff like that."

"You're a big boy now, Brian."

"Not that big, Charley. I just don't know all the ramifications, you know? It couldn't hurt to talk it over with my big brother and my girl, could it? She still is my girl, isn't she, Charley?"

"You'll have to ask her."

"I will, don't worry. And listen, man, I've still got your money, haven't I? I mean, it's not like you would've given it to me if you'd known I was going to jump bail, right? So I figure it's still yours. I want to give it back."

That almost took Charley's breath away. "I'm all for that," he said.

"Then you guys will come up here?"

"I will, yes. As for Eve, you'll have to ask her."

"Don't worry. And listen, Charley, fly up as soon as you can, okay? I mean, like today."

"As soon as I can, right."

Brian then asked him to put Eve back on, and Charley gave her the phone. She spoke a little more about the girl, evidently Stephanie's Terry, then reluctantly agreed to fly up with Charley.

"Yes, as soon as we can," she told him, digging a pencil and paper out of the phone-stand drawer. "All right, go ahead . . . But

why not just give us the address? . . . All right, noon and six, yes."
She wrote down his directions and said good-bye.

After hanging up, she shook her head in disgust. "We have to
meet him in some goddamn park. Noon or six. Isn't that cute?
He must figure we'll arrive with the FBI."

"Me, probably, not you."

"I wonder."

"So we'll meet him in the park."

Eve's eyes were heavy with concern, even dread. "I really don't
like this," she said. "It's like I've finally reached shore, and now
I'm being told to turn around and swim out into the deep
again."

"I know the feeling," Charley said. "But Brian did tell me he'd
give my money back. And he wants to discuss turning himself in."

"Do you believe him?"

"I want to." Charley took her in his arms, and she hugged him
back, hard. "It'll be all right," he told her. "We love each other,
and nothing's going to change that."

# chapter eleven

Eve had been in Seattle five other times: twice with her parents, once with her ex-husband, and twice with Brian, the last time staying overnight with him on an old friend's yacht moored in Lake Union, which lay virtually at the city's center, probably no more than a mile from where Eve was now, standing at a window in her and and Charley's tenth-floor suite in the Olympic Four Seasons Hotel. It was after four in the morning, and she had been awake for over an hour, having no dearth of things to worry about, things she was trying hard to put out of her mind.

Instead she concentrated on the street below, which looked scrubbed and fresh, like everything else in the city, especially the Olympic. She had stayed at the hotel once before, on the trip with her ex-husband, so she was not surprised at how tastefully elegant the old place was. That time, however—old Bernie not being quite as free with his money as Charley was—they had stayed in a simple, average-size room with a double bed, no sitting room or whirlpool bath or banks of windows running along two walls, no thirty feet of wool carpet separating her from the king-size bed where her new lover softly snored.

Turning, she looked over at him now, barely able to make him out in the night light, just his tousled head showing above the covers. And again she entertained the thought that their love affair would be a short-lived thing, entertained it like a long, sharp icicle impaling her skull. For she had fallen so hard for him that she actually hated his wife, just for living. And hated his life back in Illinois, and of course now hated Brian too—all the things that she knew would inevitably pull her and Charley apart.

With Brian, though, the problem was that she also still loved him, or at least still felt bound by the *habit* of loving him, of living and sleeping with him. Because of this ambivalence, she had no idea how she was going to handle things when they were all three together again. What was she to do, stand midway between them or cling to Charley and stick her tongue out at Brian? At least she knew she wouldn't do the reverse of that, not in this lifetime.

She was still amazed at the difference Charley had made in her life, not just the fact of being in love with him, but being actually, consciously, *happy*. Until now—until Charley—she hadn't realized how easy life could be, how much more fun, if you weren't in a constant state of anxiety, always wondering what your lover was brooding about, wondering just when he would blow. Even though Charley and Brian were alike in many ways, for instance having the same warm, easy smile, the same good looks and hard bodies, they were at bottom totally different. When Charley made love to her, there was no button pressing, no feeling of being manipulated. Rather, he was was simply so straightforward passionate, so ardent, that the buttons seemed to press of their own accord, and all at the same time, with the result that her only problem was in trying to make the experience last as long as she could, a "problem" she had never had before, not with any man.

Mainly, though, it was the other things, the daily little things, out of bed, that had won her heart. Charley was unfailingly considerate and made no attempt to hide how he felt about her, least of all in the way he looked at her. Yet there was never anything cloying in his attentions, probably because of his wry sense of humor, his ability to laugh at himself—and at both of them— in ways that never hurt or denigrated. Above all, she loved how comfortable he was, both in his skin and in his world. And it was a contagious comfort, making her feel more relaxed and confident than she had in years.

Still, the icicle remained where it was, stuck in her head. This was not the real world, she kept telling herself. Not her world anyway. It was a vacation. It was a honeymoon. And honeymoons always ended.

Late the next morning Charley and Eve were sitting over lattes in the bright sunshine of a sidewalk cafe in Pioneer Square Park. The scene they looked out on was almost as charmingly picturesque as it was depressing, for though the park was a lovely little place, it was crowded at the moment with some markedly unlovely people. Except for them and the cars driving past, it could have been a scene from a century earlier: the worn brick walkways and the old park benches and cluster-globe streetlights, as well as an ornate iron-and-glass pergola, a streetcar stop of long ago. There was also a kiosk and a totem pole and a curious little fountain-cum-statue of the Indian chief for whom the city was named, all lying in the shade of handsome trees. So it didn't surprise Charley that street people had taken over the park, runaways and drunks and petty hoodlums, one of whom was amusing himself and his buddies by dribbling spittle onto the face of an old man sleeping on a bench.

Noon came and went, without any sign of Brian or the girl Terry. And since workers on their lunch break were lining up for tables, Charley and Eve decided to leave. For over an hour they walked the downtown streets, most of the time holding hands, with Charley pulling Eve along, frustrating her apparent need to stop and study every shop window they passed. Charley, on the other hand, was more interested in the throng of passersby, who soon convinced him that Seattle was the true home and natural habitat of the yuppie. Not that there weren't more of them in larger cities, but here their preponderance was overwhelming: a virtual army of well-dressed young people of both sexes, bright-eyed and rosy-cheeked from their morning workouts and ready to take on the world, or if not that, then at least a good, low-calorie, high-priced lunch at some chic little eatery, places with names like the Burger and Spirits Emporium and the Great American Food and Beverage Company. Even the oldsters on the street seemed to share in the general attitude of bustling self-satisfaction, everyone evidently considering it something of an accomplishment to be living in Seattle instead of elsewhere.

It was an attitude Charley had no problem understanding. Just flying into the city, gliding in past postcard-perfect Mount Rainier and circling back over the downtown, with snow-capped mountain ranges in either direction and Puget Sound at the city's front door and huge Lake Washington at the back, he could understand a certain smugness on the part of those who lived amid such natural splendor. At the same time, he certainly didn't envy them the pace of their lives or the racket they had to endure.

By the time Charley and Eve reached the hotel, they were in need of food and drink. So after a quick visit to their suite, they returned to the lobby and went into the Garden Court, as it was called, a room of such size and elegance that most of the patrons spoke as if they were in church. Beyond a bank of greenery, including some sizeable trees, there was a row of two-story Palladian windows revealing across the street a sparkling white skyscraper that was beveled in at the bottom, as if Paul Bunyan had taken a couple of whacks at it before deciding to let the thing stand—precariously.

Though Charley was wearing a sportcoat, he gathered from the waiter's subtly patronizing look that he was too casually dressed for the room. But he went ahead and ordered anyway: a daiquiri for the lady and an Asolut martini for himself.

"If you only want to drink," the waiter suggested, "there is the Georgian Terrace. You'll find it—"

"No, we'll imbibe here," Charley told him. "And later, we may even eat."

Eve smiled as the young man left. "That's not like you, Charley—being short with a waiter."

"Well, he was short with me. About five nine, I'd say."

Eve graciously ignored his joke. "He looks a little like Brad Pitt."

"Brad's snooty little brother."

"Maybe you should kick him when he comes back."

"Or bite him maybe. I could practice on you." He picked up her hand as though to bite it, but kissed it instead. "Now, don't think this means I'm going to kiss his hand."

"You're sexist," she said.

"That's for sure."

After their drinks were served, Eve gave Charley a woeful look. "What happens if we keep going to the park and Brian doesn't show?"

"Then we stop going there."

"We could go out looking for him."

"In a city this size? How would we go about that?"

"Well, I told you about our last trip here, staying with one of his old friends on the guy's boat in Lake Union."

"Only you don't remember the man's name or the name of the boat."

"No, but we could go looking in that general area."

"It wasn't the *Seagal,* huh?" Charley had already told her about his run-in with Chester, sending him on what he'd thought was a wild goose chase, looking for Brian on a Seattle boat called the *Seagull.* And he'd told her about the fax Donna had sent him later, the picture of Brian and a friend back in the seventies, standing at the stern railing of a yacht named *Seagal.*

"I just don't remember," Eve said now. "As I told you, we only stayed the one night, then went on to Sun Valley and stayed a few days with some other friends of his."

"Well, if Chester Einhorn didn't turn around and go home, maybe we'll run into him. We could join forces, looking for the *Seagal.*"

"That would be fun."

"Wouldn't it, though? Little Chester with his great big guns."

Eve smiled. "When I think of you tossing him down a mountain—well, I just wish I'd been there."

Charley blew on his fingers. "Yeah, when it comes to handling little-bitty guys, I'm a tiger."

Eve wasn't buying. "Oh, I don't know. I think you could hold your own against just about anybody."

"You think so, huh?"

"Yes, I do."

Charley gave her a salacious look. "In that case, would you like to come upstairs and feel my muscle?"

Smiling, she took a sip of her daiquiri. "After one more of these and some food—yes, that might be arranged."


**A**t six that evening Charley and Eve again waited for Brian on the edge of the tiny Pioneer Square Park, but again he did not appear. Afterwards, they had dinner at a very noisy but excellent steak house, and then they went walking in Pioneer Square, which turned out to be an entire area of the city and not just the tiny park they had been watching, an area where century-old buildings and streets and parks had been carefully preserved and restored. And they were not alone. It seemed as if half the city's work force had chosen to stay downtown and wander with them along the tree-lined streets, past the old brick and stone buildings with their many cafes and bars and shops. For a change, though, yuppies appeared to be in the minority, outnumbered by neighborhood bohemians and street people: lost kids, hookers, winos, and aspiring hoodlums, a veritable Rainbow Coalition of teenage males standing around in small groups, flying their gang colors and staring at every passing couple as if they were potential crime victims, which in some cases they probably were, Charley reflected uneasily.

Holding hands, he and Eve wandered into a block-square park with numerous trees and benches and a wide brick walkway leading past some kind of iron shelter or bandstand into a handsome minisquare with kiosks and sidewalk cafes and a view, in the distance, of the city's domed stadium. Taking one of the tables, they ordered after-dinner drinks and sat there for a time watching the passing parade of strollers in the fading light. Brian was not among them, however, and Charley had the feeling that he and Eve could have sat there through the fall and winter and they still would not have seen him.

That didn't bother Charley in the least, however, not with Eve sitting with him in the twilight, wreathed in cigarette smoke, her eyes looking vaguely troubled, even as she smiled at him.

"I kind of like this town," she said. "Maybe when all this is settled and done, I'll move here. Open up a boutique."

"All by yourself?"

"Why? Do you know someone who might join me in such an endeavor?"

"It's not exactly my line."

"How about a construction company, then?"

"That sounds better. You could be my secretary, and I could sexually harrass you."

"I don't know. I think I like the boutique idea better. I could be the boss and harrass you."

"What would you sell?"

"Maybe naughty underwear, like Frederick's of Hollywood."

"You'd do better with raincoats. Remember, it's supposed to rain here three-fourths of the time."

"Just a rumor. Look at that sky. Not a cloud."

"Mark Twain said the worst winter he ever experienced was one summer in Seattle."

Eve shrugged. "Well, it's a great climate for sleeping anyway."

Beyond her, back in the park, there was some sort of altercation taking place next to a modernist steel sculpture, the kind Kevin Greenwalt would paid good money for.

"It's getting dark," Charley said. "Maybe we'd better be starting back."


The next day, after another futile watch for Brian at the little park, Charley and Eve walked down the steep hill to the waterfront, which was thronged with tourists shuffling along a broad walkway that bordered the city's old wooden piers, most of which had been remodeled into restaurants and shopping malls, with hot dog and gimcrack stands out in front. At other piers cruise ships were docked and sightseeing boats were loading. There were also ferry docks and concrete parks and a couple of trolley cars clanging along a rail track on the other side of the water-front street.

Charley and Eve chose a restaurant with a broad outdoor deck lined with umbrella tables, all occupied at the moment. Unde-terred, Charley made his way into the bar and, giving a ten-dollar bill to a waiter, told the man that he and his wife were on a very tight schedule. And a few minutes later they had a table, bless-edly at the far end of the deck, which gave them not only a mea-sure of privacy but also an uncluttered view of the Sound and the ships coming and going: the systole and diastole of the Japanese economy. The deck, like the entire area, was patrolled by sea-gulls so huge that Charley wondered if he might not have to fight them for his food when it came.

Once again the day was Californian, clear and bright and dry, lacking only a certain petrochemical tang to the air. Charley and Eve both kept their sunglasses on, mindful that they probably had been on television more than they knew. Eve was wearing a light summer dress, and she had left her hair long and loose, with the result that Charley could barely keep his mind on what she was saying as the sun and sea breeze set her spectacularly afire.

"I guess we'd better face it that this has been a wild goose chase. Maybe he was here when he phoned us, but he sure doesn't seem to be now. So where does that leave us?"

"Sitting above Puget Sound. Listen, if one of these gulls tries to carry me off, you grab on, okay? Maybe he won't be able to lift us both."

Eve laughed, but not very happily. "I guess you're not going to let Brian get you down."

"Don't believe it—he already has. And in that regard, there's a certain little chat you and I have to have, but keep putting off. This morning, though, I promised myself: today we talk."

"About what? Turning ourselves in? Or I guess I should say, turning myself in."

The waiter brought their food, iced teas and caesar salads, which for the moment they ignored.

"That's about it," Charley said. "We just can't wait for Brian any longer. If we could bring him in with us, we could justify our being here together and why you've remained at large—because we wanted to convince him to stop his vendetta and turn himself in. But since we can't do that—can't even find him—then we have to go in on our own before he does, or before he's caught. Because once they have him in custody, we've got no leverage. They'll charge you as an accessory, and probably me too now, being up here with you instead of home in Flossmoor, where I promised the Denver agents I was headed."

The prospect of turning herself in obviously terrified Eve. For a time she said nothing, just sat there staring down at her salad, as if she hoped to find an answer there.

"I'll be with you," Charley said. "We'll go in together."

She slowly shook her head. "I don't know, Charley. It just scares the living hell out of me, you know? Just the idea of being arrested. Fingerprinted and all that. Probably even locked up. I'm not sure I can cut it."

"The sooner we do it, the less time you'll face."

"But how do you know that?"

"Generally, that's the way it goes. But you're right—I don't know for sure. So it would be a good idea to call your father's law office. Even if they're all tax lawyers, they can recommend a good criminal lawyer up here. He'll know what you should do."

She looked at him as though for mercy. "I just have to think about it a while, you know? I need to lie down for an hour or so and just think about it. Okay?"

"Of course. Eventually, though, I'll either have to go in alone or fly home and not tell them I was ever here."

"That way you'd be totally out of it, right?" she said. "Then that's what you should do, Charley."

"Probably. The only trouble is, I can't do it. I can't just leave you hanging out here. I can't leave, even temporarily, until I know you're square with the law."

Eve fell silent again. Then, very casually, she said, "Charley, when all this is over and done and I open my little dirty underwear boutique, will you come and visit me?"

"Of course. Twice a year anyway."

"Lucky me."

He realized then, too late, that she had just rolled a grenade across the table. He had missed it because of her sunglasses, because he hadn't seen her eyes.

Scrambling to recover, he said, "Eve, I was only joking. I love you. And if I have my way, we won't ever be apart. I won't have to visit you."

"Is that the truth?"

"It's the God's truth," he said, reaching across the tiny table and taking her hands in his. Because of her sunglasses, he still couldn't see her eyes.

"I do love you, Charley," she said.

"And I love you."

"I'm not very hungry. Let's go back to the hotel."

When they got there—by taxi—Eve did lie down, but not to think about turning herself in. Stripping immediately, she flew into his arms and wrapped her legs around him, and he carried her that way to the bed and laid her down, kissing her as he struggled out of his clothes. And they made love almost violently, so hungry for each other that Charley wondered if they would ever find quietus again.

Eventually, though, he collapsed onto her, spent. But even then, he remained right where he was, holding her in the cradle of his arms and kissing her tears and hair and everything else his lips could reach. For a good ten minutes they stayed that way, twined in the pale afternoon light, until finally Charley felt himself beginning to grow again, which naturally resulted in his starting to move again, slowly and gently. And this time there was no violence in their lovemaking, just a slow and delicious sweetness, as if the act had become a mere aspect of their kissing, the joining of their lips being their essential union. Charley was almost convinced that this time it would go on forever, or at least until he expired from an excess of happiness and pleasure.

It did end, though, with the sudden ringing of the bedside telephone. At first Charley made no move to answer it, but the thing kept on ringing. Finally, in a silent rage, he moved off Eve and picked it up.

"That you, Charley?" It was Brian.

"Yes, you bastard."

"I figured if you were in town, you'd be there—old moneybags Charley, you know. But why bastard?"

"Your little park, we've had a bellyful of it."

"Yeah, I can imagine. And I'm sorry, man. But listen, me and my friend, old C.J., we had this surprise visitor, you know? And it sort of complicated things."

"C.J., that's the guy who lives on his boat?"

"Yeah, here in Lake Union. Listen, we're going out for a little spin tomorrow morning. Why don't you and Eve come along? She is there, isn't she?" When Charley didn't respond, Brian continued. "We'll talk things over, okay? The FBI, your money, whatever you want."

"I don't want to 'talk' about my money, Brian, I just want it back."

"Whatever. So you two come on over, okay? And we'll have this little shakedown cruise."

"And who gets shaken down, I wonder."

Brian laughed. "My brother, the comedian." He went on then, giving Charley directions to the boat. Finally, he asked to speak with Eve.

Charley put his hand over the mouthpiece. "He wants to talk to you."

Eve shook her head. "No thanks."

"She's not very talkative right now," Charley said. "And for that matter, neither am I. We'll see you tomorrow."

After he'd hung up, Eve reached for him. "Where were we?"

Charley kissed the tip of her nose. "I think I remember," he said.

# chapter twelve

As he and Eve drove around the small lake, heading for Brian's friend's boat, Charley could have kicked himself for not having gone along with Eve's earlier suggestion that they go looking for the boat on their own. She had told him that it was on the north shore, straight across from the downtown high-rises, but he hadn't realized how easy the search would have been, considering that there were only a few small marinas there, squeezed in among the many lakeside restaurants and marine service companies. Charley figured that it would have taken them all of half an hour to locate the *Seagal*, and Brian. But then he wasn't about to complain. The last few days had been among the happiest of his life.

When they reached the marina, Eve went over to the locked gate while Charley phoned the *Seagal* from the car, as Brian had suggested. It was Brian who answered.

"Charley?"

"I think so."

"Sounds like you."

"Must be then. Eve's over by the gate."

"Then I shall buzz her through."

"Good of you."

As he and Eve headed down the pier between the rows of
boats, Charley gave her waist a slight squeeze and she tipped her
head toward him, so he could give her a last-minute kiss. In ad-
dition to his new deck shoes, he was wearing jeans and a T-shirt.
Eve had on shorts and a sleeveless blouse over a bikini. And both
of them had brought along windbreakers, knowing how cold it
could get out on the water.

The day was bright and cool, with a brisk breeze roiling the
lake and making the few sailboats' halyards clatter against their
aluminum masts. Charley knew that by any reasonable standard,
he should have felt just fine, given the beautiful weather and
the setting and the fact that he was about to go sailing with Eve.
But because Brian was in the picture, all he could feel was the old
sense of uneasiness and even dread. Brian had led him down the
garden path so many times before that he couldn't help feeling
that was where he was headed yet again.

But there was still the little matter of his money, which he was
determined to recover. Then too there was always the outside
chance that he could persuade Brian to give himself up, join
him and Eve in going to the FBI. And if neither of these things
developed, well, there was still the sun and the sea. Nevertheless,
as he and Eve moved along the pier, looking for the *Seagal,* he
couldn't shake the old negative feelings.

The *Seagal* turned out to be something of a surprise, not the
rotting old wood scow Charley remembered from the snapshot
but a gleaming white fiberglass forty-foot yacht with elegant teak
and stainless-steel trim. Just as in the past, however, Brian and
C.J. were standing at the stern railing, beer cans in hand. Except
for a cowboy hat, sunglasses, and a week's growth of beard, Brian
was wearing only a pair of khaki shorts. His old friend C.J. now
looked a decade older than Brian, having gone jowly and bald,
with a fringe of collar-length gray hair. Looking down at Eve and

Charley, his mouth curled upwards in a tight little smile, as if he alone were privy to some amusing cosmic secret.

Part of the hull was folded down into a kind of stepladder, which Eve climbed now, with Charley's hand on her elbow, needlessly helping her.

"See how chivalrous my big brudder is," Brian said. "He's a gentleman of the old school. And my oh my, C.J., but don't they make a fetching couple?"

"That they do."

On the deck now, Charley looked at Brian without enthusiasm. "Any more of that," he said, "and we're going to fetch ourselves right back where we came from."

Smiling still, Brian turned to Eve. "Speaks for you now, does he?"

She didn't answer.

"And what is this? We've been apart, what, an entire week, and you don't even have a kiss for Daddy?"

She started to peck him on the cheek, but he moved and kissed her on the mouth, chastely though, apparently not quite ready yet for a showdown. He then introduced Charley to C.J. As they shook hands, Charley asked the man if he had a last name.

"Beaver," C.J. said. "And don't ask what the initials stand for. I'm just C.J."

Brian laughed. "If I get a little high tonight, Charley, I just might tell you."

"And get tossed overboard for your trouble," Beaver said, as if Brian couldn't have manhandled him with ease.

Charley had some extra things for himself and Eve in a flight bag. He asked Brian where he could put it.

"You mean, where's your cabin?"

"Something like that."

"Well, right now the bow cabin's occupied by our new arrival, who's sleeping off a fairly heavy one last night. Man never had mai-tais before."

"I take it he knows about you?"

"You mean my fugitive status? Yes, he does. But he still chose to stay on, at least for this little outing. You two can meet him later."

Charley held up the flight bag, reminding Brian.

"For now, just toss it in the main cabin there, what C.J. calls the salon. We'll work out sleeping arrangements later." Saying this last, he looked at Eve, his expression ironic and playful.

But Charley hadn't missed the term. *"Sleeping arrangments? I* thought this was to be a little spin out in the Sound. We're not going if it's overnight."

Brian was still looking at Eve. "I repeat, Charley speaks for you now, does he?"

"In this instance, yes."

"Well, I should have said napping arrangements," Brian explained. "Don't worry, you two will be home by beddy time."

"You're really cute today," Charley said.

Brian smiled. "I do my best."

Beaver reached for Charley's flight bag. "Here, we'll just put this in the salon. And later, if you two want to lie down or just escape from the rest of us, there's the main stateroom. And then of course there are the couches right here in the salon."

As Beaver led the way into the main cabin, or salon, Charley saw Terry sitting on a stool at the galley bar, picking at a bowl of potato chips. She was wearing jeans and a Sonics basketball T-shirt. Across from her was the main helm. Behind her was a curving stairway going below, and beyond that jalousied doors leading to the bow cabin. The girl barely looked up. Eve went over and said hello, asked her how she was doing.

Terry shrugged indifferently. "Okay, I guess."

"Your mother's really worried about you," Charley told her. "Have you tried to call her yet?"

The girl looked at him as if he'd just crawled aboard from the bottom of the lake. "Are you serious? The FBI would trace it and come after Brian. You want to see him locked up?"

Brian gave Charley an amused look. "Well?"

"No, I don't," Charley said to Terry. "But I gather he's pretty keen on the idea."

The girl did not even smile.

At that point Beaver said that he was going up top to start the engines and that Brian and Terry should get ready to cast off. But Charley intervened, saying that he wanted to have a few words in private with his brother before they got underway.

Beaver shrugged. "Sure. What's a few minutes?" He motioned for Terry to follow him, and they went out onto the rear deck, followed by Eve, who gave Charley an enigmatic smile as she closed the glass door behind her. Brian made a face, benign but bored.

"This really ain't necessary, Charley. I know just what you're going to say, so you can save your breath. Yes, I've got your money with me. And yes, I'll give it to you before we get back. Also, I'll be ready then to turn myself in to the FBI or the CIA or whoever else wants me. You can be the go-between, okay?"

Charley was surprised, almost stunned. He smiled wryly. "Well, I must say, that does save a bit of breath. There is one other question, though."

"Shoot."

"Why is this little spin so important? Why not just forget about it, give me my money, and let me find a lawyer and start negotiations with the FBI?"

Brian shrugged. "I don't know. Maybe because I just want this last free afternoon out in the sun, you know? And with my

brother along, and my lover, or ex-lover—whatever she is now."
He said this last without any emphasis, as if it held no special pain
or meaning for him. "Is that so hard to understand?" he added.

Charley shook his head. "No. So I guess we might as well get
underway."

Brian laughed. "Hey, you're beginning to sound like C.J., the
admiral."

Charley smiled. "Man the hatches and belay the halyards."

"Aye aye, captain."

They went back outside then, where Terry was perched near
the stern line, waiting. Brian went forward, taking the catwalk
alongside the cabin. Beaver had already climbed up onto the
bridge, where there was another helm. Charley went over to Eve.

"Is everything all right?" she asked.

"I think so. At least, he said all the right things."

"Good."

One of the engines suddenly kicked in, and Charley looked up
at the bridge. "Let's go up there too," he said.

Eve smiled, but shook her head. "No, you go. I think I'll just
wait here."

Still waiting to cast off, Terry sat watching them. So Charley
limited himself to giving Eve a lingering touch on the arm before
he clambered up the metal ladder to the bridge. He accepted it
that she had to be alone with Brian, that there were things they
had to say to each other in private. Still, he couldn't pretend
that he felt no pain or anxiety, wondering how she would react,
being alone with Brian again. At the moment, though, there
were other things to divert his attention.

When both engines were idling to Beaver's content, he signaled to Brian and Terry to cast off the moorage lines, which
they did. Beaver then eased the gears into reverse, and the huge
boat started backwards, with the throttles still on idle. He then

eased one gear back into neutral, and the yacht turned, backing around like a car. Once out in the waterway, he put both engines into forward gear and eased the throttles forward. The *Seagal* was on its way.

Charley and some of his friends had gone coho fishing a few times on Lake Michigan in a similar boat, so he was not totally unacquainted with the feeling of riding on the bridge of a motor yacht. It was a little like sitting on the roof of a small two-story house floating out to sea, only in total comfort, sitting in a soft, leathery seat. Unlike the Lake Michigan boat, the *Seagal*'s bridge had no canopy, So Charley and Beaver were sitting right out in the sun. And Charley liked it that way, for the air was dry and the sun felt almost cool. At the same time, it was so bright it had turned downtown Seattle into something like Ronald Reagan's "shining city on a hill."

"Nice up here, huh?" Beaver said.

Charley nodded. "It's *great* up here."

Flying in over Seattle, he had been surprised to see that the city was essentially an isthmus lying between Puget Sound and the twenty-mile-long Lake Washington. At the city's waist, a ship canal ran from the lake to the Sound, on the way passing through the smaller Lake Union and finally the Ballard Locks, which dropped the *Seagal* almost twenty feet to sea level.

Before they got that far, though, Beaver had put on a smart white windbreaker and a captain's cap, neither of which did much to alter his appearance as an aging hippy. For a while he chattered amiably, making small talk about the points of interest they were moving slowly past. Eventually, though, Charley was able to steer the conversation to more pressing matters.

"Brian says he's going to turn himself in when we get back."

Beaver nodded, but said nothing.

"Which is a little puzzling," Charley went on. "I mean, why

bother? Why take the chance? If you had boat trouble and the Coast Guard found him aboard, it could get kind of dicey, couldn't it? Harboring a fugitive and all that."

Beaver shrugged. "I'm not worried. The *Seagal*'s running just fine. And Brian keeps a pretty low profile. Right now he looks like a cowboy, don't you think?"

"Or a beachboy. But tell me, do you think he's really going to turn himself in?"

"Who knows? It's up to him." Beaver got out a cigarette and lit it. "You gotta remember, Charley," he said, "me and Brian go way back. Whatever he wants is okay with me, 'cause he's pulled my fat out of the fire plenty of times."

Charley smiled ruefully. "I wish I could say the same."

"Well, you two kinda went separate ways, right?"

"You could say that."

"And anyway," Beaver said, "this whole thing, it just ain't right, big movie companies thinking they can twist the the truth around any way they want and call it history. I go along with what Brian's doing. I say he's got a right."

"Well, I just thought I'd mention it," Charley said. "You're really sticking your neck out for him, and I wanted to be sure you knew the risk."

"Don't worry—I wasn't born yesterday. But you want to know something? This is the first time in years I'm having fun. That's the great thing about Brian. When he comes around, things tend to get lively."

"That's for sure." Getting up, Charley gave Beaver a friendly clap on the shoulder. "Anyway, I think Brian's lucky to have a friend like you. And for that matter, I think you're pretty damn lucky to own a boat like this."

Beaver gave a dry, mirthless laugh. "Well, at least part of it anyway. A few nuts and bolts at least."

Since he didn't elaborate, Charley assumed that the man was merely saying that the boat was not yet paid for.

They were just then emerging from the ship canal into the Sound, and for a few moments Charley continued to stand there on the bridge, holding onto a seatback as he took in the scene around him: the shining city off to one side and the dazzling expanse of water stretching to the deep green of the Olympic peninsula with its high, jagged mountains running snow-capped across the sky. Closer, a pair of large, modern ferries were speeding across the Sound in opposite directions.

As Charley turned, about to take the ladder down to the stern deck, he saw that Brian was already on it, halfway up, only his head and naked torso visible. He was smiling, not very pleasantly.

"Well, our guest is finally up and around, Charley," he said. "Are you ready for this?"

"Ready for what?"

In response, Brian swung backwards, extending his arm out like a circus ringmaster. "Ta da!" he sang. "May I present none other than Mr. Chester Einhorn in the flesh!"

And so it was. The little cowboy was standing down on the stern deck, blinking in the bright sunshine, trying to look up at Charley on the bridge. And for a moment, Charley almost panicked, ready to fall to the floor or jump behind something to protect himself, thinking his brother had lost his mind over Eve and somehow had found Chester and enlisted him to carry out his revenge. But then Charley saw that the cowboy was unarmed, was just standing there in his boot socks, with his wiry little arms hanging loose at his sides. He was wearing just what he'd had on the last time Charley saw him, the same blue-checked shirt and stovepipe jeans, ripped now at the knees and seams, and not as a fashion statement either. Then there was his expression, his look of utter lostness, like a monkey in a spaceship.

Charley then saw Eve on the catwalk, peering around the corner of the cabin and looking every bit as alarmed as Charley had felt a moment before. But catching her eye now, he gave her a look, a shrug, of reassurance. Then he turned to Brian again.

"Well, if you'll get off the goddamn ladder, I'll come down," he said.

Brian did so in a single move, jumping off. Charley quickly followed, not wanting to give the little cowboy his back any longer than he had to. As he turned to the two of them, Brian laughed out loud.

"Hey, man, you should see your face. You look like you're about to shake hands with a rattlesnake."

Exactly, Charley almost said. Only he wasn't about to shake the man's hand. Instead, he just stood there absently looking down at Chester while Brian explained how the little cowboy happened to be there, how two days before, he and Beaver had noticed "this little bum" loitering around the gate.

"Well, we go to investigate, and who do I find but Chester Einhorn in the flesh! Been hitchin' and hikin' all the way from Colorado, lookin' for the *Sea*gull, thanks to your advice. And by God if he didn't find us, and in short order, I might add. Figured we just didn't know how to spell *seagull*, right, Chester?"

"Yessir, that's about it," Chester said. In his stocking feet, he looked smaller than ever, yet somehow just as menacing. And his lipless grin did nothing to add to his appeal. "Well, old Charley!" he said, forcing a laugh. "You really did me, din'tcha? I shore didn't know you was that stout, no siree. Picked me up like some kinda mutt and sent me scootin'. Like to kill me, you shore did."

"You didn't give me much choice," Charley said.

Chester wagged his head. "Man, I thought I wasn't never gonna reach bottom. That was some mountain, lemme tell ya.

Like I told Brian, I went skiin' is what I done, only without no skis. And without no snow." Again he laughed and shook his head, as if he really admired the way Charley had almost taken his life.

Meanwhile Eve had come out from behind the cabin. Moving cautiously, she came up behind Charley and laced her fingers through his.

"Well, it's all in the past now," Brian said. "No reason you two can't be friends, same as me and Chester."

The cowboy nodded agreement. "That's a fack. Charley was jest doin' what he had to do, and I was doin' what I had to do. No reason we cain't bury the hatchet."

"For now, you mean," Charley said.

"Naa, fer good. Hell, Brian 'splained it all to me, how what happened to Belinda was her own damn fault much as anybody's. And then trickin' me the way he done, he never figgered I'd shoot the bastid, didja, Brian? So it's all over and done. Right now all's I care about is helpin' him git his own back."

Brian laughed. "Whoa there now, Chester! You don't want these nice people to get the wrong idea, do you? I've already 'got my own' back, remember?"

Charley looked at his brother. "You better have. Otherwise, we're jumping ship."

Brian's grin was doleful and wry, as if it were an old cross he bore, dealing with unbelievers. "Don't worry about it," he said.

**E**arlier, after the *Seagal* had gotten underway, with Charley and C.J. up on the bridge, Brian had taken Eve by the arm—not very gently—and ushered her into the main cabin, closing the glass door behind them. He took off his sunglasses and cowboy hat, sailing the latter across the room.

"Okay now," he said, "let's get down to business. *What the fuck is going on?*"

Eve was steeling herself, telling herself that for once she wasn't going to let him get to her, wasn't going to let him intimidate her or seduce her.

"I think you know," she said.

"And just what is that supposed to mean?"

She felt vulnerable standing there with him directly in front of her, half-naked, so goddamn powerful-looking. She edged onto a bar stool and lit a cigarette. "Well, after you took off with your teenage sidekick, I didn't know what to do or where to go."

"So you called Charley."

"No, that's not how it happened. He'd got Stephanie's address from one of your old friends. And he showed up just after you'd left for Greenwalt's place."

"And since then?"

"Well, he thought I should go to the FBI. Turn myself in. He would have gone in with me. I knew it made sense, but I just couldn't do it. And I still can't."

"So you tell him about Aunt Maureen's, and he takes you there."

"Well, she's in Europe. I couldn't think of any other place. God knows where you'd gone, you and little Terry. And after the Greenwalt thing, I figured I probably wouldn't see you again until you were in custody—which didn't seem to bother you all that much—I mean, carrying out your vendetta with no thought as to what it meant for us."

Brian put his fingers to his temples, as if he'd been presented with a daunting intellectual challenge. "Just what is this I'm hearing? Let me think. You know, it sounds oddly like some kind of rationalization, don't you think? Like someone did something wrong, and knows it, but is trying real hard to make it sound okay. What could it be, I wonder."

"You ought to know," she said, "you being such an expert at it yourself."

"Well, maybe I'm just thick this morning. Why not just tell me? Just spit it out."

"I think you already know."

Brian sat down in an easy chair, throwing out his arms and legs like a teenager. "Well, let's see. I know you and Charley were together in Santa Barbara for three or four days, right? And I found out from the desk clerk at the Olympic that you were staying in the same suite, registered as Mr. and Mrs. Charles Poole, I think he said."

"So?"

Brian jumped up then, coming over and taking her jaw in his hand and turning her face so she had to look at him. "So what's going on, baby? Just what the fuck is going on?"

Eve forced herself to continue looking straight at him. "We're in love, Brian. Charley and I are in love."

Brian let go of her face then and stepped back, just standing there for a few moments, looking at her and frowning, as if he couldn't believe what he was seeing. *"In love!* What the devil are you talking about? The last I knew, it was me you loved. That last night at Stephanie's, isn't that what you told me while we were fucking? Isn't that what you said for the ten thousandth time?"

Eve did not answer.

"And then there's dear old Charley. I seem to recall he has a wife and kid—he bother to tell you that? When he's putting the wood to you, I take it he don't talk much about old Donna, huh? Or his asshole kid Jason? Huh, babe? Come on, I can't hear you. What about them, huh?"

Eve managed to nod. "Yes, I know about them. And I'm

sorry about them. But that doesn't seem to change anything."

"Why, Christ no! Why would it? A primo dish like you up against that cold bitch Donna? Old Charley must think he's died and gone to heaven, right?"

"You'll have to ask him."

"So that's it, huh? I'm on the run from the feds, and you get itchy, so I'm history. Is that it?"

Eve was grateful for the phrase. Brian loved to sound hip, whereas Charley would rather have taken a beating than use those same words, *so I'm history.*

"I didn't say that," she told him. "All I know is that Charley and I are in love. And while I still love you too, Brian, it's not the same anymore."

"Oh, I see. Now that Charley's in the picture, you love me the same way he does, like a brother. Is that it?"

"I didn't say that."

He went back to the chair again and sat down, this time dropping into it, as if he were exhausted. "Jesus, Eve, I can't believe how much this hurts. I know I'm a flake and that I've put you through an awful lot, but I always just accepted it that you'd be there for me, that you loved me no matter what. And now . . ." He shook his head in despair. "Jesus, I feel like someone cut out my heart."

By then Eve's eyes were streaming. She got off the stool and went over to him, getting down on her knees, the only way she could put her arms around him and hold him. "Brian, I'm so sorry. We never meant to hurt you. It just happened, you know?"

He didn't respond to her embrace. "Don't bother," he said. "You're Charley's now. And I don't cheat on my brother."

**A**s soon as Charley was able to get Eve alone, he asked her how things had gone with Brian.

She shook her head. "Not so hot. I wish he'd gotten mad and called me names, or even slugged me. Instead he was nice about it, in the end anyway. Nice and brokenhearted."

They were on the catwalk at the time, reasonably private. Charley took her in his arms and kissed her. "What did you expect?" he said. "If I lost you, I'd wrap the anchor chain around my neck and go for a swim."

She looked at him, still unhappy. "I just hate coming between the two of you."

"You haven't, Eve. There's always been plenty of stuff between him and me—chasms for one. So don't blame yourself. I don't figure I've lost him, I've gained you, as in-laws say. Or at least I hope I have."

"What does that mean, you hope you have?"

"Just that."

"Jesus, Charley, I think you'd be sure of me by now."

"God knows I want to be. But I can't help it. I keep thinking of my one week with you, balanced against his three years."

She said nothing for a short time, just leaned there in his arms, her pelvis tight against him, her beautiful face solemn, the lovely green eyes gravely regarding him. "I keep thinking my real life began this week," she said.

Grateful for the words, Charley embraced her tightly and kissed her again, slowly, deeply. "I do love you," he said.

Smiling now, she gently pulled away, in the process giving his erection a playful squeeze. "I love you too. But you'd better lose that before you join the others."

"I've got a suggestion," he said.

She laughed. "Big surprise. But if I take you up on it, it'll have to be up front, on the bow, where the whole world can watch. I'm going sunbathing."

Charley watched her as she moved toward the bow, swinging

her hips provocatively. "Sometime today," he croaked hopefully.

In answer, she just raised her hand and waved a casual bye-bye, his absolute ruler.


**C**harley returned to the bridge just as Beaver was giving the wheel over to Chester, who lasted about thirty seconds before he jumped up, shaking his hands as if they had caught fire.

"I jest cain't do it!" he bawled, giving the wheel back to Beaver. "I jest cain't! I ain't cut out for water and that's all there is to it."

Brian naturally had a bit of fun with this, teasing his new little buddy. "Maybe if we got you a saddle to sit on, or if we smeared some cowshit on the wheel—maybe that would help."

"It jest might. You never cain tell."

Once out of the Seattle harbor, Beaver opened up the throttles and pointed the *Seagal* north. He said that they were going to take the Saratoga Passage, a protected waterway between long Whidbey Island on one side and Camano on the other. The engines, two Cat diesels, produced almost as much noise as they did power, making conversation almost impossible outside the cabins. So Charley had to wonder in silence what the big hurry was, considering that they were supposed to be out for a mere spin into the Sound.

Still, he had to admit that despite his misgivings, he was beginning to enjoy himself. Under the pleasant onslaught of the sun and sea, his worries and anxieties seemed to slip away. Even the air conspired against him: not winelike, according to Beaver, but margaritalike, intoxicating and salty at the same time. Above all, there was much to see, especially later, after they had made their way through the white water of Deception Pass and continued north into the San Juan Islands: solitary beaches and rock walls rising sheer out of the water, with pine and fir and cedar running along the top, and old settlements at the mouths of harbors and half-hidden coves so beautiful they looked as if no man had ever dared enter them. On the more distant islands one could see upland meadows and farmland and small mountains, and beyond that, far to the east, the long white ridge of the Cascades, with Mount Baker towering over the rest, and described by Beaver as being "out today," as if it were on a par with the sun and moon.

With each headland they passed, there were bald eagles watching from the dead branches of the highest trees. Every now and then one of the birds would swoop down and have a look at the *Seagal* and then indifferently drift off into the sky. There were also Canadian geese and great blue herons and countless gulls as well as tiny flotillas of ducks: mothers leading their young through the shallows in flawless formation.

And finally there was a family of sea lions that spilled off some rocks at the boat's approach and within seconds came swimming alongside, rolling and frolicking in the water. When Terry first saw them and called out from the bow, everyone hurried to the railing to look, everyone but Chester, whose interest was of a different order. But Charley and the others were watching the sea lions and had no idea what the little man was doing until they heard the deafening report of his magnum pistol and saw the lead mammal shudder in the water and plunge, trailing a cloudy streamer of blood. By the time Charley turned in shock to look at Chester, Brian was already on him, pulling him from the railing and slamming him against the cabin wall so hard his gun clattered to the deck and slid off into the water.

"*What the fuck you doing?*" Brian bawled at him. "*You crazy?*"

Chester's eyes had bugged and he was shaking. "It was jest a seal!" he explained.

"You want to bring the law down on us? You like the idea of prison, do you?"

Chester blubbered that he was sorry, that he hadn't meant any harm, that it was just a way of life back home. "A man's s'posed to shoot critters," he said. "It's jest our way."

Finally Brian let him go, and the little man sagged against the wall. Looking down from the bridge, Beaver pedantically informed him that the animal was a sea lion, not a seal, and that in any case they were both protected by federal law, that it was a felony to kill one. But Chester was not listening. By then he had gone back to the railing and was staring down into the water as if he expected his magnum to come floating to the surface.

"That piece cost me a bundle," he complained. Then he looked up and saw Charley, Eve, and Terry watching him. "What y'all starin' at? What am I, some kinda movie star or somethin'?"

When none of them said anything, he turned away in disgust and went into the cabin. Giving the others a shrug of resignation, Brian followed him inside. And Charley was puzzled by what he observed then through the cabin window: Brian crowding Chester into a corner and talking earnestly to him, as if the cowboy were a delinquent schoolboy, and Chester accepting it as his due, nodding in eager contrition, his squinty eyes filling with tears. Finally, he capped off this odd little performance by taking hold of Brian's arm, almost embracing it, as if Brian were some sort of exalted leader, a king he had failed.

Charley looked at Eve to see if she had witnessed the scene, but she was still staring down into the water for some sign of the wounded animal.

"Well, so much for sea lions," she said. "I guess they're no different than movie directors."

There were four or five other boats in the broad channel between the islands, and Charley wondered for a time whether their crews might have heard the shot and would be coming closer to investigate or lend assistance. But none changed course. Eve meanwhile went back to her blanket on the bow, still wearing her windbreaker and shorts despite the brightness of the sun. Charley sat down next to her.

"Tell me," he said. "Do you still believe we're out on a little afternoon spin?"

"Why? You think we're heading somewhere?"

"At about thirty miles an hour, yeah."

"Did you ask Brian?"

"Earlier, yes. And I'm about to again. But you know what he'll give me—the same old bullshit as before."

In midafternoon, Beaver put in at a small resort at a place he called Obstruction Pass. While he was having the boat fueled, Charley, Eve, and Brian went ashore to stretch their legs. Indifferently, not expecting any real answers, Charley quizzed his brother.

"Well, here we are, almost to Canada, I'd say, and you still maintain we're out for a spin?"

Brian threw up his hands. "Hey, man, look around you. Smell the roses. How can you beat this? On a yacht in the San Juans on a day like this? This is living, man."

"Well, I'm just a mercenary old stick-in-the-mud. I seem to remember some promises about my forty thousand."

"And you'll still get it. But on the way back, just like I said."

Charley turned to Eve. "What'd I tell you? Ask and it shall not be given unto you."

Brian laughed. "My God, what's that? Sounds like we're back in Sunday school. And of course Charley was always the star there too. Show her, man. Quote some more holy stuff for us."

"Jesus wept."

"Oh come on, you can do better than that. How about this? Thou shalt not steal thy brother's ass, or his manservant—or his girl."

"What's that from, the Book of Brian?"

"That's enough," Eve said, turning and heading back for the boat.

When they got underway again, Brian spelled Beaver at the cabin helm for a time, while Terry served a lunch of cold cuts, bread, and potato salad. There was also a plentiful supply of soft drinks and liquor as well as beer, which Brian, Beaver, and especially Chester went at with steady gusto. After everyone had eaten, Terry dutifully put the food away and without a word went down the spiral stairs, either to the head there or to the main stateroom. Because the girl looked so troubled and unhappy, Eve followed her down, into a vestibule with doors fore and aft: the front one leading to the engine room, the rear one to the stateroom. Eve knocked on the stateroom door, and Terry asked who it was. Eve gently opened the door. "Just me," she said. "Are you okay?"

Terry was lying facedown across the bed, as if she'd thrown herself there. "Yeah, I guess so," she said. "Just tired is all. I haven't been sleeping so hot."

"That's understandable. So I'll just leave you alone, then."

"No, come on in," Terry said. "I won't sleep. And I guess I wouldn't mind a little company."

Eve sat down on the corner of the queen-size bed. Like the salon, the room was carpeted and luxurious, with its own private bathroom.

"One thing I've been worried about," Terry said. "I hope you didn't break up with Brian because of me. I'm nothing to him, really, just a kind of helper or gofer, you know? All the way driving up here, he never even touched me. I don't think he thinks of me as a woman or even a girl."

Eve smiled at her. "Or maybe he was just being a gentleman. Remember, you're still a teenager, Terry."

"You really think that was why?"

"Why else?"

Terry rolled over and sat up, running her palms over her eyes, which had moistened when she told Eve about Brian's indifference. "I guess I've really screwed up, haven't I?" she said. "I mean, being wanted by the police now, and Stephanie probably climbing the walls."

"Well, I'm afraid the FBI wants me too—helping Brian escape or whatever. Charley says that the sooner we all turn ourselves in, the better it will go for us."

Terry gave her a puzzled look. "Do you really prefer him to Brian? I mean, Brian's just so exciting, you know? I never get tired of watching him. He's like a movie star."

Eve shrugged. "Well, maybe I just got tired of excitement, or at least Brian's kind. If you knew Charley, I think you'd understand."

Getting off the bed, Terry went over to the back window and stood there looking out at the boat's boiling wake. "There's something else too," she said. "Something that really scares me."

"What's that?"

The girl made a face of self-deprecation. "Oh, I imagine it's nothing. I'm probably way off base. But I keep hearing things that Brian and the others say, and I get the feeling he's planning something, another strike against the studio, something like that."

"How? Where?"

"I don't know, but I'd say somewhere up here, on one of the islands. But I'm not sure—it's just a feeling I have."

"Can you tell me what you're heard?"

"No, I've already said more than I should have, since I don't really *know* anything." Looking peevish now—at herself or her predicament—she turned and headed for the door. Before leaving, though, she looked back at Eve. "Don't say anything, okay? I really don't know a damn thing. I'm probably just tripping on too little sleep, that's all."

Eve looked dubious. "You really think that?"

"Sure. Why not?"

Eve couldn't think of a polite way of answering that, so she moved on. "Listen, before you go, there's something else I've been wanting to ask you."

"Go ahead."

"What you did at Greenwalt's place—how did Brian talk you into doing it?"

The girl shrugged. "He didn't, really. He just asked me to follow him in the Porsche and showed me where to park it. He wanted me to wait there, and then after he came back, he was going to leave the wagon there and we'd take the Porsche home. But I said I wanted to be his lookout. And one thing led to another."

Eve smiled. "It certainly did."

"And he never told me about leaving town until we were on our way."

"He made you go?"

"Oh, God no! I loved it."

"So here you are," Eve said.

"Yeah. So here I am."

After Terry had left, Eve stretched out on the bed, wondering whether there was anything to what the girl had said about another strike. Certainly Charley was uneasy about the trip, how much more than a little spin it was turning into. But for the life of her, she couldn't imagine anything Brian could do to Wide World Studios up here in Puget Sound. In any case, the bed proved to be firm and comfortable, and she was surprised at how good it felt to get away from the sun and the wind and the water. Since it was already late afternoon, she suspected that the *Seagal* was going to spend the night in the San Juans, which in turn made her wonder where she and Charley would sleep that night: perhaps right where she was. Thinking about it, she began to ache for him, could almost feel his long, hard arms around her, his lips roaming her face and hair, his lovely cock filling her to the brim.

At the same time, she had reservations about their sleeping together at all that night, here, so close to Brian. And for that matter, she judged that Charley, being the kind of man he was, wouldn't feel right about it either, the two of them sort of rubbing Brian's nose in it.

Trying not to think about it all, she picked some magazines off the built-in table next to the bed. She had hoped for a *Vogue* or an *Elle,* pretty pictures of anorexic young things selling expensive clothes and cosmetics, some of which she sometimes bought. But there was only *Time, Fortune,* and *Business Week,* all library copies, which Eve thought odd. The first two had pictures of the ex-Australian tycoon Rupert Stekko on their covers, as well as long articles on him inside—not the sort of thing Eve was interested in at the moment.

Putting the magazines aside, she stretched and closed her eyes and wondered if she could fall asleep, considering the roaring of the engines and the boat's wake churning a few feet from her head. It didn't seem very likely.

# chapter thirteen

**C**harley was sitting alone on the stern deck, indifferent to the island slipping by on his left, green and rocky and beautiful. Rather, he was thinking about Donna, wondering what sort of state she was in by now and what she might have done about his continued absence. He regretted that when he'd phoned her from Eve's aunt's house that he hadn't told her a little more of the truth, for instance that he was with Brian's newly abandoned girlfriend, trying to help "the poor thing" out, something like that. Lies still, but closer to the truth. That way, he figured he would at least have given Donna a plausible reason for his absence, as well as a pretty good idea of what was actually going on, some real fuel for the fires of resentment undoubtedly burning in her.

Of course, it wasn't as though she previously had lacked for reasons to be critical of him. After all, was he not the incomprehensible jerk who had turned over to her the running of his business so he could play architect and carpenter with his "geriatric seven," as she called his staff? And while she was hard at work selling houses and opening branch offices and raking in the money, wasn't he likely to be found on the golf course or tennis court? None of which she ever let him forget. Mr. Donna Poole, she had said; that's what people were beginning to call him.

So he had a pretty fair idea what she was feeling, probably more anger and contempt than pain. And he had no doubt that if he didn't come crawling home soon, she and her lawyers would begin the process of picking him clean. What he didn't know, however—and what worried him the most right now—was what else she might have done about his absence, such as contacting the FBI and informing them that he was missing and that he evidently had fallen in with Brian and his girlfriend. And that scared him, the possibility that the feds might now be looking for him too, and not as a cooperating witness but as a suspect, a principal, a cohort of Brian's.

Even then, considering all that, he never for a moment questioned his involvement with Eve. Whatever trouble he was in, whatever losses he might incur, he figured it was worth it—as long as he had her.

As he sat there on the deck, he was aware that Terry had come up from below. Seeing him out on the stern, she had slipped forward quietly and now was standing at the point of the bow, holding onto the railing. Brian, Beaver, and Chester were on the bridge, above and behind her. Charley noticed that they were unusually talkative and excited, but he didn't think much about it, not even when the engines suddenly throttled down and the boat lurched sharply, slowing. Beaver then pointed it away from the shore, and there they floated, the engines idling, exhaust pipes gargling salt water.

Getting to his feet, Charley looked up at the bridge and saw Beaver and Chester hovering anxiously around Brian as he peered through a pair of binoculars at what appeared to be a luxurious resort about a half mile distant. There was one large white building occupying a wooded, rocky point, with numerous outbuildings and cottages scattered around it and in the wooded hills above as well as along the curving shore of the bay. There was a swimming pool and tennis courts and in the bay itself breakwaters that protected moorage buoys and floating docks, where over a dozen yachts already had tied up for the evening. Farther out, on the near side of the breakwater, a single boat rode at anchor, a long, handsome yacht with a dazzling white hull and a reddish, wooden superstructure.

Even before he asked the question, Charley knew that he wasn't going to like the answer. "Brian, what's going on?"

Just then Eve came up from below, evidently wakened by the boat's sudden slowing in the water. As she joined Charley on the stern deck, Brian came down the ladder, followed by Chester and Beaver. Charley sensed that his brother was trying hard to appear calm and relaxed, but his face was flushed and his eyes were fired with excitement. He parroted Charley's question.

"What's going on? Well, Charley, I don't like telling you this, but I'm afraid you were right. We're not out for a little spin after all. No, afraid not. And that place over there, it's sort of our destination. But C.J.'s the expert. I'll let him explain."

Beaver signaled to Terry, who was still up on the bow. "You might as well hear this too," he called. "No sense having to repeat it."

But instead of explaining what was going on, all he did at first was tell them where they were and what they were looking at. The riverlike body of water they were on was the East Sound and the land on either side was horseshoe-shaped Orcas Island. In front of them was the famed Romano Resort. The main building, the mansion, was originally the retirement home of a Seattle lumber baron. Built just after the turn of the century, the house rested on bedrock and had foot-thick concrete walls as well as its own water and electric power systems. It had been turned into a resort by a subsequent owner, and now Romano offered every amenity the yachting crowd might require, "except space,"

Beaver went on, "as you can see. For instance, that large yacht over there, it had to anchor outside the breakwater. Now, for most yachts that might be a problem in rough water, but not for that one. Because, you see, that's the *Nomad,* and there wasn't any plastic back when she was built. In fact, she's one of the few great classic motor yachts left. Very beautiful and extremely valuable. And her owner—"

Brian interrupted him at that point. "Let me tell them," he said. "The owner, my friends, is none other than Rupert Stekko, the man that owns the company that owns the studio that owns *Miss Colorado.* And tonight, when it's dark and everyone's ashore celebrating, I'm gonna blow that beautiful boat to kingdom come."

The remaining hours of light went much too fast for Charley. For a time he was inclined to go along with Eve and Terry, who were trying to convince themselves that Brian wouldn't go through with it in the end and actually blow up the *Nomad.* He might have come all this way with that purpose in mind, they said, but now that he was here and could see his target—how large it was, how beautiful—certainly he would come to his senses. He might have destroyed a movie set and a collection of bad art, but this was virtually a ship. It would be just too much, too violent. It would be an act of terrorism.

And Charley thought Exactly. What else was it Brian had been engaged in these past weeks if not terrorism, albeit of a somewhat more frivolous variety? On this occasion, though, it wasn't frivolousness Charley saw in his brother's eyes so much as a kind of grim acceptance, like that of a man who had a terrible duty to perform, and try as he might, could not talk himself out of it. So Charley felt he had no choice finally except to take the man at his word, that he actually was going to try to blow up the *Nomad*. And just as Charley accepted this, he accepted the fact that he would have to try to stop him, any way he could.

Soon after Brian had made his announcement, Beaver went into the cabin helm and took the *Seagal* in about three hundred yards closer. They moved slowly past the eighty-foot yacht and then went on across the Sound to a small cove on the other side, again less than a mile distant from the resort. There they dropped anchor and began the long wait for darkness, with Chester taking the first watch up on the bridge, keeping the binoculars trained on the distant yacht.

Meanwhile Beaver pointed out that the *Nomad*'s skiff—actually a handsome old Chris-Craft speedboat—was already in the water, tied to the ladderlike stairway that led up to the deck. So one could surmise that Rupert Stekko and his guests were still aboard, had not yet gone ashore for drinks and dinner. When Charley asked what would happen if they did not go ashore at all, Brian said it was all worked out, that he and Chester would simply board the *Nomad* and herd everyone into the Chris-Craft and take them down the Sound a few miles and put them ashore in the wild, then return to the yacht and "blow it at our leisure."

"Just like that," Charley said.

"Don't worry, they'll be going in for dinner," Beaver insisted. "That's why they're here after all, to see and be seen. Later they'll probably bring some new friends out to the boat for a nightcap. Also to let them gawk at the gold hardware and priceless woodwork."

"Sounds like great fun," Charley said.

Beaver shrugged defensively. "It's a way of life, good as any other, I'd say."

They were in the salon at the time, so Brian and Beaver could fill everyone in on the operation. Brian wanted them all to know what was coming, he said, to make sure they wouldn't get in the way or get hurt. Beaver explained that the *Nomad,* despite its size, didn't have diesel engines but ones that ran on gasoline, a pair of antique sixteen-cylinder behemoths requiring an eight-hundred-gallon tank to feed them. *That* was what Brian was going to explode.

"I think I can safely say it'll go off with a bang, not a whimper," Beaver concluded, with a smirk.

Charley looked over at Eve. "What do you think now? You still think they won't do it?"

She gave him a despairing look.

"Right," he said. Getting up, he started for the rear door, and as he expected, Brian reached out to stop him, keep him from doing anything rash. But Charley did it anyway, seizing his brother by the arm while he was off balance and roughly pulled him out onto the stern deck. Beaver immediately had jumped to his feet to help, but Charley froze him with a stab of his finger.

*"You* stay put!" he said.

By then Brian had regained his balance and was standing with his back to the railing, smiling sheepishly, like a football hero bested at Ping-Pong. Meanwhile Chester had come hurrying across the bridge to the top of the ladder, eager to come to his master's aid. But Brian waved him off.

"Everything's okay," he told him. "Just keep watch."

As Chester reluctantly returned to his post, Eve came up next to Charley, facing Brian.

"You're not going to do this," Charley told him.

Brian made a face: weariness and derision. "Man, it's just a goddamn boat. A lot of wood and metal, that's all."

"If that's all it was, you wouldn't be here."

"It's important to *him,* that's why."

"*Him?* You don't even know *him,* for Christ's sake."

"I know what he does. I know his decisions affect me and everyone else. If he can make a few more million maligning me, well, that's his business."

Eve joined in. "But this is so *extreme,* Brian. It's not like the other things."

"Sure it is," he said. "Destruction of property, that's all it amounts to."

"You blow that gas tank," Charley told him, "and parts of that boat are going to be falling all over the resort."

"Should be quite a sight."

That left Charley speechless for a few moments. He just stood there looking at Brian, wondering why he couldn't bring himself to smack him one, knock the arrogance right out of him.

"I'm not gonna let you do it," he said finally.

"You're not gonna *let* me?"

"That's what I said."

Brian gave him a pained look. "Aw, come on, Charley, don't try anything, okay? If you're thinking of swimming to shore here, keep in mind the water's not even fifty degrees. A lot of people go into shock after only ten or twenty seconds in it. And even if you did make it, which I can't let you do incidentally, it'd take you an hour to find a phone and try to blow the whistle on us. So why not just relax and go with it? Like I said, it's only a fucking boat."

Eve's eyes had filled. "God, Brian, you should hear yourself. You're really over the edge this time, and you don't even know it."

"By your standards maybe. Not by mine."

"And what comes after this?" Charley asked. "Kill some Stekko stockholders? After all, they own the company too."

Brian sighed in boredom. "Look, I don't have time for all this.

I want you two and Terry to go down below and stay there till it's all over."

"We're not going anywhere," Charley said.

"Come on, man, please."

"Fuck you."

"Then just stay out of my way, all right?" Brian turned away then, starting to leave.

But Charley wasn't finished. Reaching out, he roughly took his brother by the arm again, to pull him back. But Brian came too easily, spinning, and drove his fist hard into Charley's ribs, just below the heart, knocking the wind out of him and dropping him to his knees. Unable to breathe, Charley knelt there on the deck, vaguely aware of Eve cursing Brian and crying at the same time. Then she and Terry were each holding him under the arm and struggling to help him up. Above, on the bridge, Chester was squealing happily and pounding his fist into one of the seats.

"Way to go, Brian! Way to go! Don't take no shit off nobody! Nosiree!"

In contrast, Brian's voice was level, unexcited. "On second thought, we'd better keep them in the bow cabin, where we can watch them. Down below, he might try to screw with the engines."

"Right on," Beaver said, watching from the salon. "And I'll padlock the hatch too, just to be safe."

Brian nodded. "And we'll keep the guns out here. No sense inviting trouble."

Charley was on his feet by then, with Eve and Terry still helping him. His ribs felt as if a stake had been driven between them, and every breath he took seemed to work it in deeper. Before going inside, he looked over at Brian again.

"I'll remember that," he told him.

Brian shook his head in regret. "Hey, I'm sorry, man. Believe me, it wasn't what I wanted."

"That boat won't be either."

"We'll see."

The bow cabin was not as large as the other stateroom. It had a narrow bed on either side, connecting at the front, with storage compartments below. In the back, one step up, there was a vanity and closet on one side and a head and shower on the other. Two more steps up was the louvered door to the main cabin, with the helm immediately on the left and the dinette on the right. It was there that Beaver sat watching them while Brian and Chester kept watch on the bridge.

Terry had got an ice pack for Charley's swelling ribs, and Eve had filched a bottle of brandy on the way forward, so he was not without care. Both women seemed cowed by what Brian had done, not to mention what he was planning to do. Eve begged Charley not to try anything else.

"They've got guns now," she said. "Even Chester. Brian actually gave one to that murderous little creep. So we're helpless now, Charley. We can't do *anything*. Do you understand? *You* can't do anything."

When the women were helping him down into bow cabin, Charley had been vaguely aware of Beaver getting a rifle and handgun out of a locked cabinet near the helm, and this hadn't surprised him greatly, considering what Brian was planning to do.

"Terrorists do carry weapons," he said to Eve now.

"Right. So we've got to cool it. Agreed?"

Charley didn't answer. Terry, sitting on the opposite bed, was moist-eyed and trembling, nothing like the snarling Amazon he had seen at Greenwalt's. He reached across the aisle and put his hand on her shoulder, and she immediately began to cry.

"Hey, we're going to be all right," he said. "The worst that can happen is like the man said—a boat gets blown up. That's all. We'll be okay."

"After Greenwalt's, I just couldn't stop shaking," she got out. "I couldn't believe what I'd done. But Brian was so cool, you know? Just like now, like it was his daily routine or something. I really like him, and respect him—I really do—but I guess he scares me now."

"That's his problem," Eve said, "that he's *not* scared."

"At Greenwalt's he was so cool about it all," the girl repeated. "And I thought, well, it was the right thing to do. I believed in what he was doing, and that's why I helped him. But I was so scared, I thought I'd die."

Still watching them, Beaver laughed out loud. "Christ, you three sound like you're at a wake. You ought to be grateful you're here, for shit's sake. The man's making history, and all you do is whine. You make me want to puke."

But instead of puking, he bragged. If it hadn't been for him, Brian never would have even known about the *Nomad,* he said. And he was the one who located it too. Calling himself photojournalist Roger Moon, he had phoned the home office of Stekko Inc. in San Francisco and had explained that he was doing an article on classic yachts for *National Geographic* and needed to interview Mr. Stekko and get some fresh shots of the *Nomad.* Stekko's very cooperative secretary then made a few calls and phoned Beaver with the good news that her boss had reservations at the Romano Resort through the weekend and could be reached there. She also gave him the *Nomad*'s marine phone number.

"So here we are," Beaver said. "And I might add that without my help Brian Poole wouldn't know how to blow up a balloon. For a job like this, it takes more than gasoline and a lighter. You also gotta have fuse cord and the know-how to use it. And it don't hurt to know something about boats either, like where the fuel intakes are on an old scow like the *Nomad*."

"You're a wonder," Charley told him.

"Ain't I, though?" Beaver paused to shake a small amount of white powder onto his thumb, which he then brought up to his nose and snorted, almost as if he felt compelled to demonstrate for them the source of his remarkable endurance, not to mention bad judgment.

Eve asked him if he wasn't worried about going to prison, and he made a face, dismissing the idea. "All this is under duress," he said. "Brian's forced me to do it, can't you see that? And he's the one who called Stekko, not me. That's what he'll tell the police anyway. Just ask him."

"So you'll be free to get yourself an agent and sell your story," Charley said. "Go on talk shows. Be a celebrity."

Beaver shrugged in helpless agreement. "A man's gotta live."

"And some gotta crawl."

"Aw, quit it. You're breaking my heart."

It was then that they heard Chester begin to yell up above.

*"There they go! There they go!"*

Brian immediately appeared in the rear doorway, hanging sideways from the ladder, and announced that it was time to leave. Then he went back on top. Beaver squared his captain's cap and moved across the aisle, into the helm seat, out of Charley's view. One after another, the engines kicked in, followed by the whine of the anchor windlass. Looking out through one of the cabin's slotlike windows, Charley saw in the distance the tiny Chris-Craft as it departed the long white yacht and headed around the breakwater, toward the resort's landing.

Though it was not quite dark yet, lights were burning in the buildings and over the walkways and the tennis courts and pool.

As the *Seagal* began to move out across the waterway all the lights on the boat suddenly went off, Beaver evidently having thrown a master switch of some kind. In the dimness, Eve looked at Charley, practically glared at him.

"There's nothing we can do," she said.

Charley nodded, but in his mind he was thinking of the explosion to come, pieces of the *Nomad* falling on the resort, hitting innocent people, maybe a child or two. And he was thinking that if anything were to be done, it had to be done *now*, while Brian and Chester were still up on the bridge. And all he could think to do was overpower Beaver and lock the other two out of the cabin, then turn the boat around and beach it on the near shore. Certainly Brian wouldn't shoot at him or allow Chester to. He knew full well that it would be a wildly reckless thing to try and that the stakes probably didn't justify it, since he really didn't know that anything other than property loss was involved. Yet he couldn't control the sudden thumping of his heart or the dryness in his mouth or the coiled tension in his body, the urge to do something, to *move*.

And move, he did, bounding up the three steps to the salon now and coming around the corner onto Beaver at the helm like a cat onto a mouse, not missing the man's bugged eyes or his long fringe of hair flying out as Charley seized him by the front of his jacket and, yanking him out of the seat, threw him down the curving stairway. Abruptly the boat veered to the left, causing Charley to lose a step in his headlong rush to the sliding glass door, to close and lock it. And it proved a costly step, for Brian suddenly dropped like Tarzan into the opening, having jumped down from the ladder. Instead of breaking his forward motion, however, Charley simply put his head down and plowed into his brother's stomach, sending them both sprawling out onto the deck. Then, scrambling to get to his feet before Brian, he heard Chester's feral squeal again and saw in his peripheral vision the glint of a handgun coming at him.

**W**hen he regained consciousness, Charley found himself lying on his side on the salon carpet, with his head in Eve's lap and his hands taped behind his back. He could see Terry looking out through the open doorway at Beaver handing a five-gallon can of gasoline and a large bundle of rags over the railing to Chester on the stern ladder. And beyond Beaver, Charley could see the lights of the resort, much brighter now that night had fallen. The boat's engines were silent and the only light in the salon came from the helm control panel, green and faint, but enough for Charley to see clearly the fear and concern in Eve's eyes as she held a compress to his head.

"How long have I been out?" he asked.

That made her smile. "You *haven't* been out. You crawled in here. The little bastard was going to hit you some more, but Brian stopped him."

"Brian's a prince," he said.

From the doorway, Terry looked down at him. "And Eve kept Beaver from kicking you. She practically threw him down the stairs again."

Charley felt weak and nauseated, and his head ached, to the point where he had forgotten about his ribs.

"He wasn't too happy about what you did to him," Eve said. "He was limping and his nose bled all over his little sailor suit."

"You're my girl," Charley said.

"That's for sure." She bent down and kissed him on the head.

"I take it Brian's still going through with it," he said.

"So it appears." Eve took the compress off his head and looked at it. "Well, Rambo, you've stopped bleeding. You'll probably live. So I imagine you'll be wanting to try something else now, maybe something reckless for a change."

"Not very likely."

"In case you do, you should know that I won't be freeing your hands. Beaver's orders. And he's carrying a rifle."

At that point Beaver called out over the water: "Remember! It burns at four feet a minute!"

He came over to the doorway then and told Eve and Terry to "bring the bastard" out onto the deck. "I wanna keep my eye on him," he said. "And you bitches too."

The women helped Charley to his feet. Then the three of them went outside. Beaver was gesturing nervously with the rifle.

"Over there," he commanded.

Eve helped Charley into a canvas chair at the corner of the stern railing, as far from Beaver as they could get. She and Charley were both wearing jackets, and Terry had pulled a blanket around her, yet they were all shivering in the cool, salty air as they watched the dinghy moving toward the long dark shape of the *Nomad* about two hundred yards away. Silhouetted against the brightness of the resort, the yacht had one white light burning atop its superstructure, plus some dim interior lights in the main cabin and above the outside stairway. Without these, Charley doubted that he would have been able to make out the men in the dinghy—Brian rowing and Chester huddled down, holding onto both gunwales as the tiny craft rose and fell in the two-foot chop. Charley saw that the *Nomad*'s speedboat was still gone, apparently tied up at shore while Rupert Stekko and his family and guests were enjoying dinner.

Once again Beaver wanted them all to know what a vital part of the operation he was. "I sure hope Brian remembers everything I told him," he said, going on then to explain that yachts as large as the *Nomad* often had fuel intakes on both sides of the vessel, which meant that there would most likely be a portside intake somewhere near the top of the retractable stairway. After removing the cap, Brian was going to hook a wire either into the intake or around it and attach it to a gasoline-soaked rag, which in turn would be tied to the end of one of the fuses.

"The first step," Beaver said, "will be to spread most of the rags outside the pilot house and soak them down with gas and attach the other fuse cord. Then they're gonna run both fuses down the stairway and light 'em as they take off. One way or another, that baby's gonna blow."

"How about finding out if anyone's still aboard?" Charley asked. "They gonna try to work that in?"

Beaver snorted with scorn. "Well, hell yes, what do you think? But there ain't anyone. The Chris-Craft made two trips to shore. The captain—who's probably a combination pilot, mechanic, and janitor—he took the beautiful people in first, then came back for a woman, probably the chief cook and bottle-washer. But Brian's gonna look anyway, so don't worry your busted little head about it."

As the dinghy reached the *Nomad,* they all fell silent. Brian and Chester were only silhouettes by then, one large and the other small. And though they moved with obvious stealth, Charley nevertheless clearly heard the gas can clank as the two men made their way up the outside stairway of the yacht. They disappeared onto the deck for a while, then Charley saw them again as they passed in front of the lighted windows of the main cabin. The larger figure went inside for a short time and then came out and worked alongside the other, next to the pilot house. Less that a minute passed before they retreated to the top of the stairway and went to work again, huddled figures all but invisible in the darkness. Then they went back down the stairway and Charley saw the larger figure untie the dinghy and hold it steady while the smaller man got into it. A cigarette lighter flared in the darkness, lighting the fuses, and suddenly there appeared to be two Fourth of July sparklers climbing the side of the yacht. In their flickering light Charley could see Brian scramble into the dinghy and begin to row. Eve, standing behind Charley, dug her fingers into his shoulders.

"I can't believe it," she said. "It's a nightmare."

Beaver laughed nervously. "Not yet it ain't! But it's gonna be! A couple more minutes is all!"

A couple more eternities was more like it, Charley thought, as the sparklers continued to crawl upward through the darkness. And though Brian was rowing hard, the dinghy also seemed to crawl, rising and falling with the waves, pushing ahead only a few feet with each stroke of the oars. Still, the two men had almost reached the *Seagal* when the sun seemed to rise up out of the water behind them, in an orange and yellow inferno against which the dark image of the *Nomad* appeared for a millisecond, long and elegant and somehow wraithlike, as if it were already a ghost ship. Then it disappeared in a thunderclap.

"Oh my Jesus!" Beaver cried. "Look at that! Just look at that!"

It was a sight Charley knew he would remember the rest of his life: the blazing pieces of wood and metal—parts of engines and saunas and gold faucets and ancient teak and mahogany wood-work—falling all over the bay and the resort in a gentle rain of fire. Closer to the *Seagal,* pieces of the classic yacht fell hissing into the water. In the harbor a couple of other boats had caught fire, and on the hillside above the main building patches of brush were burning. A siren began to wail at the resort and then a small fire truck appeared out of nowhere and clanged its way toward the marina. People were running about and shouting, some pointing at what had been the *Nomad,* but which now was only a pile of smoky rubble sinking into the sea.

Brian and Chester already had pulled the dinghy onto the transom and secured it to the davits there, and now the two men came up the ladder and onto the deck, Chester first, looking demented with joy. He even danced a little jig.

"We did it! We did it!" he cried. "We shore as hell did it!"

Beaver by then was looking pale and shaky. "You bet we did," he asserted.

In contrast, Brian seemed impatient more than anything else. "Why aren't the engines running?" he asked. "And the anchor's still down. For Christ's sake, let's get with it!"

As Beaver hurried inside, Brian looked over at Charley and Eve for the first time. And Charley could see, in the light of the fires, his brother's anger and frustration—why, Charley wasn't sure.

"Well, is that it now?" he asked. "Is it over?"

Brian didn't answer. Instead he came across the deck and took out a pocket knife and cut the duct tape binding Charley's hands. Then he went inside with Chester and Beaver, as the engines kicked in, followed by the sound of the windlass. And soon they were underway, the boat steadily gathering speed as Beaver opened the throttles wide. Though it was even colder now on the deck, Charley continued to sit there in the canvas chair, with Eve and Terry standing close to him, at the railing. In silence, they all watched as the lights of the resort—and the scattered fires—grew slowly dimmer.

# chapter fourteen

In time the cold and the sea spray drove them inside, into the dark of the salon, where they sat waiting like relatives at a hospital. For over thirty minutes Beaver kept running without lights, a practice he said he wouldn't recommend unless one knew the San Juans as he did, like the back of his hand. To Charley, though, the visibility did not seem that bad. There was a three-quarter moon illuminating a thin layer of clouds, which in turn seemed to light up the entire Sound, enough anyway to make out the shoreline on either side of them.

Beaver said that their goal was one of the many coves at the south end of Lopez Island and that they would anchor there through the night and the next morning, so that when they reached Seattle in the late afternoon, the Ballard Locks would be crowded with scores of boats waiting to get through to their moorages in Lake Union or Lake Washington. There was safety in numbers, he said, and he didn't want the police knowing about the *Seagal* or his "involuntary" participation in the operation until Brian gave the word.

At the the moment, though, it appeared a good deal of time would have to pass before Brian gave anyone the word about anything. Like a man under arrest, he stood with his hands pressed up against the glass doors at the back of the salon, leaning there and staring out at the night and the water as if they were old enemies of his. From his mood, one would have thought that both fuses had fizzled out and left the *Nomad* riding peacefully at anchor.

Chester for some reason had put his cowboy boots and hat back on. Despite the darkness and the motion of the boat, he kept walking about the salon, whipping off his hat and lashing the furniture with it, crowing about the firebombing and pestering Brian about television. When could he turn it on? When would the news coverage begin?

For a while Brian tried to ignore him. But when that proved impossible, he went out onto the deck, only to have Chester follow him there. And though Charley couldn't hear their voices over the roar of the engines, he could see in Chester's reaction that the exchange had not been a friendly one. Coming back in, the little man did his best to shatter the sliding glass door, throwing it closed so hard it bounced back open.

"What in hell's eatin' him anyways?" he complained. "Din't we jest do a job of work together, huh, didn't we? Who's he think I am anyways, some kinda candy-ass he kin jest chew on every time he gits the notion? Does he think that, huh, does he? Cuz if he does, then by God he's got another think comin'!"

When no one answered, Chester kicked an ottoman and began to whip the bartop with his hat. Looking uneasily over at him, Beaver suddenly slowed the boat and flipped a switch, which made the lights come on, inside and out. Chester asked if this meant he could watch television, and Beaver smiled his tight little smile.

"Why not?" he said.

The little cowboy immediately turned the set on and pulled the kicked ottoman over to it, sitting down in front of it like a caveman huddled over a fire. He kept turning from one channel to another, as if he wouldn't know for sure what he and Brian had done until he saw it confirmed on television. But there was no report of the incident, not until the regular eleven o'clock news broadcasts, and then most of the stations only reported that a large yacht had exploded and burned at the exclusive Romano Resort on Orcas Island. The Bellingham channel, though, added that arson was suspected and that the state police were looking for a suspect.

None of this satisfied Chester. He wanted to *see* the explosion, he said. And what about all the fires they had started, on the other boats and up in the trees? And what about Stekko himself? Chester wanted to see the man. He wanted to hear him piss and moan.

"Them candy-ass reporters," he groused. "They jest ain't doin' their job. Why, they ain't even got enough smarts to connect it all with Brian. Shit, we prob'ly got to do it ourself—phone in nominously and tell 'em."

Brian, watching from the doorway, said there would be no phoning in, not until they reached Seattle.

"Why not?"

At the helm, Beaver gave a weary sigh. "If we phone from the boat, they'll know who we are. We have to wait till we can use a pay phone, and not an island one either."

Chester again whipped the TV with his hat. "Well, shit, that means we jest gotta sit here and stew. I don't like it."

"You don't have to," Brian told him.

A few minutes later, Beaver throttled down and headed the *Seagal* into a cove where several other boats were already anchored for the night. As usual, he seemed to know just what he was doing, maneuvering the yacht around into the wind before dropping anchor, then reversing a short distance, making sure the thing dug into the cove's bottom. He then killed the engines and jumped up from the pilot seat, announcing that it was time for champagne and food.

"I'm so hungry I could eat dirt," he said. "Terry, why don't you get the stuff out of the fridge while I break out the bubbly."

Charley didn't want to have anything to do with any of them, Beaver the same as Chester and Brian. But at the moment he was too hungry to stand on principle. Eve, though, wondered if he should have anything to eat at all, considering that he might have suffered a concussion.

"Don't they recommend no food for twelve hours or something like that?" she asked.

"I feel fine," he told her.

"The devil you do." She took him by the hand and led him forward. "Come on, I want to look at that head again. And your ribs."

On the way, Charley asked Terry to bring their food and drinks to the bow cabin. "And you stay with us tonight," he added, not wanting to leave her to the vagrant impulses of a drunken Chester. The girl nodded eagerly.

Charley followed Eve into the head, where she had left the boat's first-aid kit. Sitting on the toilet, he leaned sideways over the sink as she cleaned the cut with soap and water. After drying it, she daubed on antibiotic ointment, complaining that his hair was too thick for her to see the cut properly.

"Sorry about that," he said.

"Well, you should be."

She had him stand and hold up his shirt and jacket while she delicately fingered his swollen ribs.

"What d'ya think, Doc?" he asked.

"That your brother's a maniac, that's what I think."

"So does he, I gather."

"It's a little late. Tell me, does it hurt when you breathe deep?"

"Hell, yes."

She looked worried. "That could mean a punctured lung, couldn't it?"

Letting his shirt and jacket fall back into place, he put his arms around her. "I'm not coughing blood. I'm not wheezing. And probably haven't even got a cracked rib, just bruised ribs, like quarterbacks get every Sunday afternoon. So stop worrying, all right? I'll be fine."

She looked at him through sudden tears. "You bastard, Charley. Why would you take a chance like that over a *boat?*"

"At the time it seemed easier than doing nothing."

"But to go up against *all* of them!"

"It was stupid."

"It was *insane.*"

He shrugged. "Yeah, but it worked, didn't it?"

"How can you joke about it?"

"I don't know. I guess I'm still pretty numb. I can't believe he actually did it."

Eve sagged against him. "God, when I think of trying to tell it all to the police—*explain* it, you know?—why we're here, with him again. They'll think we're either crazy or lying. It's just too much."

Holding her close, Charley began to kiss her lightly, working from her forehead down to her lips. "It'll come out all right for us," he said. "We'll get a couple of decent lawyers and tell them the whole story, that we were stupid and incompetent but never participants, never co-conspirators. And they'll make a deal for us, probably get us suspended sentences if we turn state's evidence against Brian and the others. Something like that. It's done all the time."

"Could you do it? Testify against your own brother?"

"I don't see why not. After all, he spray paints his name at the scene of the crime. In fact, the more I think about it, the more it seems all this isn't about *Miss Colorado* anymore, or his reputation. If he didn't make his point in Colorado, then he sure as hell did in Bel Air. So I think blowing the *Nomad* was simply a matter of fun and fame. He's already had his fifteen minutes, and now he wants a full hour at least."

Eve sighed. "I hate to say it, but you're probably right. About testifying, though, what about Terry? In L.A., she *was* a participant."

"Yeah, but she's only eighteen. And I gather her mother can afford Johnny Cochran. She'll come out okay."

"I hope you're right."

"Me too."


**J**ust about the last thing Charley wanted to do that night was spend time with his brother, the mad bomber. But ever since Brian had come back from the *Nomad,* Charley had sensed in him a certain unraveling of the spirit.

"He's out on the deck again," Terry had said. "Sitting alone. He didn't want anything to eat."

So Charley eventually picked up the bottle of brandy Eve had gotten for him earlier and went back through the salon, where Beaver sat trying to watch television in spite of Chester, who was still camped about a foot away from the screen, flipping from one channel to another. Charley closed the glass door behind him and drew another deck chair over to where Brian was sitting, with his feet up on the railing. After taking a pull on the bottle, he held it out to him.

"Here, something to warm your tootsies."

Brian declined the offer. "Who needs it? I can live with me, even if no one else can."

"Well, good. Leaves more for me." Charley took another pull. "Communing with nature, are we?"

"Not that I'm aware of."

"Too bad. There's a bunch of it out there."

The cove itself was about two hundred yards across at the mouth, a horseshoe of rock walls topped by a palisade of fir trees that looked hauntingly beautiful against the moonlit cloud cover. On the strand of beach below, a wood fire flickered at the base of a column of blue smoke, and the sound of voices came softly across the water, including the peal of a child's laughter. Two cruisers, smaller than the *Seagal,* were anchored together— *rafted,* according to Beaver—and like the fire, their lights reflected off the cove's dark surface, forming lanes of coruscating copper and silver that ran straight to Charley. An owl's hoot only added to the peacefulness of the scene, putting it even further at odds with the reality aboard the *Seagal.*

"I guess you and Eve both think I'm crazy now," Brian said.

"You really give a damn?"

"Well, I know I don't feel so hot about what happened to you. Christ, I can barely remember the last time I swung on you. It must've been in grade school, in self-defense."

Charley set the brandy down on the deck. "It's been even longer since anyone pistol-whipped me."

Brian laughed despairingly. "Goddamn Chester. I still don't know how he got there so fast."

"I guess he figured he owed me one."

"Yeah, but he would've done it anyway—you know that. He probably would've whacked you ten more times if I'd let him."

"I'm indebted to you."

Brian wearily shook his head. "Look, you don't have to bother, Charley, I know how you feel. I'm a total asshole and what I've done is ridiculous and pathetic. Right?"

"Not pathetic. I wouldn't say that."

"That's decent of you."

"Just one question, Brian. Why in God's name did you have to drag me and Eve into this thing? You didn't need us. In fact, we made it a lot more difficult for you. I keep thinking about it, but I never come up with an answer."

For a time, Brian made no response. He just sat there with his arms folded and his feet propped up, his eyes focused off in the mist somewhere. "I can't say for sure," he said finally. "Could be, when I called Santa Barbara and found out you two were together, maybe I just wanted to get back at you. Involve you. Hurt you both. But I'm not sure. Maybe I knew this would be my last strike, and since you were the two people I cared most about, maybe I just wanted you to be there and see it. Maybe I just wanted to have you around these last hours before I take off again, for good."

"That's what you're going to do?"

"Why not? I'm already a fugitive. If they nab me now or in five years, the punishment will probably be pretty much the same."

"Not if you went in voluntarily."

"Maybe not, Charley. But I ain't going gentle into the slammer, or whatever they call it now." He picked up the brandy bottle and took a short drink, then another, before giving it back to Charley. "Hey, brother, I almost forgot," he said, getting to his feet.

Under the gunwale there was a row of built-in storage cabinets, one of which he opened now. He got out a package wrapped in plastic and gave it to Charley.

"The money, just like I promised," he said. "And I wish it was all there. But I had to spend some of it, and C.J. took ten for his contribution and the use of the boat. Incidentally, he's broke. Finally went through his entire inheritance, even the boat. Once we're back, he's got to turn it over to the bank and live like the rest of us, maybe even go to work."

"Poor fellow."

Sitting again, Brian shrugged. "Well, he's been a friend a long time. And he helped a lot with this thing tonight."

"So he told us."

"I can imagine."

Though Charley wondered just how much was in the package, he decided not to ask, figuring that whatever figure Brian gave him probably wouldn't prove out anyway.

"The ten thousand you gave C.J.," he said. "You realize I'm gonna have to go after it."

"Good luck."

"While we're on the subject, just what the hell does the C.J. stand for?"

Brian smiled. "The J I forget. But the C stands for Christian. Christian Beaver."

Charley laughed. "That's great. Christian Beaver, huh? From now on, I call him Chris."

For a time, the two brothers continued to sit there in silence. The people on shore had put out their fire, and Charley could hear them as they rowed toward their yachts. One voice, a man's, came so clearly across the water he could have been sitting on the other side of Brian.

"I ain't ever going back," the voice said.

A woman laughed. "Not until tomorrow anyway."

Charley got up then, about to go back into the cabin. But he paused long enough to lay his hand on Brian's shoulder. "For what it's worth," he said, "you still got a big brudder."

Though Brian said nothing, he reached up and covered Charley's hand with his own.

**A**s Charley stepped into the cabin, a television bulletin cut into a late-night movie review program. A clean-cut young newsman excitedly announced that there were two new developments in the yacht explosion story at the Romano Resort in the San Juan Islands. Knowing that Brian would want to hear the bulletin, Charley called out that he was on the tube again. Then, leaving the glass door open, Charley moved out of the draft and sat down. Eve and Terry evidently had heard too, for they came hurrying up from the bow cabin as the newsman's voice read on, over stock footage of the resort by day and helicopter shots filmed soon after the blast, not much but darkness and electric lights and a few scattered fires on the hillsides.

"Earlier tonight the luxurious eighty-foot yacht of communications tycoon Rupert Stekko was blown up in the exclusive resort's harbor. Authorities at first thought the explosion was accidental and involved no loss of life, but a few minutes ago San Juan County Sheriff Keith Butler reported recovering the body of the yacht's cabin boy, a teenage Filipino. No name was given."

By then Charley was barely breathing. Though he wanted to turn and see if Brian had heard the terrible news, he did not. He just sat there and watched as the newsman, on camera again, announced that there was increasing speculation that the notorious fugitive Brian Poole was in the area and might have been responsible for the firebombing.

"We go now to Harry Shaw on Orcas Island. Harry?"

The picture cut to two men standing in the floodlit darkness, with the channel's white helicopter parked directly behind them.

The reporter, a balding young man in a flight jacket, was holding a mike, moving it between himself and a tall, slim man in an elegant tux, with the jacket unbuttoned. The man had long iron-gray hair, dark, close-set eyes, a large nose, and wide mouth: the face of a wolf.

"John, I'm standing here with Rupert Stekko, owner of the firebombed yacht," the reporter said. "Sir, I understand that you have reason to believe that this terrible act may have been the work of Brian Poole, who's already committed a number of terrorist acts against your movie company, Wide World Studios."

Stekko smiled thinly. "Well, I make it a point not to deal in reckless speculation. All I can tell you is that Kevin Greenwalt—"

"The man whose great art collection was destroyed by Poole last week," the reporter interrupted.

Stekko nodded. "Yes, the man who runs Wide World—"

"Which is just one part of your empire."

The tycoon looked at the reporter as if he'd just belched loudly, then casually reached over and took the mike from him. "Which I own a controlling interest in, yes. Anyway, Mr. Greenwalt phoned me two days ago with the news that the car Poole used in his escape from Bel Air—an old nine-eleven Porsche with California plates—had been briefly spotted by the Seattle police. That's all I know. I will add this, though, that if Mr. Poole is responsible for destroying the *Nomad* and killing this very fine young man, he will have to pay for his crimes. And I'll do everything in my power to see that he does."

Finished, Stekko handed the mike back to the reporter, who was stammering. "Well, I g-g-guess that's it from here, John. As yet, no real proof yet, who's responsible for the bonfiring . . ." Catching himself, the reporter whinnied and shook his head. "The firebombing, that is. Back to you, John."

Having come all the way into the cabin, Brian now reached down and turned off the TV. Then, without saying a word, he went out onto the deck again. Chester was the only one who followed him.

"Hey, Brian, come on!" he said. "It wasn't none of our fault, man! No way! You went inside and checked, din'tcha? And nobody answered, did they? So it's this gook's own goddamn fault—not ours."

Brian had climbed up onto the bridge by then, and when Chester tried to follow him there too, Brian shoved him off the ladder. And Charley heard him speak then, his voice sounding oddly weak and strangled.

"Keep the hell away from me," he said. "All of you."

# chapter fifteen

**C**harley was finding it almost too much to deal with, not just thinking about the youth who had died and wondering what effect his death would have on their own lives, but also knowing that Brian was alone up on the bridge, lying out in the cold and the damp right above their heads, trying somehow to deal with the knowledge that he had killed.

Crying openly, Terry had gone back to the bow cabin and crawled into her bunk as if she might never leave it. Eve was sitting next to Charley on the built-in couch, snuggled tightly against him, her tears wetting his neck and shirt.

"We've got to go to him," she kept saying. "We can't leave him alone up there. He can't deal with it, Charley, I know him. He's going to dive off the boat and not bother to come up."

But Chester would not allow anyone else to go up. Producing the gun Brian had given him before rowing to the Nomad, he had taken charge, telling them all what to do, which essentially was nothing.

"If anyone's goin' up top and talkin' to the man, it's gonna be me. We the ones who blew the goddamn boat, and I'm the one with this li'l goddamn peashooter," as he called the .25 automatic, which appeared perfect for his tiny hand.

Beaver meanwhile was going at the champagne as if it were water, this on top of another lung-rattling snort of cocaine. Bitterly, he lamented that he had ever been fool enough to get involved with "a fanatic and a psycho," a word choice that brought Chester to his feet, in fact up onto his toes, with his chest puffed out and his mouth in a snarl as he yanked Beaver off his stool and began to shove him about the salon, berating him every step of the way.

"Jest who you callin' psycho, you candy-ass motherfucker? If you done yer job right, we'd of knowed who was in that goddamn boat, and nobody'd be dead now. And Brian wouldn't be layin' up there stewin' like he is—you hear me?"

He finished by shoving Beaver down into the pilot's seat and telling him to watch his mouth from then on if he knew what was good for him. With that settled, Chester began to pick at another sore.

"And jest who the fuck Brian Poole think he is anyway? Too big and important to even talk with a guy? I put my ass on the line fer him today, and this is how he pays me back, huh, like I'm some dumb shitkicker or somethin', not worth his precious time? Well, lemme tell ya, this shitkicker has jest about had it. And that's a fack."

For consolation, he returned to the television set, again flipping compulsively from one channel to another, as if he had to hear the story many times before he could get it straight in his head, exactly what it was he had done. There was film of the *Nomad* during some sort of yachting festival in San Francisco: Stekko and his wife and crew looking spiffy in blue and white, accepting an award of some kind, while in the background, under an airbrushed halo of light, was the smiling face of the victim, a dark young man in a servant's uniform. And there were interviews of the San Juan County sheriff and of a dockhand at the resort who had seen a new white yacht, a forty-footer, lying off-shore in the early evening and running without lights later on, after the explosion.

"She acted kinda peculiar to me," the dockhand said. "Usually they just come in and tie up, or move on. But not that one."

The newsman said that the Coast Guard was already checking boats of that description throughout the San Juans.

Meanwhile, Chester had found a bottle of tequila in the liquor cabinet and was tipping it up to his lipless mouth with breath-taking regularity. This whole thing wasn't any fault of his, he said. If Brian hadn't ruined his baby sister's life and tricked him into taking a shot at that "fag movie director," he would have been home on his ranch at that very minute, snug as a bug in a rug. Yet here he was now, wanted by the police and FBI and "Jesus knows who else" for crimes he never would have commit-ted if it hadn't been for Brian Poole.

"Goddamn his ass, it's all his fault," he mourned. "I only went along cuz I figured he was real people, you know? But he ain't. He's jest some damn celeberty, that's all. Ain't got no time for common folk, no sir, So the only one I'm lookin out for now is old number one, that's who. Me, myself, and I."

He asked Beaver if it might not be a good idea to go ashore and hole up on the island somewhere, and Beaver told him that he was free to do whatever he wanted. As for himself, things were different now, Beaver said. There was no sense trying to take the boat back into Lake Union. Instead he was going to stop in Everett for fuel and leave the thing right there at the gas pumps and take a cab on down to Seattle.

"Let the fucking bank go looking for it. It's theirs now anyway, not mine. And I gotta talk to my lawyer. I was the patsy in all this, you know."

"The hell you was," Chester scoffed. "You're a growed man. You knowed what you was gittin' into, same as me."

"Well, it hardly matters now," Beaver said. "Only important thing as far as I can see is to get some sleep." To that end, he got out some Quaaludes and washed them down with more champagne. He even offered some to Chester, telling him that he would be wise to relax and get some sleep himself. "We can't do anything till morning," he said.

Though the little cowboy grumbled, he took the pills.

In time, when Chester and Beaver began to nod off, Eve kissed Charley on the cheek and got up.

"I'm going up there, Charley," she said. "I have to be with him."

Charley nodded agreement. "Sure," he said, and was about to say more, but she was already on her way, taking a blanket with her. Knowing it was misty outside, he got a yellow slicker out of the closet and followed her, climbing only high enough on the ladder to hand it to her. Then he went back into the cabin, again sitting down on the couch. And over the next hour Charley could almost feel his life draining away, like a man with a leaking bag of gold dust. Though he knew Eve was only doing what was right—what she had to do—he couldn't control his feelings of loss and dread. The more he thought about it, the more he was convinced that the woman he loved had gone to be with the man she loved. And it hurt. It hurt more than he would have believed possible. His split scalp and bruised ribs seemed like pinpricks compared to what he was feeling now.

During the rest of that night, he checked on them twice, quietly climbing the ladder and peering ovr the edge of the bridge, just to see if they were all right, he told himself. The first time they were sitting on the floor, at the front corner, barely visible in the cloudcover light. Eve had covered them with the blanket and slicker and was holding Brian like a child as he snuggled down against her breasts. She was talking to him, but so softly Charley could not hear what she was saying.

The second time, hours later, he found them stretched out on the bridge floor, apparently asleep, only now with Eve lying in Brian's arms. Charley then had made his way back down the ladder as quietly as he could, feeling oddly weak. He figured he had already lost the life he had in Illinois, such as it was, and now he had lost this new one too, this still-amorphous, but somehow shining, beautiful new life he was to have had with Eve. And it bewildered him. He couldn't imagine how he could have been so sublimely stupid, so monumentally self-delusional, as to think that such a stunning, marvelous young woman would prefer him, a glorified carpenter, over his dashing if slightly wacko younger brother; and especially now, with Brian all gussied up, virtually transfigured, in the glad rags of romantic tragedy.

Back in the cabin, Charley grimly surveyed his companions for the night: Beaver drunk and asleep, slumped over the wheel, resting his fringed head on his hands, and Chester snoring in front of the TV, spread-eagled in an armchair, the gun resting on his flat gut. Looking at them, Charley figured that the least he could do was put an end to it all, the whole, long, improbable mess.

Not even trying to be deft, he picked the gun off Chester's belly and the little man reacted as he'd been impaled by an electric cattle prod, practically jumping straight up from the chair, his arms flailing. The gun was so small Charley had only palmed it at that point, so that was how he hit him with it, a cold-steel hand slap, knocking him to the floor.

Across the salon, Beaver looked up to see what had happened. Charley beckoned to him with the gun.

"Get your duct tape and come over here," he said.

Beaver did as he was told. Charley had him tape Chester's feet together and his hands behind his back. Then he prodded Beaver back to the helm.

"I want you to radio the Coast Guard and give them our location," he said. "Then give the mike to me."

Beaver had the look of a man wetting himself. "You sure about this, Charley?" he asked.

Charley smiled. "Damn sure, Chris."


**W**aiting for the Coast Guard to find them, Charley wanted to make sure he stayed awake. Instead of stretching out on the couch, he arranged the cushions at one end so he could just rest there, propped up, able to keep an eye on Chester and Beaver, who himself was now securely duct-taped, even over the mouth, for he had objected vehemently to the whole idea.

Charley had tried to explain as much as he could to the Coast Guard, but he sensed that it was too complicated for the man on the other end of the line, or airwave, so he'd simplified.

"There are good guys and bad guys aboard. The bad guys are all incapacitated—out of action—so don't arrive with guns blazing."

"Copy that," the man had said.

So Charley waited now, fighting sleep, mourning his loss and cursing his foolishness. The one thing that didn't bother him much was the situation at home, the certain breakup of his marriage. He'd lain awake more than a few nights these past years wondering just how it was that love died and whose fault it was, his or Donna's or just the times, the infinity of possibilities open to the successful American. Whatever, at least now there would be no argument. It would be his fault entirely.

Picking at his wounds, old and new, he eventually dozed off, for how long he had no idea. And when he began to wake, he discovered that a cold, damp body was snuggling against him, burrowing into his arms while trying to pull a blanket around them at the same time.

"It's only me, darling," she said. "I'm afraid I'm sopping. It's so foggy out there you can barely see your nose."

Charley was befuddled. "Eve?" he said.

She smiled and kissed him. "Yes, Eve. Remember me?"

"I thought you and—" He stopped there, beginning to suspect now that he had been even a greater fool than he had thought.

"I did what I could," she said. "I held him and talked to him, almost like he was my child, you know? And I think he's going to be all right. He's sleeping now. And it's beginning to get light, at least the fog is."

"You're shaking," he said.

"I know, I know. I need some dry clothing. Where's Terry?"

"Asleep up front."

"Did you duct tape her too?"

Charley smiled. "No, just Curly and Moe there. I've radioed the Coast Guard. They should be here soon."

"You've been busy."

"I was lonely."

She gave him a look of mock pity. "Poor fellow. Listen, I'm going to see what Terry has, maybe a pair of sweats."

As she started to get up, Charley suddenly found himself and pulled her back down, hugging and kissing her as if she had just emerged alive from a cataclysm, something on the order of the *Nomad*'s last seconds.

"Jesus, girl!" he said. "Jesus Christ Almighty but I do love you!"

When she caught her breath, Eve laughed and smiled. "Well, I love you too, Charley. You hadn't forgotten that, had you?"

He nodded sheepishly. "Maybe for a minute or two."

"Idiot," she said.

**A** half hour later Eve was down in the bow cabin, talking earnestly with Terry, probably repeating the same things Charley had told the girl a short time before, reassuring her, telling her that the Coast Guard would be coming soon and that it would be all right, because he and Eve were going to help her all they could. They would explain to the authorities that she had no part in blowing up the *Nomad*.

Charley used the head, gargled some mouthwash, then went out onto the stern deck after first picking his way past Beaver and Chester, still duct-taped, occasionally squirming violently. Unconsciously holding his breath, Charley went part way up the ladder and surveyed the bridge, breathing again only when he saw Brian stretched out on the rear bench seat under the yellow slicker. His face and hair glistened with moisture, and though his eyes were closed, Charley suspected that he was not really asleep, just faking it in order not to have to talk. Whichever, Charley was content to live with the silence. Coming back down the ladder, he looked around him at the cove still slowly coming out of darkness, its surface steaming in the cold air. Tatters of fog drifted over the beach and hung in the trees, and in a high, dead fir a lone bald eagle was perched on a barren limb as if it had been keeping watch over the cove through the night. Even as Charley was squinting up at the bird through the mist, he heard the sound of a diesel engine, far off still, but growing steadily louder.

Just then Eve came out onto the deck, wearing jeans and a

sweatshirt now, holding a blanket around her shoulders. She too quickly checked out the bridge, then came back down.

"Thank God," she whispered. "He's still asleep."

"Not for long, though," Charley said. "Hear that?" At her look of panic, he took her in his arms. "Come on, you knew they were coming. It's going to be all right."

"If you say so." Shivering even with the blanket wrapped around her, Eve turned in his arms so she too could watch the mouth of the cove, where the sound of the diesel was coming from, clearer now.

"I don't like the way it sounds," she said. "It's so . . . brutal."

"That's how a diesel sounds. Remember, we've got a couple of them right under us."

"Well, I still don't like them."

Just then the boat came out of the mist, about the size of the *Seagal,* all white except for the broad red stripe of the Coast Guard slashed across its bow. Eve reflexively dug her fingers into Charley's arm.

"Oh God!" she cried. "I don't like this at all."

Charley made no response, his attention now locked on the patrol boat as it slowed into the cove and began a circular route that took it between the *Seagal* and the two smaller cruisers. Her engines cut to an idle and the boat virtually stopped dead in the water. Charley could see an officer in the pilot house studying him and Eve through a pair of binoculars.

"We should signal to them," Charley said, raising his arm and waving.

At that same moment, on the low-slung stern of the boat, a crewman pointed at the Seagal's bridge. And Charley, turning, saw that Brian was on his feet now, calmly observing the patrol boat.

"Well, I guess this is it," Charley said to him.

Smiling slightly, Brian looked down and nodded. Then, turning away from the Coast Guard boat, he stepped up onto the side of the bridge and dove into the water a dozen feet below. Eve dropped her blanket and hurried across the deck.

"No, Brian!" she cried. "No! Don't!"

Immediately the engines of the Coast Guard boat revved and the craft started forward, heading around the *Seagal.* Charley followed Eve to the opposite railing as the patrol boat thundered into view again, moving slowly still, its pilot obviously taking care not to run over the swimmer. Two of the crew had gone forward on the bow, one to watch out for their quarry while the other readied a life raft to throw overboard. But Brian swam on, heading for the mouth of the cove, as if he planned on swimming out across the entire Sound.

The Coast Guard had other ideas, however. Moving in close, they forced him to work against the wash of the boat, which was considerable. At the same time, one of the crewmen eased the doughnutlike raft into the water and slipped down into it, extending a boat hook out to the swimmer in the apparent expectation that he would give up and take hold, let himself be pulled to safety. But Brian didn't reach for the hook, nor did he seem at all bothered by the boat's wash or by whatever it was the officer was shouting at him through the bullhorn. He simply went on swimming, and the patrol boat patiently plowed along next to him, until they were both out of the cove and heading into the Sound.

Eve had wrapped herself in the blanket again and was leaning back against Charley, trembling in the circle of his arms. He could tell by her breathing that she was trying hard not to cry. For himself, he felt angry more than anything else, reflecting that even now, at the very end of his tether, his brother had to put on a show, do it *his* way.

Finally, though, just as Brian and the Coast Guard boat had begun to fade into the mist, Charley saw him reach up and take hold of the boat hook. Quickly then he was pulled aboard, first into the raft, then into the boat itself.

Eve shivered violently. "Oh, thank God! Thank God! I was afraid he'd just dive under and disappear!"

"Me too," Charley said, though long experience had taught him that Brian loved life—and himself—far too much to choose death over surrender.

As the patrol boat headed back towards them, Eve turned in Charley's arms. "Hold me tight," she said. "And don't ever let go, okay?"

"Never?"

"Never."

Charley's arms tightened around her. "You've got it," he said.